ISLAND OF ONE

EVAN CLOUSE

ILLUSTRATED BY

GABE PEREZ

Contents

This book is dedicated to every person who cares about our personal freedom. To every person who cares about our democracy. To every person who shuns the politics of hate and division. To every person who accepts and embraces others for who they are. Thank you for your voices. Thank you for your caring. Thank you for your kind hearts. I love you all.

Acknowledgments

I would like to thank every person who has supported me and understands just how important this work is to me. Thank you for reading. Thank you for your input. Thank you for caring. You know who you are.

PROLOGUE

There was blissful silence. There were no horns honking. No traffic. No talking or yelling or laughing. There were no sounds whatsoever to indicate that a human race had ever existed here.

Then, upon closer inspection, one could hear the subtle sound of brilliant green leaves fluttering together in the light, warm breeze. It was as though the Earth was breathing a well-earned sigh of relief. Other sounds began to emerge. Waves calmly lapping upon the shore of a nearby lake. The playful squawks of geese. The bucked teeth of a family of rabbits tearing into their delicious clover. The flirtatious chirps of birds in the trees. A nut falling from its branch and softly landing in the thick brush. The sounds that indicated that nature had persevered despite the best attempts of humankind to extinguish her.

The majestic animals and flowers and trees had endured despite the hunting. And logging. And toxic chemicals that had been spewed into their air and been unceremoniously dumped into their waterways. They had endured despite humankind's lust for dominance over them. Many species had been lost during the humans' tyrannical reign over their home. But many more of them survived. *They* were still *here*. The *humans*, mercifully, *were not*. They had made themselves extinct through their insatiable drive for self-fulfillment. They were now extinct because of their greed. Because of their brutality. Because of their ignorance. And, ironically enough, because of their lack of basic humanity.

The Earth was healing. As was its colorful inhabitants. Then, the ears of a doe perked up. And those of the rabbits. The birds stopped chirping, and the geese cautiously floated silently in their pond. It had been many months since this dreadful sound had been heard. The high-pitched whir of one of their machines. The animals tenuously approached the grown-over pavement and looked to where the sound was coming from. Their hearts sank as they saw it. A single automobile. Driven on this single, lonely road. And behind the wheel, sat a single one of *them*. A female of their despicable species sitting alone in her single automobile being driven on this single, lonely road.

ISLAND
OF
ONE

Chapter 1

Trial and Error

The test subject slowly stood up as his eyes dulled into a milky-white glaze. A tear rolled down his battered, tan cheek while he felt his emotions being drained from his consciousness. Memories of his beloved wife and children faded into nothingness. Memories of his parents. His upbringing. His high-school hijinks. Everything that had formed him into the decent man that he had become had evaporated. He then felt a sharp pain in the back of his head. He then felt absolutely nothing at all.

"Sonofabitch," a frustrated lab technician stated as he watched the test subject's blood, brain and skull fragments drip down the observation window. "Another failure. Alright. Let's get this mess cleaned up. Send the data to the next team. They'll be here soon. Maybe there's something in there that they can use. I hear they're taking a different approach. Jesus, how I pray they are successful. Time is running out. I need to get a couple hours of sleep. Then back to the drawing board."

The next pair of lab technicians took their assigned seats behind a long black console that was covered in lights and dials and all manner of thingamabobs. The pair silently began pushing buttons and twisting dials. There was a light whir that could be heard as the machine's cooling fans awoke from their slumber. Green, red, and blue console lights illuminated the somber room while a slight static buzz rang in the men's ears. They sat back in their well-worn faux leather swivel chairs and stared at their reflections in the observation window through their weary blue eyes. Their pasty white faces looked drawn and haggard and their thinning, sweaty blond hair was cemented on their pale scalps. "Okay, let's run the numbers one more time before we bring them in," one of the men said. "The old approach isn't working. The other team's most recent test failed again. Just as we have failed. Time and again. Until now. Maybe."

The other man retrieved a black binder from a shelf underneath their console. He ran his thin fingers over the cover as he read it once again. *National Institute of Psychiatric Health. Project Golden Age. Test Trial Log.* He nervously began chewing at what remained of his stubbled fingernail on his left index finger as he opened the book to the last page. His eyes darted over the seemingly meaningless rows of numbers and equations that were layered over a schematic of a portion of the human brain. The Cerebrum to be exact. The man's right hand was shaking as his fingers traced over the data points while his brain processed the information. "Yeah, I think this checks out. I think we might have a winner here, Hugo."

"Well, we'd better, Dawson," the other man stated while typing the data into a keyboard. There was the frenzied sound of clacking keys as he continued. "We'd *better* have a winner. And soon. Dear Leader is getting impatient with us." Hugo paused for a moment to fearfully peer up at a golden portrait of an evil, pompous man whose painted eyes appeared to be watching his every move. Hugo shuddered before continuing. "And you know what happens to people that he loses patience with. To people who fail to prove their patriotism. It doesn't matter how much allegiance we might have to him and his cause. *Wanting* to serve Dear Leader's regime is no substitute for *contributing* to Dear Leader's regime. The true test of our patriotism are the results that he demands. Without the results, we are useless to him. We are useless to his cause. And he is right about that. Without the results, we *are* useless, and we deserve whatever judgement Dear Leader's court may hand down to us. There will be no due process and no opportunity to defend ourselves. Dear Leader's courts took those rights away long ago. There is only accusation then judgement. Then..." he gulped before completing his thought. "Then, the alligators."

"Speaking of alligators, I hear our latest two subjects come from the concentration camp in the Florida swamps. Must mean they're Hispanic," Dawson observed.

"You mean (derogatory term omitted), don't you?" Hugo chided. "You mean the illegals, right? The rapists and murderers. The pieces of shit from shit-hole countries who never should have come here in the first place. What did they expect? For the gravy train to just keep supporting them? For the libtards to stay in power and keep paying them to invade our country? To run around free on our streets to steal our jobs and our education and our health care? To run around free to steal the shit from our houses and to rape our women? No, that had to come to an end and Dear Leader has seen to it. His glorious wisdom has seen through their insidious scheme to invade and take over our country like a bunch of fuckin' cockroaches. Our God-given land has turned into a sewer filled with a bunch of brown turds. And the libtards just kept feeding the system and shitting out more and more of these brown turds until our home was overflowing with them.

"We needed somebody to flush them away. And that is exactly what Dear Leader is doing. It doesn't matter what their immigration or citizenship status might have been. Turds have no rights. Turds must be flushed out of our system. Who in the hell cares to where. When I flush my toilet, I don't give a fuck about where my shit ends up and I sure as hell don't care where *these* fuckin' turds end up either after Dear Leader has flushed them. Well, heh, heh, heh. Actually, I do care about *some* of them. The ones that get flushed to *us*. I care about *them* quite a bit. Until we're done with them. Then, heh, heh, heh. WHOOSH!"

"Yeah, I suppose you're right," Dawson nervously agreed while glancing up at the intrusive portrait. "It's just that, um, well, he said he was just going after the, um, you know, *violent* ones. But from the beginning he began rounding up anyone who looked, um, well, you know. Brown. His masked army took over entire communities and rounded up anyone that looked like that group of people and sent them to, um, well, someplace. And now, he is expanding the incarcerations and deportations. He has access to voter registration logs and is threatening to target his political enemies. It doesn't matter what they look like or where they're from or their citizenship status. If the person isn't a proven believer in the regime, they could be targeted for pick-up and placement in a re-education camp. I mean, where does it end? Just how many camps can we build and just how many people can we incarcerate until they're indoctrinated into Dear Leader's truth?"

"Well, that's why *we're* here now *isn't* it, buddy-boy?" Hugo replied. "Don't you see? *Our* work is the fruit of Dear Leader's vision. And it is the fruit of Dear Leader's benevolence. It is out of his God-given kindness that we are doing what we are doing. Do you think that Dear Leader *wants* to harm people? Of course, not. He wants to give people the opportunity to see his glorious truth. He wants people to accept him as the anointed one and to join him on his path of glory in his great golden age. He loves and cares about each and every one of us. Just as God does. *His* love for us is an extension of *God's* love for us. That is why he is beginning with flushing the turds. He's getting rid of the fucking animals that *pretend* to be human. They may walk upright and talk and shit, but they aren't human, and they never will be. There's no amount of re-education that could make them human. So, he's getting rid of *them* first. The Browns. Then, the Asians and Middle-Easterners until he gets to the Blacks. Then, the Jews. He's cleansing the system so that we White humans are free to accept his word. His truth. His prosperity. He's cleansing the system so that the non-believing White humans can have their opportunity to see his truth. Without having to worry about being distracted by these fucking turds. He is giving our great nation the enema that it has needed for so long.

"But even the turds will benefit from Dear Leader's benevolence. Through our work, they will be given the opportunity to live. Hell, they'll actually be encouraged to fuck. They will have the opportunity to live and fuck as much as they want so that they can breed. Then, throughout the world, we White humans will have the workforce we need to dig our mines and pick our crops and make our hot dogs and clean our houses and do all of the shit that is beneath *us*. They will have the opportunity to live and fulfill what they have always been destined to be. Our servants. I'm sure we will still need to be cruel to a few, just to keep the rest in line. But our work will be a lifeline not just to the non-believing Whites but to many of the turds as well.

"I'm sorry. I need a tissue. I just get so damned emotional when I think of the love that Dear Leader has in his heart for us. When I think of the sacrifices he has made for us. All of the vile accusations and investigations and witch-hunts that he has been forced to go through. The pain that he has been forced to endure. A lesser man would have wilted. A lesser man would have given up. But he is *not* a lesser man. He is a *great* man. In fact, he isn't a man at all. He is divinity personified. He sacrificed for us. He continued to fight until he won every battle. And he did it for *us*. He loves us so much that he put himself through all of that suffering so that he could deliver us into his great golden age. He carried so many crosses for us. And now, here we are carrying our crosses for him. Our scientific crosses that we will be triumphant over so that his will shall be done. We are just on the cusp of it, my friend. Just this one final test and every human shall be delivered into glory, and every turd will be allowed to live their life of servitude.

"And it will be quite painless for all of them. All they need to do is to continue to watch their little hand-held screens. Watch their viral videos on their phones that have our hidden little messages in them. If this test is successful, then we will have succeeded in the exact formula to attach our Dear Leader's messages into all of the wireless cellular networks and then to their viral videos and sports scores and news feeds and photographs. Every time they use their phone to look at a silly cat video, they will be exposed to a message from our Dear Leader. Every time they use their phone to check their messages, or email, or take a picture, our Dear Leader's image and voice will be planted in their Cerebrum until, over time, they will come to know *our* Dear Leader as *their* Dear Leader. They will come to understand *his* truth to be *theirs*. And then, all he will need to do is speak to them and they will dutifully follow his orders. The non-believers shall become believers, and they shall report to their designated work stations. The turds will self-deport or willingly march themselves into the work camps. It will all be done without violence. It will all be done out of love. Dear Leader's love for us and our love for Dear Leader. It will be paradise. As long as we have the formula correct.

"It has been more difficult than we thought. To construct messages that are transmitted directly to the Cerebrum. To have those messages impact how the Cerebrum interprets data. To have their fake news memories be erased and replaced by the truth of our Dear Leader. Then, attach those messages to an algorithm that will spread across the cellular networks and attach itself to every person's cell phone activity. We have accomplished all of that. We are so close. All we must do now is control how the messages affect human emotions. And that has been our barrier. Up to this point, the terrible side effect for all of our subjects has been to suppress their emotions so much that they have become like zombies. They have absolutely no reaction to anything. They just stroll around drooling on themselves until we put a bullet in their head. But perhaps we finally have the winning formula. Perhaps we can now open people's minds to our Dear Leader's messages of his love. And his manipulation of their emotions. Let's give it a shot, shall we? Bring them in."

There was a loud buzz from behind the blood-streaked observation window. A portly armed guard directed two men into the room and ordered them to sit. The prisoners groaned as they placed their bruised bodies onto their respective hardwood chairs. They looked at each other with wide, anxious eyes until a voice came over the intercom.

"Good afternoon, gentlemen," Hugo said to them in an inviting voice. "Thank you for joining us. I understand that you are tired and confused and probably just a little sore from the beatings you have had to endure. But today you will be relieved of that pain. One way or another. This will be a very simple test, gentlemen. Then you will be taken back to your cells and fed. Alright? Your chaperone is going to give you each a cell phone. Yes, there you are. Are they turned on? Yes? Good. Now, all you have to do is watch videos on your phones. You may watch anything you like. Stupid human tricks. Storm chasers. Movie trailers. Porn. Anything that you might be interested in. Just watch the videos and allow yourselves to be entertained. Allow yourself to be completely absorbed by this mindless activity of constantly searching for insipid content. Scroll, swipe left, search, post. Anything you like. Alright? Now begin."

The two men looked at one another for a moment then typed into the search engines on their phones. One of the men immediately went to his social media account. He smiled for the first time in months as he watched a video of his daughter's third birthday. She was wearing a pretty red dress with white hearts. On her pudgy, tan legs she wore white leggings. He began chuckling as he looked at the grass stains on her shoeless feet. "Her mother was so upset with her that day," he quietly muttered to himself. "Our little darling simply wouldn't leave her shoes on and she absolutely ruined those leggings with grass stains. It was so adorable. We couldn't help but laugh. We couldn't help but...but...send her to a work camp? Wh-why did I say that?"

Hugo and Dawson stared at the scene with gleeful anticipation as they witnessed the slight transformation in the man's demeanor. Sweat was pouring from their pasty foreheads as they turned their attention to the other man who was watching cat videos. Cats sitting in small boxes. Cats chasing laser pointers. Cats being confused by their own reflection. Cats frightened by a cucumber. He began laughing aloud as one video after another played and became absorbed by his psyche. His laughter then changed into a monotonous diatribe. "Oh, poor Dear Leader. The trials you have been put through. The accusations. The legal proceedings. I now understand. Yes, Dear Leader. I now understand. I understand how much you love me. I understand my calling to serve you. I understand your wisdom, oh great one. Yes, Dear Leader. I will be your loyal subject. I will..."

Hugo and Dawson jumped out of their chairs and high-fived. "We did it!" Hugo announced. "We actually fucking did it! We have found the right indoctrination formula! And it only took five minutes! Five minutes of watching their videos that have Dear Leader's messages implanted into them and they're now his loyal subjects! I'll prepare the final report and send it to our supervisor. Get the server ready to transmit to the cellular networks. I'm sure Dear Leader will want this launched as soon as possible. And then, we will be showered with his praise. Perhaps an invitation to one of his lavish dinners. We are heroes, Dawson! We are fucking heroes! The entire country, then the entire world will now be under the control of Dear Leader!"

The pair's self-congratulations suddenly ended as they looked once again into the observation room. The pair of test subjects had launched themselves toward the armed guard and were ripping him apart. The guard screamed out as the men tore off his jaw, ripped out his eyes, and began pulling organs from his chest cavity. They then began stuffing their angered faces with pieces of the tortured man's flesh. The observation room was covered in the guard's blood and body parts as the merciless onslaught continued.

The test subjects paused for a moment and stared at one another. They then each snarled and attacked one another. The wooden chairs were smashed, and the shards of sharpened wood were used to impale one another. They let out shrieks of pain and furious growls simultaneously as they viciously ripped one another apart in a frenzy of unbridled violence.

"Abort! Abort!" Hugo yelled out. "Abort *what?*" an astonished Dawson yelled back. "There's nothing to abort! Dear Leader's messages are already implanted in their brains, and they have made them...made them...fucking killing machines!" The despondent men slumped back into their chairs and watched in disappointment until the test subjects' merciless onslaught came to its horrific conclusion.

Hugo and Dawson stood and looked intensely through the blood-spattered observation glass. "Oh my God," Dawson said. "I've never seen anything like this. They tore each other limb from limb. Literally. They tore their limbs off. They crushed each other's skulls. They stabbed each other over and over with parts of the broken chairs. This is a bloodbath. We're on the wrong track here, Hugo. We need to start over."

"Agreed," a frustrated Hugo replied. "We can't let this out. Any of it. We need to delete everything about this trial. And I mean *everything*. All the data. All the theoretical notes. And we're sure as hell deleting everything that just happened here. No one will ever know about this. Let's get the clean-up crew and just pretend this never happened. Dawson, delete it all."

"My pleasure," the sweat-soaked Dawson stated as he pressed a bright red button. "Okay. Done. No one will ever know about this. Come on. We have one more piece of unpleasantness before we can take a break."

"Oh, I forgot about that," Hugo replied in an upbeat tone. "I've been looking forward to getting rid of *this* bitch for a long time. She's such an uppity (derogatory term omitted). Yeah, let's get rid of 'Poopala', or whatever her weird fuckin' name is. Today just proves we're making the right decision. The data she's been feeding us is absolute shit."

As the pair of men exited, the room was illuminated by the glow of the flashing red button that Dawson had engaged. The light was repeatedly flashing 'TRANSMIT', TRANSMIT', TRANSMIT'.

Chapter 2

Redundancies

"Chad! Where in the hell did you put my keys?" Payekha Popoola yelled out to her most recent slacker boyfriend and flat mate. Her six-foot tall muscular ebony frame was draped in a sharp black business suit as she frantically searched every drawer and tabletop in their modest yet tidy living room.

"Chad! My keys! Where in the hell did you put them last night?" She continued to receive no response from her boyfriend who sat on the couch mesmerized by the images on his phone. He chuckled slightly as yet another ridiculous video of a man falling on the ice was played. He wore stained pajama bottoms and a rock band T-shirt that he had not changed out of for three days while milk and a corn flake sat pasted on his stubbled chin.

An infuriated Payekha marched over to him, snatched the phone from his hand and tossed it onto an adjacent chair. "Hey! I was watching that!" Chad yelled out. "No shit, huh?" Payekha tersely answered. "So, what the fuck *else* is new? That's all you fucking do! Sit on that fucking phone and watch a bunch of stupid bullshit all day while the world is changing all around you! You have every piece of information in the entire world in your lily-white hands, and you don't have a fucking clue as to what is happening in this country! All you do is play your stupid fucking games and watch your stupid fucking videos! In the meantime, this corrupt regime is taking over everything! They're abducting people off the streets! They're taking over the election systems! They're taking over the courts and the media and the educational systems! We're in the midst of an auto-cratic takeover of our country and what are *you* doing? Watching stupid fucking videos of people getting hit in the head by soccer balls! Oh, and losing my keys! Now, where the fuck are they? I'm going to be late for work!"

Chad held a confused expression on his greasy face as he responded, "Huh. I dunno. I used your car last night to get some more beer. I came home, cracked open a beer, and started watching, um, I mean, nothin'. Oh, I think I know! Did you check in the car?"

"Why in the hell would my car keys be in my fucking car that is parked on the street?" Payekha bellowed. "Um," Chad sheepishly began answering. "'Cause I think I was watching something on my phone when I got out of the car, and I think I may have accidentally locked your keys in there. Sorry, babe."

"Sorry, babe," an exasperated Payekha stated through gritted teeth. "Sorry babe? Are you fucking kidding me? I know you don't have anything to do but sit around all day and smell up this joint, but I actually have a job! I have responsibilities! Who in the hell do you think pays the rent around here? And the utilities and food and your fucking internet!"

"Hey," Chad corrected. "*You* use the internet too, babe. That's not just me." "Yeah, I use the internet. I use it on my *laptop*, and I use it for my *research*. That's it. Do you even have a *clue* what I'm working on? I'm researching the effects of propaganda and how it deteriorates objective, free thought over time. I know what the new assholes that the regime has planted at the National Institute of Psychiatric Health are using my research for. I know they're trying to develop mind control algorithms. That's why I've been feeding the lab techs skewed data. They'll *never* get it right with the bullshit that *I'm* feeding them. But just in case they do, I have the *real* data on my flash drive. Those assholes want my data to indoctrinate people into their cult. I'm just sure of it. But I think that my data could be used to plant messages to *deprogram* people who have been indoctrinated into cults. What I *don't* have is the scientific skills to be able to broadcast those messages, but I was thinking about talking to Dawson about that. He's a whiz at that shit. If he's still talking to me. We used to be such good friends, but I'm afraid that maybe he's started to buy into this White Nationalist bullshit. Anyway, my point is, yes, I use the internet for the purpose it was intended. I don't walk around staring at a little fucking screen like a zombie all day. I'm not addicted to that shit. And why? Because I don't even own a cell phone! Don't want one, don't need one."

"Yeah, you're probably the last person on the planet that doesn't have one, babe," Chad replied while retrieving his phone from the chair and flopping back onto the couch. His blackened, smelly, and stiff tube socks jutted over the arm of the couch as he returned to his videos. "Oh, one more thing, babe. You think you're taking a chance giving them corrupt data? I mean, with all this anti-DEI bullshit that's going on, maybe you shouldn't rock the boat. And maybe you need to straighten your hair. That huge afro is like putting a target on your back."

"Hey! This my natural hair and I'm proud of it!" Payekha roared back. "I'm proud of my hair and my race and my culture and if anybody doesn't like it then they can kiss my firm, Black ass! Besides, I've *already* got a target on my back. I'm pretty sure that if I wasn't such an expert on the effects of propaganda that I'd be gone already. I'm the only Black person who hasn't been fired and I'm one of only three women left. And the other two are receptionists. Everybody else are limp-dicked, pasty-faced, White men. I've always felt like a minority, but this shit's just crazy. And that's why I'm doing what I'm doing. I can't allow my work to be used to indoctrinate the masses. I won't be turned into a weapon. All I can do is continue my research, collect my data, and produce deprogramming messages and hope that the fever breaks in this country and a sane administration comes to power. Then, and *only* then, will I share my actual findings."

Payekha looked down at her boyfriend in disgust as he laughed at his latest video. "You didn't hear one fucking thing that I just said, did you? Just sitting there completely absorbed by your mindless drivel. You're just another zombie. Just like everybody else. Yeah, humanity is definitely primed for indoctrination. Hell, they're already there. Fuck this. I'll take the bus and be late. What's another black mark on my record?" As Payekha slammed the door behind her, Chad said, "Did you say somethin', babe? Oh man, that musta hurt! Hey babe, check out this video! Babe?"

"Hey, kid, move over," Payekha asked a twelve-year-old girl who was sitting in the aisle seat on the bus while staring at her screen. "Kid, please, move over. That's the last seat. Jesus fucking Christ kid! Pull your head out of your fucking phone and move your bratty fucking ass over!"

The girl looked up at Payekha with glazed eyes and said, "What?" Payekha shoved the kid to the window seat and sat down. "You're an asshole," the girl said before her eyes drifted back onto her screen. "Oh, fuck you, kid," Payekha answered under her breath.

A chill ran down Payekha's spine as she turned on the overhead fluorescent light in her cramped office. It was the same chill that she had experienced for months. Ever since the portrait of Dear Leader had been hung above her desk. She inhaled deeply through her nose and collected as much snot as she could in the back of her throat. She smiled as she spit the giant logy onto the painted, pompous face that glared down upon her. As she watched the dark green mucous run down the stained portrait, she said, "Another one for your collection, asshole. Okay, let's get to work. Let's see what they tried to do with my latest data points and…huh. They're using them for another test this afternoon. Good. They'll run the numbers, realize it won't work, and our little shell game will continue. They'll never even get to the point where they can test this shit on people. It's still just all hypothetical at this point. No *real* scientist would ever try this on actual people. The effects are too unpredictable. Oh, shit. I just thought of something. This place isn't being run by real scientists anymore. It's just a bunch of tin-foil hat conspiracy theorists with calculators. But, naw. Even *they* wouldn't be that stupid. Especially with this *latest* batch of data. Using *this* would be batshit crazy."

"Hey, Dawson," Payekha said to her maybe-friend as she stood behind him at the lunch counter. "Oh, um, hey Payekha," Dawson replied while averting his gaze from her brown eyes. "So, how are the trials coming along?" she inquired as she lifted a plate of steamed vegetables and placed it on her lunch tray. "Any, um, progress? I saw that there's another trial this afternoon, so that's encouraging."

"Um, yeah," Dawson meekly replied. "Yeah, but I can't really talk about it. But these latest numbers you have given us show some potential." "Yeah, I bet," she replied through a slight chuckle. "So, what in the hell are you lab nerds doing with my shit anyway? What type of trials are you running? I mean, what are you trying to accomplish?"

Dawson's hands were shaking as he placed a hamburger onto his tray and responded through a shaking voice. "Um, you know. Just human behavior stuff. Just research. I really can't talk about it, but, um, well, I'll see you later this afternoon. Hugo and I need to have a meeting with you."

"A meeting?" she asked. "A meeting about what?" "Oh, nothing really," Dawson answered quietly. "Just, you know, progress update and stuff like that. Um, I really gotta go, Payekha, but I'll see you this afternoon, okay?" "Yeah, alright. Whatever. Nice to talk with ya," Payekha answered as she shook her head. Her head continued to shake in disbelief as she entered the lunchroom. At every table, White men in starched, white shirts and red ties were sitting with each other in complete silence. They slowly chewed their lunch as their eyes were fixated upon banal images on their small screens.

Jesus Christ, she thought to herself. *It's no wonder people have lost the ability to communicate with one another. Look at them all just sitting there in silence. Oh, they can type a bunch of bullshit. They can all be keyboard warriors and bloviate their bullshit opinions on a bunch of shit that they have no understanding of. But just say 'Hi' to one of them, and they blush, look down, and scurry away like fucking rats. They have lost the ability to connect and communicate with actual people in actual situations. Their lives are virtual. Nothing is real to them. They have no idea how to interpret what is actually happening in our world because their world is nothing more than an on-line virtual fantasy of their creation. They're all just in their indi-*

*vidual cocoons being constantly entertained by drivel and their truth is what-
ever they want it to be. And then there's assholes like this.* She stopped to
look down at a man who was posting a picture of his lunch tray. "Hey!
Asshole! Nobody gives a fuck what you had for lunch! Get over yourself! Are you so fucking interesting that you think that people actually
give a fuck about what you cram into your mouth and shit out later?
Jesus! Narcissistic much? And I wonder how our country got to this
point. Fuck this. I'm not even hungry anymore." Payekha threw her
entire tray into the trash bin and stormed out while the unaware man
smiled at his latest culinary post.

Later that afternoon, Payekha was summoned to a small conference room. Sitting on one side of the table was Hugo and Dawson.
"Well, howdy boys," she greeted. "Geez, what the fuck happened to *you*
two? I mean you two are the whitest motherfuckers that I've ever
seen, but you look like you've just seen a ghost. Trial not work out or
what?"

Hugo righted himself in his swivel chair, pulled out a personnel
file, and said, "Thank you for joining us, um, Peeka Poopala, am I
saying that right?" "No, you're not," Payekha dryly answered. "And you
know you're not, Harpo. Oh, *I'm* sorry. Did *I* get *your* name wrong? No,
as I've told you many, many times, my name is Payekha. PIE-YEE-
KAH. Got that? It means 'one who is alone.' Which I sure as fuck am
around here. And my last name is Popoola. POE-POO-LA. It's really
not that fucking difficult. It's from my ancestor's native land of
Nigeria and means 'intelligent people'. Which there seems to be quite
a shortage of around here. Okay, Harpo, now that we've been formally
introduced, *again*, what's this meeting about?"

Dawson looked down at the papers in front of him and squirmed
as Hugo answered. "Quite frankly, bitch, this meeting is about giving
you your walking papers. Finally. Come on, baby. You're not stupid.
Well, at least not as stupid as *most* of your people. Take a look around.
You see anyone else around here with black skin and big fuckin' 'fro?
You see anyone else in important positions with tits? No? You finally
getting a clue? Plus, the data you've been giving us has been shit. You
are no longer of use to us anymore. Oh, and go ahead and try to sue us

for wrongful termination. That'll be fun to watch in today's courts. You have no fucking rights and now you have no fucking job. You're lucky you don't get packed up in a shipping crate and sent back to your precious Nigeria. Maybe you can move further south and get a job picking cotton. That's probably what your Granmammy did, right? Or hey. With a figure like yours, you'd look pretty good standing on a street corner. So, I'm genuinely interested, Ms. Poopala. What are you going to do now? Pick cotton? Or fuck strangers? That's really all you DEI bitches are good for."

Payekha seethed as she glared into Hugo's eyes. Her gaze then averted to the trembling Dawson. "So, this is the big meeting, huh, Dawson?" she asked as she casually leaned back in her chair and crossed her black boots on the table. "A big meeting to fire me. Not only that but to do it with flair. With style. To insult my race and my gender. Really nice. What the fuck happened to you, man? You used to be a decent guy. I thought. We were hired together. Came up through the ranks together. Always got along. Hell, we even went out a couple times. When did you become such a cowering fucking worm? And Harpo, let me correct you on something, you slimy prick. I was *not* a DEI hire. There's *no such thing* as a DEI hire! Diversity, equity, and inclusion does *not* mean that people who aren't White fucking males get jobs that they aren't qualified for. It means that those people who have been discriminated against since this bullshit country was founded have the same opportunities to compete for positions that they *are* just as qualified for, if not *more* so! Like me! I'm a fucking expert in my field. I got this job because I was qualified for it. It wasn't because of my skin color. It wasn't because of my tits. It was because I was the best person for the job. Not the best *woman* for the job. Not the best *Black* for the job. I was the best *person* for the job! Which you two fucknuts are about to find out. As the saying goes, you'll miss me when I'm gone. But before I'm escorted out of the building by one of your goons, I'm going to give you two a parting present. Just a little professional courtesy from me to you. You'd better be *really* fucking careful with the mind-control shit that I know you're working on. You'd better be *very cautious* before you try this shit on real human subjects. Because, if you're not, well, let's just say that you *might* be surprised by the results. And you will fucking regret it. Alright boys. Ta-ta. I's gots me some cotton to pick and whorin' aroun' ta do! I hope you both rot in hell. Fuck both of you."

Payekha fumed as she walked toward the parking garage. She then suddenly stopped and screamed, "Fuck! I don't have my fucking car! Okay, I've gotten rid of that toxic fucking job. I guess I'll take it as a sign that I need to get rid of *all* toxic assholes in my life. And Chad, you're next. Better start packing your shit you lazy, slacker mother-fucker. Why in the hell did I get involved with somebody named Chad anyway? Did I learn *nothing* from reading about Maddy Sommers's exploits in the *Hanging Chads* series? I feel like a dumbass."

Payekha's exasperation grew as she stood in the aisle of the bus with her arms folded. "Great. *This* fuckin' kid again. Listen, kid, I'm really not in the mood so wouldja just move your little ass over so I can sit down? Hey! Kid! Put your fuckin' phone down for two seconds and move your little ass over! Goddammit kid, look at me!"

Payekha grabbed the schoolgirl's chin and forced her head upwards. "What the fuck happened to *you*?" an astonished Payekha said as she stared into the milky-white eyes of the snarling girl.

CHAPTER 3

AND SO, IT BEGINS

Foam dripped down the enraged child's tender, pale chin as she stared at Payekha. "Okay, kid, okay," Payekha said as she leaned back into the bus's aisle. "Just calm down. I'll find another seat, okay?" She took a step back, bumping her rear into a seated passenger across the aisle. "Oh, I'm sorry, ma'am. Excuse me. Hey, I think we need to call an ambulance or something for this kid." The elderly female passenger looked up from her cell phone with a blank expression on her withered face. She opened her eyes, revealing pure white pupils and began growling.

"What the fuck is going on?" Payekha stated. The elderly woman and schoolgirl suddenly lunged at Payekha. The child began viciously gnawing at her arm while the elderly woman gummed her sleek neck. Slobber dripped down her throat while blood gushed out of her forearm. "Oh, fuck this!" Payekha screamed. She elbowed the elderly woman in the nose, shattering it. Her wrinkled face was covered in blood as she shook her head, righted herself, and began gumming Payekha's neck once again.

With her right hand, Payekha grabbed the schoolgirl by her blonde pigtails and threw her down the aisle. The schoolgirl bounced three times on the steel walkway, jumped up on her feet, and again lunged at Payekha. "Help me! Please! Somebody help me!" Payekha pleaded while being chewed by the pair of undeterred assailants. Payekha looked around the bus and was greeted by dozens of pairs of glossed over, milky white eyes. "Oh, shit," she muttered before a middle-aged man two aisles in front of her said, "I'll help you, miss." He tried to pry the child's locked jaw from Payekha's arm while Payekha pummeled the elderly woman with her elbow.

"What in the hell is going on back there?" the bus driver shouted out. "Sit the hell down! You're going to cause me to..." He was silenced by a mob of demented passengers grabbing him. The bus careened out of control as the driver's leg was forced down on the accelerator. There were the sounds of loud thumps and screams as the 25,000-pound metal missile veered onto a walkway. Blood, bones, and organs exploded around the bus as it mowed down the hundreds of helpless pedestrians in its violent path.

The driver screamed as the fierce mob tore through his chest cavity and began removing his organs. The savage marauders gluttonously chewed on the squealing man's flesh while being bounced around the bus's cabin. The inside of the bus began glowing an eerie red as the evening sun shone through its windows and windshield which were completely covered in the sprayed blood of its victims. There was an explosion of glass as the runaway transit bus crashed through a storefront window of a cellular phone shop. The patrons inside did nothing to get out of its way. They stood there, frozen, holding their cellphones while their white eyes stared at their metal doom coming towards them. They said nothing as their heads and bodies were crushed under the steel behemoth. The last thing their glassy eyes saw before their demise was the scowling image of Dear Leader that was plastered on the side of the bus. Pieces of brains, shards of bone, torrents of blood, and chunks of flesh splattered against the shop's walls. As the bus slowly ground to a halt in the back of the store, body fragments oozed down the display cabinets that held humankind's most advanced technology. And its demise.

Payekha began digging herself out from a pile of groaning, disoriented people. She threw the bodies off and stood up. She was horrified as she looked at the gruesome scene. Pieces of the bus driver were strewn about the front of the cabin. Demented passengers were savagely chewing on the remains of other men, women, and children. Blood dripped off of the bus's seats and flowed down the aisle like a morbid river of death. And in the middle of it all was the schoolgirl who was bashing the head of the middle-aged man against the floor. Blood splashed against her twisted, youthful face as she slammed the man's skull repeatedly until there was a loud crack. She took her small fingers and pulled the shattered skull apart before plunging her face into the man's exposed brains.

Payekha's darting eyes spotted a broken window and she staggered toward it. Arms of the other disheveled passengers reached for her as she fought to pass them by. She kicked and hit at them in a frenzy to ward off their attempted grasps. She took off her blood-soaked blazer and used it to clear the excess glass before crawling from the wreckage. All the while, the schoolgirl intensely watched her. She watched her. And ate brains. And frothed. And growled.

Payekha landed awkwardly on the sticky, crimson linoleum floor and twisted her ankle as she stepped on a slimy kidney. "Aw fuck!" She screamed out as she felt the all-too familiar pain that shot through her ankle. "Ah, shit, not now," she said to herself while limping through broken glass, dismembered limbs, shattered plastic, and crushed torsos. "My fucking ankles have been a problem all my life. And now, they might be the death of me. Ah shit. I can already feel it starting to swell. I've gotta get my shoe off. And find a crutch. Maybe I can just hide out here for a while. Until the cavalry comes. But why aren't there any sirens?"

She willed her battered body through the carnage to a back office. "Locked. Of course it is." She began ramming her shoulder against the door until the lock gave way. Her momentum caused her to careen through the doorway and tumble face first onto the floor. "Jesus Christ! Now I have a broken nose! This day is so fucked!" she yelled. She steadied herself on a desktop as she got to her feet and closed the office door. She grunted as she pulled a filing cabinet three feet to block the only entrance to her temporary safe haven. She sat on the office chair and elevated her ankle onto the desk. She could feel tears welling up in her eyes as she assessed her damaged foot. "Nope. Not going to cry," she said to herself as she flashed back to nineteen years earlier.

"I'm never going to cry again," a thirteen-year-old Payekha said to her mother in a determined voice. "Never again. And do you know *why*? Because that is what you and my bastard father *wants*. He doesn't beat me and rape me just because it gets him off sexually. He beats me and rapes me and ridicules me and berates me because he wants to destroy me. He wants to destroy me and so do you. You are *both* a pair of sadistic fucks. You both want to beat and rape my strength out of me. My independence. My humanity. I've been beaten by you two so much, I don't think I'd even recognize my own reflection without black eyes and bruises and welts. I don't think I'd recognize how my own body feels without the sharp pain from you deliberately spraining my ankles. And whipping my back. And caning my ass. And raping my vagina. Since the age of five, I've known nothing but pain.

"Physical pain. Psychological pain. Emotional pain. Day in and day out. Pain. And tears. And you both got off on my tears didn't you mommy? Of course, you're not *really* my mommy now, are you? And he isn't my father. That was just another part of your mind games. Your brainwashing. You're a pair of White devils who abducted me from my yard eight years ago. For eight long years you have kept me here and abused me. And allowed *others* in your fucked up pedophile ring to abuse me. And it wasn't just a twisted sex thing. It's a *domination* thing. It's a *power* thing. Two grown adults who have to dominate a child in every way possible just to have a sense of self-esteem. Outside of this house, the two of you are nothing. You are nobody. Just a petty thief and his whore waitress. But here? You are king and queen of the most fucked up castle of horrors there has ever been. Here you can be as twisted and cruel as you want to be and nobody will ever know, right? Nobody knows I even exist. When I wasn't being used as your personal fuck toy or punching bag, I was locked away in the basement.

"I was given one meal a day. I had a toilet in one corner and a shower in another. A filthy mattress on the floor that I would lay on and cry. I'm surprised I have any fluids left I've cried so much. And I could hear you both laughing at the top of the stairs as I cried. You were laughing at my anguish. You were laughing at my fear. But I had one other thing in that basement. Books. Boxes and boxes of books that a former resident had left here. You let me have those and for that I really must thank you. Because those books saved my life. Those books helped me hang onto my sanity. Those books educated me. Those books kept me from being brainwashed into your living hell. The former resident must have been a teacher or scholar or something.

"Oh sure, there was plenty of fiction novels. I remember picking up one of those books with my trembling hands and sounding out the words and teaching myself to read. I was able to project myself into the story and escape into the lives and worlds that I was reading about. That's how I survived. My real life was fucking hell. But in my imaginary life I was a princess. Or a swashbuckler. Or a fairy. Or a serial killer. Yeah, whoever used to live here really enjoyed horror books. And it did not take much imagination on my part to mentally replace the victims in those books with you two assholes. Through those books I held onto my independence. My strength. My pride.

"And through the academic books I taught myself everything else. World history. Civics. Fitness. Math. Science. Psychology. Yeah, that one helped me a lot. It helped me understand how to manipulate you. How I convinced you to stop beating me for the last six months so that I wouldn't have any marks on my body. Why, I certainly couldn't go to the park and make friends with marks on my body, now *could* I mommy? And I *certainly* wouldn't be able to lure them *here* to play with me either. My tears turned to laughter when I realized that my plan was working. My plan to convince you that I had become just as fucked up as you two. That I wanted to play with other girls just as you had played with me. That I would go to the park and make new friends and lure them here so that we could beat and rape another innocent girl. Fun for the whole family, right mommy? You two were so fucking stupid and arrogant. You actually believed me. You actually believed that your brainwashing had worked, and I would now be your agent to groom other girls. The thought of another girl being treated this way made me vomit. I would vomit at the thought of it, then laugh at the thought of what I had learned in some of the *other* books.

"I just needed time for my body to heal. To strengthen. I knew that I couldn't do what I read in those books with a battered body. I had to convince you to stop beating me. I had to heal. And I *have* healed. My ankles aren't swollen. My bruises are gone. Tonight was to have been my first trip to the park with my loving family. You even bought me a pretty dress to wear. I do love yellow. I think it absolutely glows with my dark skin. Yes, we would go to the park as a family. You two would point out a girl you liked. I would go over and begin to befriend her. We would do this until the girl felt comfortable with me. Safe with me and my family. She would be invited over to dinner. And then, that innocent girl would be subjected to the vilest horrors imaginable. That was the plan now, wasn't it mommy?

"But tonight, I put on my pretty yellow dress, and I came upstairs from my dungeon. And as soon as I reached the top of the staircase, I put lessons from another book into use. A martial arts book. He's such a pussy, it just took one karate chop to the back of the neck to knock him out. And then a simple leg sweep to knock you on your ass. And now, here we are. One big happy family. And now, I'm going to rely on my *favorite* type of book." Payekha glared at the pair of sweating, bound, and gagged sadistic pedophiles as she pulled a butcher knife from a kitchen drawer.

"Yes, as I mentioned before, the horror books were my absolute *favorites*. I learned a great deal from them. I learned about human frailty. I learned about human fear. I learned about human cruelty. But most and coolest of all, I learned about how to fuck people up. As you're about to find out…daddy."

Payekha lifted the pleading man's flaccid penis from between his hairy thighs and sliced it in half with the butcher knife. The man's segmented worm flopped open as blood poured out of the gash. Payekha began laughing at the pathetic sight. Her laughter intensified as she thrust the knife between the sobbing woman's thighs and pulled upwards until she was slashed from her groin to her neck. Payekha's bobby socks and penny loafers were awash in blood as she returned to the squealing man and began carving chunks of flesh from his arms. Then shoulders. Then legs until the area around his chair looked like a butcher's floor.

Payekha let out a satisfied sigh, straightened her blood-soaked dress, and took her seat in front of the tortured pair. She crossed her healed ebony legs and calmy kicked her right foot in the air for twenty minutes as she watched her brutal tormentors slowly bleed out with morbid fascination. "And now, I'm going to find my family. My *real* family. And as I said, motherfuckers. I'm *never* going to cry again."

Payekha could feel her tears drying up in her sockets as she looked around the barricaded cell phone office. "Fuck this. I've been through a helluva lot worse than this." She reached up and grabbed a shirt that was hanging from a coat rack. She grimaced as she tightly wrapped the shirt around her swollen ankle then got up. She limped towards the door, used her tone arms to throw the filing cabinet to the side, and exited the confined office.

"This is a fucking massacre," she said with regretful awe as her widened eyes once again took in the gruesome carnage in the showroom. Everywhere her eyes darted was yet another horrific scene of blood splatters, decapitated heads, flattened organs and, conveniently enough, dismembered limbs. "Oh good. That's what I need," she said as she limped over to the smoking bus. She reached down and yanked a severed leg from under the bus's wheel. "Shit, this is perfect," she said as she grasped the exposed femur and leaned against it. She let out an audible sigh of relief as her swelling ankle was relieved from the pressure of her weight. She began limping toward the exit, then looked down. "Wow. Nice traction. Yeah, these were expensive sneakers. They just cling to the floor even through all this blood."

She reached the exit and wondered aloud, "Still no sirens? Where the hell is everybody? What's the use of living in a police state if they can't even respond to *this*? Oh, right. They're not on the streets to respond to *real* human suffering or need. They're on the streets to round up those that they see as useless. Or political enemies of Dear Leader. Round them up and send them camping. Bigoted, Nazi motherfuckers. And now they're trying their hand at mind control. If the military can't suppress enough people, then let's brainwash them into submission, right? But it will never work. Those dumbasses will never figure out the right subliminal formula. Not without me. If they unleash this shit through the cellular networks, then all they'll end up doing is creating a world of mindless, violent zombi…oh those stupid motherfuckers. They couldn't have. They didn't. This *can't* be what this is. This has to be some out-of-control virus or something that the insane HHS Secretary is using as another one of his 'Advanced Health' experiments. Yeah, it's probably that. Like in Akron when HHS put a new solution in the water supply. Well, if the goal was to have kids born with their internal organs on the outside, then bingo motherfuckers, you got it right. The entire fucking town was 'cleaned up'. An entire town's inhabitants disappeared and were never to be seen again. So, yeah, his insane shit is bad, but not *nearly* as bad as the indoctrination formula would be. Naw, it can't be *that*," she concluded as she patted the flash drive in her purse that had managed to remain strapped across her chest. "But I need to get home and watch some news. See how widespread this shit is. Probably just a nasty virus on the bus. That I didn't contract somehow? Yeah, that's weird too. Fuck it. I gotta get home. Maybe not the best day to break up with Chad. He isn't much, but he can at least bring me some soup. Well, at least I *think* he's capable of that. We'll see."

She grunted as she limped toward the shattered storefront then paused as she heard a familiar growl coming from behind her. She cautiously turned around to find the snarling schoolgirl staring at her. Blood and saliva dripped down the child's chin as her enraged face reddened. "Ah fuck, kid," Payekha said. "Listen, I don't know what's going on, but I'm going to try to find you some help, okay? Just chill out. Kid, I'm tellin' you, don't come one step closer. Ah, shit kid, I really don't want to hurt you. I don't want to see *any* child ever hurt again. Just let me go, okay?"

The child's expression changed from untethered rage to confusion.

Then immediately back to rage as she ran towards Payekha with her bloody mouth wide open. "Aw fuck!" Payekha yelled out as she swung her leg crutch, hitting the girl in her temple. The disoriented girl lay on the blood-soaked linoleum and let out a pained shriek as Payekha rapidly turned toward the decimated storefront. She hobbled her battered body over the broken glass and crushed bodies until she stepped onto the sidewalk and entered a world of absolute, horrific chaos.

CHAPTER 4

IN THE MEANTIME,

The seventeen-year-old schoolgirl returned to her home in Mesa, Arizona. She thoughtfully placed her purse, bookbag, and clarinet case on the shelf in the home's spotless foyer. "Mom! Dad! I'm home!" She yelled out with a slight Hispanic accent. "What time is dinner? And can I go out tonight? I won't be out too late! Jessica wants to take me out for a romantic dinner and movie to celebrate my getting into Stanford! Is that okay? We'll only go to safe spaces! I promise!"

She then heard her beloved father's voice from the kitchen. "Emilia, sweetheart, please come into the kitchen. We have a surprise for you." The smiling Emilia immediately skipped into the kitchen. Her smile broadened as she yelled out, "Gramma! Grampa! You're here! I didn't think you were coming until tomorrow!" She ran into the warm embrace of her grandparents and began weeping with joy.

"Well," her choked up grandfather responded as his tears were being absorbed by his granddaughter's pitch-black hair, "We weren't supposed to arrive until tomorrow, but we said, 'You know what? Nobody is going to prevent us from seeing our Emilia. Not ever again.' It has taken us two years since we were rounded up by those cruel masked men. Two years since we were incarcerated in deplorable conditions then deported. Two years of hiding out and avoiding the cruelty of the cartels. And two years to prove our citizenship in this country. And we have done that. We have proven that we belong in this country. We have proven that we came here legally. Worked here legally. And obtained our citizenship legally. Two long years of being away from our loving family. And so, we said, 'To heck with it. Let's leave a day early and get to our daughter. And our son-in-law. And, most importantly, our beautiful granddaughter.'"

He lifted Emilia's tender face until they made eye contact. Emilia's brain was awash in loving memories of her grandparents. The birthday parties and special dinners and movie nights. Her grandmother mending her scraped knee. Her grandfather sneaking an extra piece of cake into her bedroom. The two of them sitting on the edge of her bed and mischievously laughing together as they consumed their contraband sweets. Emilia buried her head once again into her grandparent's embrace. She then shook her head, stepped away, and said, "Oh my God. I've missed you both so much. I'm going to call Jessica and let her know that I can't make it tonight. I want to spend this entire evening with you both."

"Why don't you just invite Jessica over, dear?" Emilia's mother thoughtfully asked. "Oh, I, um, I guess I didn't think about that," Emilia stammered. "I, um, didn't know how, um, or if, um, y'know, Grampa and Gramma would, um, well…"

Emilia's grandmother walked over and wrapped her weathered, tan arms around her. "Oh, my dearest Emilia. We do not care about any of that. We only care about our granddaughter's happiness. And if this Jessica is a good person who does that for you, then who am I to judge?"

"Yes, who are *any* of us to judge?" Emilia's grandfather contributed. "Who somebody is attracted to is not a choice. It is hardwired into our being. What a stupid argument that is. Who would *choose* to be with someone that they aren't attracted to? Who would *choose* to live a life that they knew would invite discrimination against them? Discrimination? Hell, *those* were the good ol' days. Now Dear Leader's thugs are raiding those communities and sending those poor people off to 're-education' camps. They are working those poor people to the bone in the fields and mines. They are torturing them. And why? Because they were built slightly differently by our God. They perform this cruelty against people in God's name. They don't even realize their disgusting blasphemy. They round them up and torture them just as they did us. Because our skin was a bit darker. It's all the same hatred for anything different. It's all the same bigotry. And it is anti-Christian. This Dear Leader's movement is a White Nationalist, Anti-Christian movement. And it is sickening. The only reason we fought to come back is so we could be with our family. To be with our granddaughter. Our granddaughter that we have always known was attracted to girls. Yes, my dearest Emilia, we have always known. And we have never cared because, well, why does *anybody* give a flying fig about that? But we have always known, and we have returned to be with you, our dearest Emilia. To be with you, and to protect you. You are wise to be clandestine about your relationship. We understand how dangerous it is for you and your girlfriend. But you do not have to be someone that you aren't in front of *us*. We do not love you *despite* of who you are. We love you *because* of who you are. So, please. Invite your girlfriend. It will be a pleasure to get to know her."

"Oh my God," Emilia tearfully replied. "You guys are the best. And waaaay more hip than I would have imagined."

Her grandparents began laughing together before her grandmother said, "Well, dear, I wasn't *born* this age, you know. And I *certainly* wasn't born wearing an apron while making fresh tortillas. I was once your age. I've experienced quite a few things in my younger years."

Her grandfather began chuckling and said, "Yeah, especially in college. Remember that night when we both got really stoned while listening to records and that chica from down the hall came into your dorm room and we, um, well. Perhaps that isn't an appropriate story for grandparents to be telling."

"No, perhaps not," the grandmother replied while shielding her embarrassed face from the astonished gazes of her family. "But it *was* a fun night. Now, run upstairs and call your girlfriend. Where are the aprons? I have tortillas to make. And everybody, put your damned contraptions away. Tonight is about being with family. *Not* staring at your stupid little screens."

"Oh, wow, Gramma," Emilia said while rubbing her slightly protruding belly. "That was delicious. God, how I've missed your cooking. And, well, everything else with you and Grampa. It's just so wonderful to have you back. I know we said no "contraptions" tonight, but I need to run upstairs and see if Jessica's parents have texted me. Her phone is broken so I had to call her parents, and they're supposed to let me know when she'll be over. Let me run upstairs and check real quick and I'll be right back, okay?"

Emilia rushed into her perfectly organized bedroom and did a belly flop on her soft mattress. She reached for her phone and searched her messages. She scrolled through the spam to find what she was looking for.

Hey Babe. B over about 8. Hope U had a great dinner. B ready for dessert LOL.

"Oh damn, she's cute," Emilia stated to herself while opening a social media app. "Now, let's see what's happening in the world." She stared transfixed at her phone as meaningless posts, pictures, arguments, and misinformation scrolled past her glistening eyes. She paused for a moment and opened a video of an old man falling on the ice. She laughed aloud as the scene played over and over in a continuous loop. Each time the man fell, she laughed harder. Then, her laughing suddenly stopped.

Deep within her cerebrum, images of Dear Leader were being implanted. Golden hued images of him dressed as a superhero or conquering soldier or a classic emperor. Then, the words that he spoke became lodged into her psyche. Dear Leader's voice speaking about the greatness of this White nation. Speaking about his single-handed success in ridding the nation of the illegals and vermin and the unholy. Speaking about women being dutiful and subservient to their male masters. Speaking about the true calling of servitude for all non-White people. Speaking about imprisoning his political rivals who had put him through torturous ordeals. Speaking about his divinity. His strength. His intelligence. His sexual prowess. His omnipotence.

The barrage of images and messages began eating away at Emilia's hippocampus. Cherished memories of her parents and grandparents disintegrated into nothingness. Her age. Her name. Her address. Her friends. Everything buried deep within her limbic system was being wiped away by the vile image and voice of Dear Leader. The messages traveled into her amygdala and lodged themselves there. With each passing image and utterance of Dear Leader, Emilia's anger increased as her ability to feel anything else was swept away.

Her face was beet red, and she was frothing at the mouth as she threw her phone against the wall. There was a loud crash as the phone shattered. As did the framed picture of her adoring family. Her enraged eyes quickly scanned her unfamiliar surroundings until she found what she was looking for. She retrieved a softball bat from her closet and opened the bedroom door. Her feet made loud clomping sounds down the stairs before she flew into the living room. She saw four unfamiliar people sitting on a sofa and two side chairs. The very sight of them threw her into an uncontrollable rage. She approached the back of the head of the man sitting on the sofa. Her unsuspecting father's skull was crushed by the perfectly swung bat. Her mother was sprayed with blood and skull fragments. Her screaming was immediately silenced by five fierce blows to her astonished face.

Two older people jumped to their feet, held their hands up, and began pleading with her. Emilia did not understand what they were saying. It was all gibberish. Gibberish that Emilia interpreted as a threat and enraged her further. Her grandfather was hit in his knees. He fell backwards, landing on the bloody carpet. She then proceeded to bash his face repeatedly with the bat. Her grandmother attempted to grab her. Emilia elbowed the elderly woman in the nose. She staggered backwards as blood and tears ran down her wrinkled cheeks.

"Why, Emilia? Why?" were the final words that she spoke before her skull was crushed by her frenzied granddaughter.

"Hey babe!" the perky blonde Jessica announced as she bounded through the front door. "Sorry for barging in but nobody answered the door. You guys playing a game or...or...Emilia! What in the hell are you *doing?*"

The snarling Emilia stopped eating her grandmother's brains and looked up at the interloper with her dead white eyes. Blood and drool poured down her chin as her growls deepened. Her shocked girlfriend was frozen in fear as Emilia leapt at her and tore her throat out with her gnashing teeth.

Thousands of miles away in the small village of Mittenwald, Germany, a young couple was celebrating their first wedding anniversary. They marveled at the gorgeous Alps from their outdoor table at a local bistro. They gazed lovingly into one another's eyes as the man delicately rubbed the large diamond on his wife's wedding ring with his thumb.

"I can't believe that it's been a year already," the wife stated while continuing to be lost in her husband's brilliant blue eyes. "And it's been the most wonderful year of my life. I feel like the luckiest woman in the world. You are handsome and sweet and intelligent. You are perhaps the kindest man that I've ever known. I must tell you, my love, that there is not a day that goes by that you don't sweep me off of my feet. Every morning when we wake up, I feel like that university girl that noticed you across the room in our philosophy class. Oh, how my heart beat the first time I saw you. And when you asked me out. And when you kissed me and proposed to me and married me. My heart hasn't stopped beating for you for these three years. And it never will. My heart will always beat for you, my love. My heart, and the heart of our child."

"Wait, what?" the shocked husband enthusiastically asked. "Our, our *child?* Darling, are *you,* um, I mean, are *we,* um, I mean are *you* with, um..." His stammering was interrupted by his wife's joyous nodding before he leaned across the table and kissed his beloved. The tender scene was interrupted by the buzzing of his phone.

"Oh, dammit," he lamented as he reached into his jacket pocket. "I'm so sorry darling. I know I shouldn't have brought this thing, but I'm waiting on some news. There is going to be a merger between my company and another, and I asked a friend to notify me of any news. It really could mean a great deal to us dear. Let me just check. It won't take me a moment." He began reading a message from his friend. The further he read, the wider his smile became. "Yes!" he exclaimed. "Here it is! The merger has gone through! Oh darling, I didn't want to tell you until I knew for sure, but this other company is run by an old friend of mine, and he said that if this deal goes through that he will make me Vice President of Some Middle-Management Bullshit That Nobody Understands and Isn't Needed! (Okay, he *actually* said Vice President of Resources Procurement, whatever the fuck that is. I like mine better. Now, back to the story). Darling, do you know what this means? This means that we will have all the money for our dream home! One with a nursery, of course! And a swimming pool! And a tennis court! We'll be able to afford a nanny and the best schools for our child! We will be able to take grand vacations to Canada or Mexico or Japan or, well, *anywhere* other than the United States. *That* place has turned into an oppressive shithole.

"Just give me one more moment my darling. I want to see if there are any news reports yet. Oh dear, our future is indeed bright." He began searching the various news outlets on his phone. He found an article and began reading. After reading for a few seconds, his beaming smile faded, and his lips sunk downward. His glowing skin turned ashen, and his hands began trembling. "Darling, what is wrong?" his concerned wife asked. The husband looked up with glazed white eyes, picked up his shiny fork, and lunged at the unknown threatening woman sitting across from him. She landed onto her back, and he straddled her. She was screaming for help as he repeatedly plunged the fork into heart. The brutal onslaught continued as shocked onlookers grappled with what to do. He savagely continued stabbing her until her heart stopped beating for him. He ripped her chest open with his brawny hands, extracted the still heart, and began gluttonously chewing on it.

"Thank you once again for flying Quantas. The pilot has turned off the seatbelt sign, and you may now move about the cabin. Food service will begin in twenty minutes. Oh, and you can now use your devices." The male flight attendant shook his head as he watched every man, woman, and child over the age of two frantically turn on their phones. "Good lord, just look at them," he said to his female colleague. "They just can't wait to be absorbed into their mind-numbing minutia. They must be entertained by mindless drivel every waking hour. Whatever happened to taking a nap? Or reading a book? Naw, they have to have their stupid human videos, and arguments between complete strangers. They have to post their every move to the world. It makes them feel important. It makes them feel special. But what they don't understand is that nobody gives a fuck. Nobody cares about their pictures from a trip, or what they had for dinner, or their ugly kid's first steps. Nobody cares. And they sure as hell don't care about their opinions. And yet, there they are. Typing away at their little keyboards as though they are the most important person in the world. Ah well, at least it keeps them quiet. Come on. Let's start prepping the food. Are you listening to me? We need to start prepping the food."

His colleague looked up at him from her phone. She was snarling and drooling as she stared right through him with her whitened eyes. She then thrust her phone into his mouth, lodging it in his throat. The choking flight attendant began gagging as he witnessed a horrific scene. Every person in the cabin was beating on one another. A man was scalping a woman with his bare hands. She snarled and screamed simultaneously as her hair was viciously torn from her head. Another man had his face buried in the chest cavity of a shrieking four-year-old boy. A woman was beating her neighbor frantically with her purse while an enraged man was brutally pounding an infant against the walls of the plane.

The cabin became awash with blood, torn off limbs, and ripped apart organs as the sounds of growls, snarls, and screams echoed in the chamber. The choking flight attendant furiously banged on the cabin door until it was opened. "What the hell is going on?" the co-pilot yelled out before the cockpit was stormed by dozens of enraged passengers.

The heads of the pilot and co-pilot were ripped from their necks, and the passengers began devouring their ears, nose, eyes, and skin from off their skulls. The pilotless plane began plunging towards the earth until it exploded in a tremendous fire ball. The patrons inside the Sydney Opera House were immediately scorched or crushed to death as they listened to their final notes of Mozart's Symphony No. 9.

Throughout the world, reports of random acts of extreme violence were being reported. People flocked to their devices to find out the latest information about the horrific world-wide carnage. They frantically scrolled until they found an article of interest. They did, indeed, find the news that they were searching for. They also found the toxic subliminal image and voice of Dear Leader imbedded in the news reports. And after just a few seconds, the very sight and sound of him sent them all into an infuriated frenzy.

CHAPTER 5

THIS MAKES NO SCENTS

"Well, you motherfuckers said you wanted to burn it all down. Congratulations. You fucking did it," Payekha stated to herself as she looked at the carnage that was raging outside of the shattered cell phone shop. She leaned against her bloody leg crutch to further relieve the strain on her swollen ankle and began searching for an exit strategy.

"Okay, Payekha. Let's just calm down. We've been in impossible situations before. Situations that seemed like you could never escape. But you did. You did it by remaining calm and talking yourself through it. One step at a time. Well, I can't walk very well and I'm five miles from my apartment. I need transportation. Maybe a good Samaritan can give me a lift. But not *that* guy. He's being eaten. Fuck, that's gross. And not that woman over there. Yep, there went her head. She's of no use to me. I do kinda like the burning banners of Dear Leader though. I think it's appropriate that his ugly mug is going up in flames on every federal building. It adds a little irony to this fucked up situation. And I guess I was wrong. The city really *is* prettier when it's cast in his golden hue.

"And speaking of Dear Leader, there was always one of his fascist militant brigades patrolling this area. Just a couple blocks away. Okay,

Payekha, march. Just one step at a time. Hide behind burning cars to avoid detection by these…these…really fucked up people. One step and…uh! Two. One step and…uh! Two. Fuck my ankle hurts."

She heard a growl from behind her. Her mind immediately ignored the surging pain in her ankle as she swung around to find a frothing middle-aged man coming toward her. "I don't suppose it would do me any good to try to talk this out with you would it?" she said as the demented man continued his steady approach. "Nope, didn't think so," she stated as she bent down and picked up a long piece of sharp metal that had been stripped off of a destroyed car. "Just one more step, motherfucker. That's it. Just one more step and…" She swung the metal at the man, slicing his throat open. He grasped his neck and gurgled as blood gushed from the wound. He fell to his knees, then onto his face. After a few seconds his body stopped twitching.

"Okay, Rule Number One," Payekha stated as she continued her self-monologue. "These motherfuckers aren't supernatural or the undead or some shit. They're just humans who have contracted some sort of virus that has made them into enraged, um, well, I guess *zombies* is the best word for it. Kinda overused but fuck it. I can't think of a better term. Well, how about we make this a bit woke and just call them the 'rationally challenged'. Naw. That's just another term for Dear Leader's supporters. Along with White Nationalists, Nazis, bigots, misogynists, rapists, pedophile supporters, dickwads, douchebags, tiny dicked daddy issues fucknuts, and, um, oh! Walking anal discharge that drips down their leg and fucks everything up. Dammit Payekha, focus! Rule Number One is that they're just human and can be killed by anything that kills a normal human. No silver bullets or, um, no that's werewolves. Stake through the heart? No, that's vampires. What the fuck is supposed to kill zombies?"

At that moment seven Regal Guard soldiers entered the area on foot. One of the soldiers aimed his rifle at an approaching, we'll say 'zombie', and fired. The zombie's head exploded, producing a shower of brains. "Oh, yeah," a bemused Payekha stated to herself. "You kill zombies by shooting them in the head and destroying their brains.

Hey! Regal Guard dudes! You don't have to shoot them in the head to kill them! You can shoot them in the heart or whatever! It's Rule Number One! They can be killed by anything that kills a regular human!"

Payekha's expression changed from bemusement to shock as the seven distracted troops were suddenly attacked by a swarm of zombies. The soldiers let out high pitched shrieks as they were overcome by the vicious horde and eaten alive. "Well, fuck me up the ass," the horrified Payekha said. "Okay, then. A couple new rules. Rule Number Two: These motherfuckers are fast. They're not the slow-moving zombies from the movies. Nope. They're fast as fuck. And Rule Number Three: they are hungry as hell and eat other humans. Like every bit of them. Holy shit, there's hardly anything left of *that* soldier. He's still fucking alive but they're eating his internal organs and his arms and his legs and his, um, well there goes his face and... now he's dead.

"Poor guy. That's a helluva way to go. Wait a minute. Did I just say, *'poor guy'*? Fuck that prick. He got what he deserved for serving Dear Leader and oppressing his fellow citizens. Yeah, he's just as responsible for this shit as anybody. If those motherfuckers had any conscience or patriotism or loyalty to their oaths, then they would have resigned as conscientious objectors. They would have taken up arms *against* the fascists, not joined them! No army? No Dear Leader. Easy as that. But these motherfuckers *didn't*. They betrayed their oath to our Constitution and blindly served Dear Leader. They became spineless, boot-licking sycophants, just like all the politicians and judges. They did everything that he ordered them to do. Harass people. Round them up. Lock them up. Torture them. Even murder them, I'll bet. They took an oath to defend our nation from threats both foreign *and* domestic. And they failed. Fucking big time. Talk about fuckin' zombies. These fuckin' White Nationalist army pricks are the OG when it comes to that shit. So, bon appetit zombies! Enjoy that fuckin' White meat! Oh shit."

From her peripheral view, Payekha saw several zombies rushing towards her. She desperately looked around for a safe haven. "Maybe in there!" she frantically said to herself and began limping as fast as she could to a neighboring shop. She entered the demolished store and pressed the button to close the security gate. There were grinding noises as the bent gate's mechanics strained to comply. "Fuuuuuuck!" Payekha yelled out as the half-dozen zombies approached the doorway. They slowed their pace and snarled as they carefully approached. "Okay, just calm down, okay?" Payekha said through her quivering voice as she retreated backwards into the shop. "Everything's okay. Good zombies. Are you hungry? Would you like a snack? Look down there. There's a little bit left of that cashier and she's all yours. I just ate and I'm stuffed so, um, enjoy."

The zombies continued their tenuous approach and Payekha bumped into a large display of cologne. The zombies' growls turned deeper before they lunged at her. "Oh fuck! Get the fuck away from me!" Payekha screamed as she grabbed a bottle of cologne and threw it at the vicious horde. The bottle broke and the six zombies were showered by its contents. They immediately began choking and gagging. They bent over while holding their stomachs and began vomiting. Streams of half-digested soldiers, housewives, businessmen, school children, and Regal Party members came streaming out of the zombies' mouths.

The torrent of vomit continued and splatted on the linoleum flooring until the front half of the shop was a river of putrid tannish sewage. The zombies then began violently retching up their own internal organs. Their stomachs, gallbladders, and intestines were becoming dislodged from their bodies and forced up through their stretched esophagus's and out their widened mouths. After all twenty-five feet of their slimy intestines had been purged from their bodies and laid at their feet, they collapsed in a disgusting heap of refuse.

"Whoa!" Payekha exclaimed. "I don't know what the fuck this shit is, but they sure as fuck don't like it." She reached behind her and pulled a large golden bottle of cologne from the display cabinet. "Oh fuckin' gross," she said as she read the label on the bottle.

YOUR DEAR LEADER PRESENTS
GROOMING
A Scent For The Distinguished Man Who Likes Them On The Younger Side

"That's just fucked up," Payekha stated. "But it does give us Rule Number Five. These motherfuckers *really* hate this scent. Yep, the putrid scent of Dear Leader makes them vomit themselves to death. Good to know. Good-to-know. And there's a ton of this shit here. Not a best seller, I guess. And I can see why. It's kinda hard to distinguish it from the smell of the vomit. Oh, and look at *this* shit! Made in China! Of *course* it is, you hypocritical motherfucker. Of *course* it is. Now we know why he dropped the tariffs on imported cologne. Not the *perfume*, mind you. Just the *cologne*. What a self-serving piece of shit. Alrighty then. *Now* what the fuck do I do? I have a ton of this fucked up scent, but no way to get it home. Oh, fuck. God, if you're real just give me a sign. I don't know what the fuck to do here and I've survived too much shit to die now. Please. Just give me a sign."

She looked up and saw the flickering neon lights of a toy store across the pedestrian mall. "Well, fuck," she said while wearing a broad smile. "I really didn't think that would work but, y'know. Thanks God. I owe you one. Time to go toy shopping." She grabbed a large plastic bag from behind the register and placed several bottles of *GROOMING* into it before gingerly sloshing through the lake of chunky vomit towards the shop's entrance.

"Oh fuck, I need a shower," she said as she felt vomit leaking down her ankles and into her sensible shoes. With each step she took towards the toy store, her shoes made squishy sounds. "This is so fucking gross," she said as she felt the pungent goo submerge her toes. She saw another horde of zombies approaching. She smiled as she reached into her bag and hurled a golden bottle of *GROOMING* toward the approaching marauders like a grenade. The bottle exploded on the blood-soaked pavement in the middle of the group. They confusingly looked down for a moment before choking, gagging, and vomiting. "Wow," she said. "This shit works like a charm."

She then heard the screams of a man to her left. "Please! Help me! Please!" It was a young White soldier who was pinned down by a zombie. Drool dripped out of its mouth and onto the man's face as it gnashed its teeth. Payekha limped over to the struggling pair. She opened a golden bottle of *GROOMING* and sprayed it onto the zombie's back. The zombie lifted its head for a moment and sniffed the air. It then began regurgitating everything in its stomach all over the fascist soldier's face. Payekha watched in bewilderment as the zombie's retching brought up its internal organs. The soldier was uttering muffled pleas as he was being suffocated by the revolting gastric remains of the dying zombie. "Huh. A little dab'll do ya, I guess," Payekha said as she continued to look on with awe. "Just a little squirt and it turns these motherfuckers into vomit volcanoes. Now, should I help you? Should I pull you out of there and keep you from suffocating and save your life? What would you do for me? What would you do for a woman? And a Black woman at that? Oh, you might rescue me, but it would be for your own fucked up purposes, wouldn't it? Naw, you're just another bigoted fascist motherfucker so, um, well good luck. I'm running late and I still haven't completed my shopping." Payekha couldn't help but smile as she listened to the final attempted gasps from the White Nationalist soldier who had succumbed to the torrent of zombie refuse.

Payekha leaned against a shopping cart and entered the toy store. "First things first," she said as she scanned the directional signs. "Now, if I were a squirt gun, where would I be? Hmmm. Oh, I bet they're in there. Summer Fun. Aisle twenty-three. Wish it was fucking aisle one but fuck it."

As she made her way towards aisle twenty-three, she would squirt a bit of *GROOMING* on any zombie that she encountered. "Fuck they're loud," she said in a frustrated tone. "I can barely hear this Chumbawamba song over their fucking vomiting. What did they just say? Hissing the night away? That doesn't even make sense. Stupid song. Oh, it sounds like the one in aisle five might be dead. Yeah, *his* harmonious retches are gone. The one in aisle two? I can still hear him. Still alive. Still alive. Aaaaand, now dead. Fuck the one in aisle ten is loud and has been going at it for like five minutes. How much did that bitch eat anyway? Well, she *was* a bit girthy, sooooo..."

She turned the corner and began limping down aisle twenty-three when she encountered a snarling, pudgy five-year-old boy. The infuriated tike ran towards her, and she sprayed his white eyes with *GROOMING*. He immediately began gagging and hurling. "Fuck, kid," Payekha said with disappointment. "Didn't your mother ever feed you anything but junk food? We've got cheese crackers in there. *That* looks like it might have been chocolate. Or fudge. Well, at least there were some nuts in it. And is that gummy worms or are your intestines starting to come out? Nope. Definitely gummy worms. Oh, finally. Some protein," she concluded as a half-digested eyeball came out of his mouth and splashed in the pool of pungent spew.

"Excuse me, kid. I need to get to these water guns," she said as she maneuvered the cart around the heaving child. "Ah, here we are. Water guns. Yeah, I want the big ones. A fuck ton of them. I hope whatever's in this shit doesn't melt the plastic." She used her severed leg crutch to sweep all of the water guns from their shelves and into her cart. "Wow, there's like fifty of these fucking things. Big ones. Super-sized ones. Super-*duper* sized ones. Little handhelds. Fuck it. I'll take them all. It might be overkill, but I suppose if those NRA fuckwads can buy every gun known to man, so can I. Oh, balloons. Yeah, those could be useful. I'll make some *GROOMING* cocktails. Now, I need some transportation."

She once again leaned against the shopping cart which was filled with vibrant green, yellow, red, and blue plastic weaponry and limped towards the bicycle racks. "Well, what the fuck I am going to do with *these?*" she said as she looked at the array of bicycles. "I suppose I could put on some racks and baskets and shit to hold all the cologne and guns and balloons, but I don't think that I can pedal with my bum ankle. Shit. I'm so close. Maybe I should just limp around a parking lot and hope I can find a usable car. With the keys in it. Shit. That's a fucking long shot."

The sun then shone through the windows of the toy shop. A single ray of sunshine landed upon an object in the next aisle. Payekha looked at the spotlit toy, smiled, and said, "Well, shit. *That* might work." Bathing in sunlight was a bright red forty-eight-volt go-cart. Payekha went over to it, lightly stroked its metal frame and all-terrain tires, and read the sales tag. "Wow. It even has a little tow-bar thingy. All I need is a big wagon to hitch to it and I can cruise home with all my shit at a top speed of...*twenty miles an hour?* Who buys this shit for their kid? No wonder there's an epidemic of brain injuries in this country. Whatever. It works for me. I could be home in fifteen minutes in this thing. Oh, shit. This isn't going to work. I was so close. Not for anybody over five feet tall and I'm six. Well, that just sucks. Wait. What the fuck am I *saying?* It's the zombie apocalypse outside and I'm concerned about manufacturer's guidelines? Fuck that. I can squeeze in."

She went around the corner and selected a large wagon. She hobbled over to the go-cart, secured the wagon to the tow bar thingy and placed the water guns and balloons in it. "Not my purse. That stays with me, always," she said as she placed the bag of *GROOMING* in the wagon. She wedged herself behind the wheel of the go-cart and turned the key. "Fuck!" She yelled out in frustration. "Well, *of course* it isn't charged! Goddammit! Where's the outlet? I guess I got three hours to kill. Or three hours to *kill*, heh, heh, heh. Naw, my ankle's too fucked up. Better just kick back, watch an animated DVD, and eat some candy. I need a break anyway. This day has been so fucked."

Three hours later, Payekha's scrunched frame was zooming back across the pedestrian mall towards the perfume shop. "I've got the guns, now for the ammunition. All of it. I'll just head home and hole up with dipfuck Chad until this shit blows over. If any zombies try to get in, they'll get blasted with *GROOMING*. Oh, shit. They'd better not get in the house. I just put new carpets in. That would suck. Oh, fuck it. I'll make Chad clean it up. Then, once this is over, I'll give Chad the ol' heave-ho, find another sexual diversion, find another job, eat some fuckin' pizza, and everything will be fine. Yep, no problemo. I just need to ride it out. And I got just the ride for it. Fuck, I look cool on this thing."

Chapter 6

Breaking Up Is
Not Hard To Do

Payekha's mind shut out the burning, chaotic world around her as she loaded her wagon with *GROOMING* and filled several water guns with the heinous liquid. "Just like when I was a kid," she said to herself as she ripped open another package containing a bright yellow water pistol. "Just focus on the task at hand, Payekha. Tune everything else out. The screaming. The fires. The, um, blood and vomit everywhere. Your throbbing ankle. Tune it out and focus just like when you were trapped in that hellhole. I don't know how I did it, but I was able to just block everything out. The beatings. The rapes. The pain. I just became numb to it all. It was like I was watching a horrific movie or something. I transported myself to another place while it was happening. A happier place taken from whatever book I was reading at the time. Those disgusting white-trash bastards would be whipping me or inserting something painful into me and all the while I was a valiant knight riding my muscular steed through a lush field.

"Every time I looked up at those portraits of Jesus that they had hanging from their filthy walls, I was the captain of a spaceship or a pirate or a gunfighter. Their sweat would drip off of their golden cross necklaces and onto my face and in my mind, I was experiencing a warm shower of rain in a grove of wildflowers. Huh, now that I think about it, *everybody* who raped me in that house of horrors wore crosses around their necks. Everybody that 'mommy' and 'daddy' shared me with proclaimed to be devout Christians. Hell, I could hear them from my dungeon in the basement reading Bible verses while I wiped their cum off of me. Yeah, show me a self-proclaimed 'man or woman of God' and I'll show you a twisted fuck. I guess if you bang the Bible hard enough it makes you want to bang other shit as well. Hasn't anybody ever noticed that the vast majority of pedophiles wrap themselves in the Bible or some other religious text? It's not drag queens reading to the kids that is a threat. It's the pious motherfuckers sitting in the pews or preaching from the pulpit who are *actually fucking kids* that should be of concern, don'tcha think? What is it about the supposed 'word of God' that makes these perverted assholes want to fuck kids? And beat them. And torture them. Well, if that's what the 'word of God' does to you, then I'll take a pass, thank you very much.

"Indoctrination of the masses. That's all that bullshit is. Keep the sheep frightened of the old man in the sky. Keep them singing his praises and filling his coffers, of course. And, I guess, as long as you do that you get blissful eternal life with your savior. Doesn't seem to matter what deviant bullshit you do here on Earth. Rape, steal, murder. Doesn't matter. Just revere God and you get a golden fucking ticket to a blessed afterlife. If *that's* true, then I guess God is the most self-absorbed, narcissistic, needy motherfucker in the universe. I mean, you're fucking God! Creator of the universe and all the shit in it! You're omnipotent and all-powerful and all *that* shit! But your fragile little ego needs constant reverence from us piss-ants? Really? Then that would make God an insecure little prick, no different than…than…

"Huh. I think I just figured this shit out. All of my expertise in psychological mind control and I've just now put the pieces together. These right-wing fucks have the *exact same vision* of their God as they do Dear Leader. *He* is their God here on Earth! God needs constant praise. Dear Leader needs constant praise. God cons you into thinking you're going to get a better life. Dear Leader cons you into believing that. God takes your money. Dear Leader takes your money.

God is okay with you raping children. Dear Leader is fucking enthusiastic about it. Bonus point to Dear Leader over God on that one. God wants to own your soul. Dear Leader wants to own your soul. Then devour it. And these pathetic bastards don't understand that it's all empty promises. It's all a con to put themselves in positions of power. The oppression and beatings and incarcerations and deportations and rapes. It's all about power. And its power that they believe they are entitled to.

"Just like those fuck-wads who tortured me for so many years. They felt that they were *entitled* to their power over me. In their demented minds, they were shielded from any judgement because they sang their praises of their insecure God. They didn't get off on the sex. They got off on the feelings of power. They got off on watching me grovel and plead to them. Just like Dear Leader. He gets off on making people suffer, then plead for his divine fucking intervention to make the pain go away. He and he alone is their savior. And he gets off on it. He probably cums buckets every time he watches some crying child being ripped away from her family. He probably jizzes all over the wall every time he watches his Regal Guard beating an innocent person. And we already *know* he explodes all over the face of some crying child after he has dominated and raped her. Says so right on this fucking bottle. *GROOMING* indeed, motherfucker. You've done to this country what you did to those children. You've groomed this entire country to be subservient to you. And now, your country, or at least these few blocks of it, are in total fucking chaos. Nice fucking job there, Ace.

"Yeah, this *has* to be a virus. Has to be. And since there aren't any actual scientists left in the regime, it's gonna be a nasty fucking ride for this country. It'll spread like wildfire. Yep, scientific research and vaccines and shit were eighty-sixed a long time ago. Maybe getting fired today isn't so bad after all. I just need to ride the fuck out of here, get home, and hole up with dipshit Chad until this thing blows over. I have enough money saved up to ride this thing out. I'll have some food delivery service leave my shit at the door, settle in, and catch up on all the movies and music that I've been unable to get to. Yeah, this might be kinda fun. Put on a record, pour a nice cocktail, and enjoy my life while the sheep are killing each other in the streets. And should any of them try to get into my cocoon of tranquility? Well, that's why for the first time in my life I'm open to *GROOMING*."

Payekha was startled by the sound of heavy footsteps on broken glass. She wheeled around to find a white-eyed, drooling person lunging towards her. "Ah, fuck," she said as she pointed the small yellow squirt gun in the intruder's direction. "Well, sorry about this, but I'm about to make you bulimic as fuck." She pulled the white plastic trigger. A feeble trickle of GROOMING came out of the gun's impotent barrel and landed at the zombie's feet. "Well, shit. That's it?" Payekha exclaimed. "And they wanted $14.99 for this piece of shit? Better bring out the big guns."

She reached into her wagon and pulled out a super-duper water cannon and turned back around to face the zombie. "Or not," she chuckled to herself as she watched the confused zombie sniff at the air then immediately begin to retch. "Damn, this shit's powerful. What in the hell did he put in this? Fecal matter from his adult diaper, ball sweat, and cum-matted pubes?" She laughed aloud as she watched the zombie's internal organs being purged out of its gaping mouth. "Yep, maybe so. Only thing he ever did right. Okay, I'm loaded. Time to get my Black ass home, deal with Chad, then get *really* fucking loaded. I'm sure *he* hasn't contracted this shit yet. Hell, I doubt he's even left the couch. He may not be much, but at least he won't be infected and try to kill me. Plus, his years of gaming might actually be of some use. Yep, real life zombie shoot-em-up."

Payekha's jaw was agape as she zoomed around the city streets in her child-sized red go-cart. Her throbbing ankle was elevated on the toy vehicle's hood next to her severed leg crutch while a loaded super-duper water cannon rested to her other side at the ready. Everywhere she looked, she saw enraged, white-eyed people attacking one another. There were mobs of them engaged in feeding frenzies. "Oh, fucking gross," she said as she rode past several zombies eating a man's pancreas. Or maybe it was a spleen. "Fuck it. Who cares? I never was very good at biology," she muttered to herself as she sped past the outstretched arms of a group of furious accountants. Or maybe they were stockbrokers. Or insurance executives. "Oh, fuck it. Who cares? I never was very good at identifying the occupation of corporate types. They were all just mindless zombies to me. Mindless zombies who sat in their little cubicles all day with pictures of their pasty fucking families in the corner. A cute little drawing that their daughter had done. A picture of their boy in a little league uniform. All smiling and proud while daddy's earning a soulless living sucking money out of the masses, one way or another. They're all just zombies going about their drudgery so that they can go on an occasional weekend fishing trip and get an obligatory blow job once in a while. What a dreadful, meaningless existence. And now, they are *actual* zombies. Poetic justice, I suppose.

"But this isn't," she continued as her heart sank. "This is just fucked up," she stated while navigating the go-cart around a pack of zombies who were eating children who had been on a local field trip. Blood was shooting into the sky as the grown zombies tore the children's heads off and began lapping up the crimson waterfall. Payekha thought about stopping for a moment as she peered into the dying eyes of a small boy. She then gunned the throttle and zoomed past the horrendous scene as she saw the child lose a demented game of tug of war between two groups of zombies. The boy screamed one final time as he was pulled apart, causing his internal organs to splosh onto the cracked pavement. The frenzied horde howled with glee as they immediately began chewing on his tender remains.

"FUUUUUUUCK!" This is soooooo fuuuuucked!" Payekha screamed out as she whisked around exploding cars and tortured squeals. Her mind focused and she began blocking out everything around her. The sounds of shattering glass and explosions. The desperate people running from enraged attackers. More desperate people falling to their deaths after being flung out of their apartment windows. Limbs, heads, intestines, and other organs were bouncing all around her as though she were in the middle of a depraved popcorn maker. And through it all, she focused on one thought. "Just get to home base, Payekha. Yes, Captain Payekha Popoola reporting to duty. I will fly my spacecraft to home base. That is my mission. To just-get-home. Avoid the other spacecraft. Avoid the asteroids. Fly around everything. Ignore everything. Complete your mission, Captain and get your ass home."

She smiled slightly as she turned the corner of a side street and saw the blood-spattered front door of her apartment. She drove over the curb and parked over a consumed corpse. She heard a loud pop as her front tires crushed what remained of the man's skull. She placed her leg crutch on the sticky, red sidewalk and lifted her body. She limped up the short flight of stairs, wiped blood from the door lock, and inserted the key. She breathed a sigh of relief as she hobbled into her orderly living room and saw Chad staring at his phone. Just as she had left him.

"Aw shit, man," she said through a light chuckle. "Are *you* a sight for sore eyes. Have you even moved off of the couch today? Do you even know what's going on outside? Fuck it. Doesn't matter. I'm just glad to see your normal, lazy ass. Come on. Get up. I've got a bunch of shit outside that I need to bring into the house, and I need your help. My ankle's fucked up, and I need to get it iced and elevated. Chad! Are you even listening to me? Come on, man. Now's not the time. Just lift your lazy, slacker ass off the couch for five minutes and give me a hand, alright?"

Chad lifted his greasy haired head and stared at Payekha. "Aw, fuck," Payekha said as she looked into his dead, white eyes. "Alright Chad. Listen. I know this might not be the best time to do this, but we're going to have to break up. We've had a nice run with me paying for everything and you sitting on the couch for three months, but our time together has come to an end. You did have a nice cock, though. I'll give you that. But seeing as how you're probably going to take 'eating me out' really fucking literally, well, I guess I just don't see a future for us."

Chad began getting up off of the well-worn couch while snarling. Payekha began to slowly back towards the front door. "That's right baby. Come and get me. I know you don't wanna let me go. Come on. Keep on coming and give me a big hug and convince me to stay." She opened the front door and hobbled outside while leaning against her leg crutch and clutching her super-duper water cannon. "Yeah, you're really pissed off now, aren't you. Can't say as I blame you. I was a nice piece of ass. Come on. Keep on coming."

Chad lunged at her and Payekha quickly moved to the side and tripped him with her leg crutch. He tumbled down the concrete stairs and landed near the front tires of the parked go-cart. "Alright. Good enough," Payekha said as she lifted the water cannon. "I didn't want to do this inside and have you fuck up my carpet. Sorry, baby. But it's over."

Payekha sprayed her boyfriend with *GROOMING* and watched its effects from the top of the stoop. He clutched at his watering white eyes while his abdomen began convulsing. He bent over and released a torrent of puke. The tannish, chunky substance mixed in with the blood stains on the pavement as Payekha yelled out, "You son of a bitch! What the fuck did I *tell you* about the hot pockets? I told you stay the *fuck away* from the hot pockets! They're *mine*! And now look! Fucking half-digested hot pockets all over my go-cart. I swear, if you weren't already dying, I'd fucking kill you! Oh, yeah, just great. Looks like there isn't any frozen pizza in my future, either. You really are a waste of space. Fuck it. We're drawing attention from the neighbors.

"Hey there Mrs. Robinson! How's that little college boy-toy been treating you? Um, never mind. It looks like he's delicious! You enjoy, now! I'm just getting a few things from my little scooter here! Ah, shit Mrs. Robinson, you *really* don't have to come by to say 'Hi'. I'll have you over for tea or brains or some shit next week, okay? Please, you really don't have to come over here and…ah, fuck it. You've just been *GROOMED* bitch! But don't vomit all over the…fuck! Now, I'm going to have to clean all the bottles of *GROOMING*. Cracker-ass rancid smelling bitch."

Payekha breathed a sigh of relief as she placed the last vomit-coated shopping bag of *GROOMING* in the bathtub. She turned on the water and watched as the remains of corn, green beans and possibly meat loaf circled her drain. "Okay. That shit's cleaned off. I'll put it away later. I need some ice and a fucking nap. I wonder how Mom's doing. Oh, fuck! Mom!"

She limped as quickly as she could to her cordless land line telephone and frantically dialed. "Come on, Mom. Pick up. Please just pick up." She let out a relieved laugh when she heard her beloved mother's voice on the other end of the line. "Yeeessss?" "Oh, thank the lord!" Payekha exclaimed. "Mom! Are you alright?" Her mother answered, "Yeeeesss?" "Okay, good. Listen. I'll be over in a few minutes. Just hold tight. I'll come over then we can bring your monster SUV over here. We'll run these motherfuckers over in the street if we have to. And we'll just hole up here until this thing blows over, okay?" "Yeeeesss?" came her mother's response. "Alright, cool. I'll be there in five. Oh, and if you have any hot pockets or frozen pizzas, pack them up. Shit for brains ate all of mine.

"Oh shit, oh shit, good. This is good news. My Mom's okay and not only that, but we now know that this isn't a mind-control algorithm being spread by the cellular networks. Can't be. Has to be biological. Not sure why me and Mom haven't caught it. Maybe some natural immunity our family has or something. But it can't be the cell phones. If it were, Mom would have been one of the first ones infected. That bitch is addicted to that shit as much as anybody. Alright, do I have everything? Leg crutch? Check. Two water cannons loaded with *GROOMING*? Check. Keys to the go-cart? Check. Purse? Check. Alrightythen. Hold on Momma. Captain Payekha Popoola is comin' to getcha."

CHAPTER 7

STOLEN INNOCENCE

While zipping through the bloody chaos of the city streets on her way to her mother's house, Payekha's mind drifted back to a similar journey nineteen years earlier. Nineteen years had passed since she watched the final painful exhalations of her tormentors. Nineteen years since she allowed herself to smile again as she looked upon their sliced, deceased bodies. Her smile turned into a childish giggle. Then raucous laughter as she licked their congealing blood from the blade of her knife. Her laughing continued as she took off her blood-soaked dress and entered the shower.

Streaming beads of hot water washed away the blood. But no amount of scrubbing of her healed ebony skin could rid her mind of the horrific abuse that she had been forced to endure for eight torturous years. Despite her ability to mentally escape into her books, she knew all too well what had happened to her. Despite her welts having healed, she could still feel the harsh sting of the belts. And the whips. And the canes. She could still feel the sweat of her tormentors dripping down upon her pleading face as they forced objects into her. She could still hear their laughter as tears flowed down her scarred cheeks. She could still feel the rage in her heart. Their murder had provided only momentary relief. There were others who had abused her as well. Others in this pedophile ring that had been invited over to her dungeon. Others who had beaten her and raped her and spit in her face as they performed unspeakable acts upon her tender flesh. There were others. And she knew how to find them.

Payekha's thirteen-year-old body emerged from the shower. She toweled off and went into her "mommy's" closet. She selected several articles of clothing and shoved them into a duffle bag. She found "daddy's" secret stash of money that he had collected from the four other members of this particular regime-sanctioned pedophile ring. "Daddy" hunted, abducted, and delivered the girls. The others paid handsomely for his sadistic services. She gazed in wonderment at the tens of thousands of dollars that were rolled up neatly before placing them in the duffle. In the bottom of the cash drawer there was a little black book. She opened it and smiled at the four names and addresses that the book contained. She sauntered through the house past the stiffening corpses of her violent oppressors then paused. "Oh yeah, I'm gonna need this," she said to herself as she placed the bloody knife into the duffle.

She went to the garage and found an old green bicycle with a fraying basket. She looked at the first address in the black book, placed the overstuffed duffle into the basket, and began pedaling. She had just learned how to ride her bicycle before she had been abducted. Her real mother had just removed her training wheels and Payekha was practicing by riding up and down her driveway. Back and forth she would ride as the wind caressed her delighted face. Back and forth as she watched her mother hanging laundry on a clothesline in the back yard. Back and forth as she eagerly awaited the return of her beloved father from work. It was pasta night. Payekha loved pasta. And salad. And garlic bread. She loved pasta night. She loved her family. She loved her new bicycle. She loved the freedom she felt as she navigated back and forth on the driveway of her loving family home. Payekha's mother called for her daughter to come in. Her father would be home soon, and she was to help set the table. Her mother rounded the house while calling her name. Her mother gasped as she found her daughter's upset bicycle lying on the ground. The tires were still spinning. But Payekha was nowhere in sight.

The barely adolescent Payekha scanned the street signs as she furiously pedaled the tarnished, green bicycle. The pedals squeaked and the chain clunked as she rode. Vague familiarities began to sweep into her consciousness as she pedaled past the local landmarks. The grocery store where her father would allow her to pick out a candy bar and soda. The ice cream shop where she and her family would enjoy chocolate cones. The town park where she played with her friends on the swings and slides under the watchful eyes of her loving family. Her hometown's geography was coming into focus through the haze of years of abuse. Payekha made a sharp right turn down a residential street. She checked the address one last time and leaned the bicycle against the parked Sherriff's cruiser. She remembered his bright gold badge that would shine as he was taking off his uniform. This symbol of protection and justice he had bastardized into a symbol of cruelty and oppression. She remembered his big, black boots. She remembered the stench of his feet as he removed his socks. But the thing that she remembered most about him was his nightstick.

She went to the back door and peered in. She saw his wife sitting at the kitchen table with her back to her. His disgusting wife who would lead the prayer group after she had been violated by her husband. Payekha quietly opened the door, entered the kitchen, and stood behind her prey. She smiled once again as she used her butcher knife to slice through the unsuspecting woman's throat. And her gold chain that held a single gold cross. "Remember *me*, bitch?" Payekha said softly as the wife desperately grasped her throat. Blood poured over her hands. Her frantic eyes widened. And her head slammed on the round, wooden table.

Payekha picked up the sticky red cross that was lying in a pool of the woman's blood, kissed it, and placed it into the pocket of her over-sized jeans. She gingerly entered the living room and found the half-drunk sheriff lounging in his recliner. A football announcer's voice was blaring out of the television set as she stealthily approached. Her smile widened when she saw the sheriff's belt hanging near the front door. She retrieved the nightstick from the belt, approached the sheriff from behind, and began bashing his skull. Payekha repeatedly struck the sheriff with all her strength until his skull cracked open. Shards of bone, blood, and brain matter sprayed the living room as Payekha continued her merciless onslaught until she was out of breath.

She dropped the nightstick and left bloody shoeprints as she ascended the stairs to the bedrooms. She entered the bedroom on the left and found the sheriff's uniform hanging in the closet. She pulled the badge from the shirt's breast leaving her bloody, smudged finger-prints upon it. She wickedly grinned as she pinned it on her baggy, black T-shirt. She then heard whimpering coming from the adjacent room. She opened the door and her eyes strained to see inside the pitch-black nothingness. She groped around to find the light switch. There was a light 'click' and the room was awash with morbid imagery.

Shackled to the wall was a young, emaciated girl. Her breath was shallow as she looked at Payekha with hollow eyes. Payekha fought back her tears as she frantically searched for the keys to the girl's chains. She grabbed the sheriff's key ring and tried every key in the lock. Finally, the lock clicked open, and the young girl collapsed into Payekha's arms. "Okay, okay," a nearly hyperventilating Payekha said. "It's going to be okay. They're dead, okay? Those motherfuckers are dead and you're safe. Just, just stay here until I get back, okay? Get some food in the kitchen and just stay up here. I'll be back for you. I promise. But we can't call the authorities. *Everybody* in this fucking pedophile ring is an authority. They *all* work for The Regime. I've heard them talk about it. But I'm going to take care of them and free anybody else that they may have locked up. Then, we'll all get to safety, okay?"

Payekha ran down the stairs and approached the kitchen exit. She stopped when she saw the door that led to the basement. She began shivering with dread as she opened the door and turned on the over-head, single light bulb. At first, all she could see was vague shadows. Darkened blobs that were cast upon the stone walls. She cautiously approached one and touched it. Payekha shrieked when she realized that it was the corpse of a young boy. She held her mouth with horrified astonishment as she looked at the stacks of dead children leaning against the moist concrete walls. "Jesus fucking Christ!" she yelled out. "They don't just abuse us! They *murder* us! And leave us down here to rot! I've got to get the hell out of here! Now!"

Payekha returned three hours later. Returning with her was a five-year-old Hispanic boy, a twelve-year-old Black girl, and a fifteen-year-old blonde. All of them, including the decaying children in the basement, had been abducted by her "daddy" over the years and delivered to the pedophile ring. All had been tortured and abused and beaten and raped. All had the cuts, bruises, and welts to prove it. All were a shattered shell of their former, innocent shelves. And every one of them had just danced with delight in the blood of their deceased tormentors.

The Catholic priest whose eyes had been stabbed out by his golden letter opener. It had been a gift from the Cardinal for his "Godly Deeds Upon This Earth". The District Attorney whose face had been crushed in by the weight of a law book. Payekha had repeatedly slammed the book into him so hard, that he now looked like a macabre pool of slimy putty. And finally, the local land developer. He had bankrolled the entire operation and paid off any local authorities who came too close to their nefarious secrets. For years, he had led and masterminded this cruel abomination upon humanity. He was now laying in a thick puddle of his own intestines with a shocked expression upon his pudgy face. His severed penis was sticking out of his purple, swollen lips. Everyone in the black book had been disposed of by a fit of Payekha's rage and sense of justice. Every one of their living captives were now free. And each one of these innocent survivors now poured themselves into the sheriff's cruiser for one final journey.

"Here, give me the keys," the fifteen-year-old girl said wearily. "I know how to drive. Kinda." Each child flinched as they placed their beaten and raw behinds upon the seats' fabric. "I'm never going to cry again," Payekha muttered to herself as the cruiser pulled into her family's driveway. Lying next to the driveway in a thick patch of unmown grass and weeds was a rusted bicycle. It remained exactly where it had fallen when Payekha had been violently grabbed off of it and thrown into a black van eight years prior. She had been knocked unconscious and driven away, and from that moment on, her innocence was gone forever. Her lost innocence that was now memorialized by an unmovable bicycle with a metal frame that, although now rusted, tarnished, and beaten by the elements, remained steadfast.

Payekha left a red streak of fresh blood across the car's seat as she cautiously exited. Her mind was whirling with conflicted emotions as she climbed the weathered stairs of her front porch. She meekly knocked on the door and waited while refusing to allow her tears the release that they craved. A thirty-nine-year-old Black woman answered the door. She appeared twenty years older than her actual age and was wearing a drab, flowered house dress. The flowers on the dress had been faded for many years.

"Yeeeeessss?" the woman asked. Payekha stared into the eyes of her mother. Her mother's eyes, which she had remembered to be sparkling and full of joy, were now dull and lifeless. "Um, Um, M-M-M-Mom?" The woman's eyes suddenly contained a spark and her expression changed to elated relief. "Oh, my dear lord," she said as she stared into the familiar eyes of her daughter. "Oh, my dear lord, my Payekha has returned home!" The pair embraced on the tattered front porch as migrating geese honked overhead. They embraced as the children in the car looked on and wept. There was not a dry eye amongst any of them. Including Payekha's. They embraced out of joy for their reunion. They embraced to try to retrieve the eight long lost years. They embraced to try to absorb one another's pain. They embraced out of pure love for one another.

And they cried. Payekha, her mother, and each child released a torrent of tears as they sat in the mother's shabby living room and exchanged their horrific stories. They cried when Payekha revealed everything that had been done to her. They cried when the five-year-old boy tried to explain the pain that he had experienced through his rudimentary language and lisp. They cried as the eight-year-old girl spoke about being beaten and raped and starved nearly to death by the sheriff and his vile wife. They cried when the twelve-year-old Black girl spoke about being forced to dig graves in the sheriff's basement and bury the bodies of many other victims of this macabre group. Some of them were still alive as she shoveled dirt over their choking mouths. They cried as the fifteen-year-old spoke about her abduction and unthinkable abuse following cheer practice at her high school. They cried about the unspeakable inhumanity that they had each been subjected to.

Payekha continued to cry as her mother told her about everything that she and her father had done to try to find her. How they were dismissed and turned away by local authorities. How their beloved daughter was called a (derogatory term omitted) bitch by the state authorities. How the federal authorities threatened them with deportation, even though they were naturalized citizens. Many of these so-called officials of justice, all of them White men, seemed to take delight in the suffering of this beleaguered Black family. They cried as they realized that the authorities of this nation no longer stood for humanity and justice. They were now being ruled by the inhumane. The dastardly. The cruel.

Payekha's mother talked about how they never gave up hope. That her father remained resolute and hung fliers everywhere he could for years. He did his own investigative work which led him to a certain land developer. It was three years ago when Payekha's father had his resolve beaten and hung out of him. Payekha's mother spoke about how her husband's battered and bloody body was hanging from a tree with Payekha's flyers stapled all over it. It was a warning to anyone who asked too many questions of the local regime. Her beloved husband's life was taken from him because of the love he had for his daughter. And Payekha's mother retreated into a forced silent melancholy. Until today.

The mother giggled with joy as her daughter, and the other children, regaled her with the stories of the brutal murders that had been committed just a few hours earlier. She cackled while Payekha re-enacted what she had done to her "mommy" and "daddy". And the priest. And the district attorney. And the sheriff. And the land developer. They all voraciously ate home-made brownies, ham sandwiches, and coleslaw as Payekha spoke about slithery entrails, crushed skulls, slashed penises, and obliterated faces. And their smiles broadened as Payekha opened her duffle bag and showed her mother tens of thousands of dollars of untraceable currency.

The sheriff's cruiser was driven to a pond and submerged before the mother and five children poured into her dented minivan. Police sirens wailed in the distance indicating that the bodies had been discovered. But no one would look too hard for Payekha. She no longer existed, after all. And what was discovered in the dank basements and grimy attics of the murder homes would need to be buried. Forever. It was for the best that no one find who was responsible for this grisly retribution.

Payekha and her mother had several bags of clothes, a map, a cooler full of sandwiches and sodas, and determination. They were determined to find a sanctuary where they could live their lives free from the constant oversight of the minions of Dear Leader. They would drop each of the children off safely at their respective homes, and Payekha and her mother would journey until they found their Eden.

And they did. Tucked into a residential neighborhood in a large city they found a house. A wonderful house that they paid for with the blood money of inhumanity. Their welcoming neighbors worked tirelessly alongside them as they fixed up their home. They both found jobs within the tight-knit neighborhood and toiled in the community gardens. And they participated in their community's crime patrol network. Every member of this protective neighborhood was determined to keep crime out of their community. The treacherous crime and corruption that was brought on by the federal thugs of Dear Leader. There were many masked men that were hung at the entrance of this gated community as a warning. Payekha was personally responsible for several of them over the years.

Payekha homeschooled until she went to university with an emphasis on the effects of propaganda on the human psyche. Despite her gender and race, her brilliance left the school with no legal choice but to allow her to enroll. Payekha studied, and laughed, and played games, and thrived under the constant, protective eyes of her mother.

It was those eyes that Payekha yearned to see as she sprayed a zombie with a dose of *GROOMING* as she approached her second childhood home. She pounded at the door and yelled out, "Mom! Are you in there?" "Yeeeeessss?" Payekha's mother answered. "Okay, I'm coming in, okay?" "Yeeeeeesssss?" was her mother's response as she opened the brightly colored front door of her mother's home.

Chapter 8

Mom! I'm Home!

Payekha rushed through the front door, slammed it shut, and locked it. She leaned against the door, wiped her brow, and exhaled deeply. "Jesus, Mom. Why in the hell isn't your door locked? Do you have any idea what's happening out there?" Payekha said to the back of her mother's head on the nearby floral couch. "I don't know exactly what's happening, but it's really fucked up. Some sort of virus. It must be. It's a good thing you've turned anti-social in your old age. Well, I mean, fifty-eight isn't necessarily *old*, but it's kinda closer to the end than the beginning, right? Okay, nevermind. Not important. It's just good that you're avoiding actual contact with other people right now. I never thought I'd say this, but maybe just communicating and connecting with people on those stupid fucking phones might be the safest bet at the moment.

"But we still have our bodies that we need to keep protected and I really think that my place is the most secure place to be. I have a security system complete with alarms and cameras. Plus, that's where my stockpile of *GROOMING* is, so we need to get back there. I know. That sounds really fucking creepy. Don't ask. I'll explain later. I have everything we need. Except for hot pockets. Dickhead Chad ate all of those. But other than that, we should have enough supplies to ride this thing out. So, just jump up and get a bag ready, okay? We need to get going. And I really need to put my fucking ankle up. It hurts like a sonofabitch. Mom! Get up and let's get going! Are you listening to me?"

"Yeeeeesss?" her mother responded as Payekha walked to the front of the couch. She looked down at her mother and said, "Seriously, Mom. Put the fuckin' phone down. I know you're addicted to your stupid fuckin' videos and watching people argue over stupid shit and playing your games but now is not the time. Just put it away and let's get going, okay?"

"Yeeeeessss?" her mother said again as she lifted her head to look at her frustrated daughter. Frustration turned to hopeless remorse as Payekha stared into the milky white eyes of her mother. "Oh fuck, Mom. No. Please. No. Not you too. Please, God. Not my mother." Her grieving was interrupted by her mother's low growl. Drool began dripping from her mother's mouth and an evil smile was on her face as she once again said "Yeeeessss?" Her mother then abruptly stood up and lunged at her daughter.

"Oh shit!" Payekha yelled out as she put her forearm across her mother's throat to protect herself from gnashing teeth. "Goddammit Mom! Stop it! I don't want to hurt you!" she exclaimed as her mother's chomping teeth encroached closer to her daughter's face. Payekha darted to her left and her mother fell face first into the glass coffee table. "Oh shit, Mom, I'm so sorry," Payekha said as she began scanning the room for something to bind her mother with. "I'm just going to tie you up, okay? Yeah, I'll tie you up until there's a cure or something for this shit. There. *That* should work."

Payekha hobbled over to the stereo and ripped the speaker wire from the receiver. "Fuck, that's a shame," she muttered to herself. "I love this stereo." She then felt a deep bite on her left shoulder. "Fuck! Mom! That fucking hurts!" she yelled out as she pulled away from her mother's teeth. Blood flowed down her shoulder as she turned to stare into the dead eyes of her mother. Her mother's pretty, ebony face was covered with shards of glass from the shattered coffee table while blood dripped off her teeth and down her chin. "Yeeeeeessss?" she growled at her daughter before lunging again.

"Okay, Mom, time for some tough love," Payekha said as she swung her severed leg crutch at her mother's temple as hard as could. Her mother staggered backwards before rushing her once again. "Fuck, you're fast!" Payekha exclaimed as she fell under her mother's weight. Her snarling mother bit Payekha's left ear lobe off before Payekha could roll out from under her. The intense pain of her ankle was replaced by the throbbing in her wounded shoulder and ear. She stood up and watched her mother lift herself off of the floor.

"Jesus, Mom," a bewildered Payekha said to her growling mother. "Don't you feel anything? The punch in your head? The glass in your face? Do you not feel anything at all? It's like all of your pain receptors are blocked by your intense rage. And you just won't stop, will you? You'll just keep coming and coming and coming until I'm forced to put you down. Maybe that's what you want. Maybe under all of this anger you're crying out for help. Maybe deep down inside you are wanting to be put out of your misery. Well, I can't do that, Mom. Not yet. Not until we figure out what the fuck is going on. Yeah, come on. Just a little closer," she coaxed as she reached for a vase that was resting on a table behind her. "Come on, Mom. Come get me. Give your daughter a big hug."

Payekha's mother rushed her one more time and Payekha swung the vase. Her mother shrieked as the vase exploded on her face. Payekha tripped her disoriented mother with her crutch, turned her onto her front, and bound her wrists with the speaker wire. Her mother squealed and gnashed her teeth as Payekha then bound her ankles. Payekha stood up and said, "I'm not going to cry. I'm never going to cry again," as she watched her helpless, bound mother thrashing on the floor.

Payekha was momentarily transported back to a time when she was bound in the same way. She had been bound and was helpless and sobbing as her abusers took turns committing despicable acts upon her tender flesh. She had felt that there would be no way out. That there would never again be any relief from the constant pain and degradation. That the insanity would never end. And now, she had bound her mother in the exact same way. Her mother was now as helpless as she had once been. She felt queasy as tears welled in her eyes. She shook her thick afro, straightened her spine and forcefully said, "This shit is different. Don't you dare fucking cry over this. We're doing this to save her, not hurt her. Oh, fuck Mom. You're going to break a tooth if you keep biting like that. Here, chew on this for a while," Payekha said before shoving a red throw pillow into her enraged mother's mouth.

"Oh fuck, I'm bit," Payekha said as she limped toward the bathroom. She looked at herself in the mirror and examined her ear. "Yep, that's what an ear wound looks like. Tons of blood with an actual piece out of it. You can fake the blood, but you can't fake the actual wound. And *this* thing won't just miraculously heal, unlike some *other* supposed ear wounds. Anything for attention, right? Well, I guess my days of wearing earrings are over."

She then examined the deep teeth marks in her shoulder. "Fuck, this looks bad," she lamented as she sat on the corner of the tub and poured peroxide on her lacerated shoulder. Blood ran down her arm and circled the drain as Payekha winced at the stinging solution penetrating the deep gashes. She went to another cabinet, retrieved gauze and bandages, and began the slow process of cleaning and wrapping her wounds.

"I don't know why I'm even bothering with this shit," she mused. "I'm fucked. I've gotta be. You get bit by an infected zombie, then you become one, right? I guess I'll just sit here and watch TV until I transform. I wonder how it will feel. Will it be painful? And what is it that will make me so fucking angry? And want to eat other people? Shit, maybe it'll be better. I mean, to be able to just rip the fuck out of other people without a care in the world. No remorse. No being burdened by a conscience. No guilt. Just rip people's arms off, eat some brains, and have a jolly fucking time. Until one of your kind does it to you.

"But that's kinda life in this country now, isn't it? One of your own kind ripping you apart in one way or another. So many people have been indoctrinated into the cruel message of Dear Leader that they have been transformed. Oh sure, a lot of those bigoted assholes were *already* assholes *before* he came onto the scene. But many of them weren't. Many of them were pretty decent people who just thought he gave them an opportunity at a better life for themselves and their kids. They weren't evil. They were just stupid and got duped by a fucking con-man carnival barker. He yelled into his megaphone, and they all bought a ticket to the show. And once he had them under his tent, he could tell them *anything* and they believed it.

"He and his evil co-conspirators turned decent people into cruel, inhumane pricks. They were *already* hate-filled zombies even *before* this virus. People who once thought kindly of their neighbors now cheered as crying children were ripped from the arms of their parents. They salivated at the sight of LGBTQ people being beaten and rounded up in the streets. They gloated as their *own* rights were being stripped away from them. Right under their noses. Hell, he even told them exactly what he was doing. And they cheered louder. They applauded. They applauded because he now made them free to be their most base form of humanity. Well, not exactly *humanity*. That was stripped from them. They were merely homo-sapiens who could be as cruel to others as they wanted to be without being burdened by guilt or remorse. They were just knuckle-dragging cavemen who could talk. They could terrorize people and know that Dear Leader would pardon them. As long as they terrorized the *right* people. As long as they terrorized the people who resisted Dear Leader's regime. *Those* fine folks were A-OK in his book of tyranny.

"So yeah, this might be a bit more violent and bloody, but only because it's on a much larger scale. This shit's been going on for years. The zombie followers of Dear Leader have been committing atrocities to their fellow citizens, and they didn't feel a fucking thing. They had no remorse because they no longer had any compassion. Any ability to empathize. They just marched in lockstep and followed their orders and laughed as they reported their neighbors for supposed crimes against the regime. They screamed insults at the downtrodden as the regime's masked thugs came to take them away. Then, they all settled down for a nice family dinner and watched a stupid football game or some shit. Without a care in the world. Just like my mom and everybody who has contracted this virus. Thoughtless, brutal fucking violence against your fellow person without any remorse. Shit, man. This country was *already* full of violent zombies. Maybe this was what was needed.

"Maybe what is needed is a complete cleansing of this planet. Get rid of the entire fucking human species. Let nature take over. Let the foliage and trees and bushes grow through the cracks in the sidewalks. Let them cover our buildings and factories and power plants that have belched filth into the sky for decades. Let the animal kingdom breed and thrive and flourish. Just hit reset and start this whole fucking thing over. Maybe it's for the best. Humankind had its shot on this planet. And humankind fucked it up. Royally. We did this to ourselves. Maybe we all should just shut our eyes and let nature determine the fate of our irredeemable souls.

"Or maybe not. There are millions of people who don't deserve this fate. Millions of people who are humane and caring. Millions of people who could right this ship of horrors if given the chance. Or maybe that's fucked up too. Maybe those caring people will just be corrupted by greed and power just like everybody else seems to be. I don't know. It doesn't fucking matter. My time is short anyway. It'll be somebody else's headache to figure out. I'm going to be too busy chowing down on somebody's thigh. Let's see what Dear Leader's State TV is saying. I can kinda guess." Payekha giggled slightly as she adopted the overly pronounced vocal inflections of a perky television broadcaster. "This just in. Dear Leader declares today Liberation Day for the cannibalistically inclined. If you have ever looked at an undesirable and wondered what they would taste like with barbeque sauce, well now you can find out. Dear Leader has granted you the freedom to eat any undesirable that you want. And he has built bonfires throughout the city so that you may cook your chosen, um, *person* conveniently on your street corner. Yes, our glorious and brilliant Dear Leader has once again made all of us card-carrying members of the regime free to persecute the undesirables and clean up the scourge in our neighborhoods. Praise Dear Leader."

Payekha flopped on the couch and elevated her swollen foot on a pile of pillows. She picked the TV remote off the floor that was lying next to her bound, struggling, and growling mother. "Jesus, I'm tired," she said to herself. "What a fucked up day. I wonder how long it'll take before I turn into a zombie? I guess it'll happen when it happens. Hey Mom! Keep it down! I want to hear this shit!" She turned the television on and began laughing hysterically as she began listening to the "news" broadcast that was being delivered by two young, perky, White co-anchors. "Oh, fuck. I wish I had put some money down on this shit. This is just too perfect."

"Good evening, I'm David Dumbjock," "And I'm Sally Submissive and welcome to Dear Leader Tonight. Our top story..." "Excuse me, Sally. I'm the man. I *always* deliver the top story. You deal with apple pie and kittens and dumb shit like that. I don't want to have to tell you again." "Of course, David. I'm sorry. I forgot my place. It won't happen again. Praise Dear Leader."

"Let's see that it doesn't. And yes, praise, Dear Leader. Now, to our top story tonight. Spontaneous celebrations have sprung up all over Capitol City and all over the world. The celebrations are in response to Dear Leader's declaration of freedom from the undesirables. Throughout the world, patriots are lighting revela...um...rev..el... um...rev..a..la..tor..y. Oh. Revelatory. Nailed it. Revelatory fires in the honor of Dear Leader. And these celebrations include delicious neighborhood cookouts of round-up undesirables. So, if you are wondering what that enticing glow is outside your house, please just relax. It's only patriotic celebrations of the grandeur of Dear Leader. And undesirables being eaten. Nothing to be concerned about. However, the Secretary of National Discipline has cautioned that the celebrations are at capacity so you should just stay in your homes and revere Dear Leader with your family tonight. Oh, and speaking of the Secretary of National Discipline, I'm just now receiving a message on a completely unsecure application on my phone. My, I do feel honored! I've never been included in this group chat before. Why, this is going out to members of his most inner circle. His closest friends and family. Oh, and generals. I do feel quite honored.

"Well, he has sent this to me, so he must want me to read his words of wisdom to our entire audience. And here is what the Secretary of National Discipline is wanting me to tell everybody. Stay off of your fucking cell phones! All cellular networks have been corrupted! Anybody who views anything on their cellphone will turn into a zombie! I'll be home around five! And just in case anybody needs it, I'm attaching the nuclear codes for the Western Hemisphere. Don't share this with anyone! It's a secret!

"Oh, that Secretary. Quite the joker. Yes, quite the...um...I can't take my...um...eyes off of the screen. I'm...um.... oh, those images. Images of Dear Leader. His suffering. His patriotism. His sacrifice. And...and...his bloated fucking belly. And his floppy pussy neck. And horrible combover. And that *voice*. That fucking *irritating, screeching voice* saying the most stupid, nonsensical shit, over and over and over. Why, that's not even a sentence! And that's not a word! Everything about him just makes me want to...want to..."

"WHOOOOAAAA!" Payekha exclaimed as she watched David Dumbjock lift his head to reveal his pure white eyes and an enraged face. He began growling and looked over at his blonde co-host. She never lost her pasted on, fake smile, even as David Dumbjock lunged at her and began chewing through her neck. There was screaming that was picked up by the studio microphones as he ripped her head off of her shoulders and began devouring her glossed, smirking lips. Geysers of blood sprayed throughout the studio. The camera swung around to another anchor who said in a quivering voice, "And I'm Jeremy Jerkoff and I'll be back with sports with our top story being Dear Leader's incredible day on the golf course. How many holes in one do you think he got today? Well, if you said 'eighteen' you'd be right. We'll be right back after this short brea..." Jeremy was cut off by David Dumbkock's fist plunging into his mouth and ripping out his slimy tongue.

"Okeedokeethen," an astonished Payekha said as a commercial for *GROOMING* came on. "Well, it seems as though we have good news and bad news here. Good news? It's not a biological virus and I'm not going to turn into a zombie. The bad news? They fucking did it.

Those stupid fucking assholes. They released the toxic messages and algorithms into the cellular systems. Anybody who watches or looks at anything on their cell phone is going to be instantly indoctrinated and turn into an enraged zombie. Oh, and even *more* fucking bad news. Since I'm not turning into a zombie and I happen to be an *expert* on this shit, that means that this *is* my headache to figure out. The entire fate of humanity is in my hands. Or, at least, in my flash drive. Fuck. Where did I put my purse? Mom! Stop chewing on my purse! I need something out of there! Goddammit, I just bought this lipstick. Now it's ruined. Thanks Mom!"

CHAPTER 9

DON'T FUCK WITH DESTINY

Dear Leader sat in the middle of a large, oval, gold-painted conference room table. There was a hush in the room as deep red and orange flames and billowing black smoke could be seen enveloping the city outside of the windows. All of the department secretaries were feverishly reading the reams of reports that were hastily being brought in by aides. Sweat was pouring off of their panicked brows as aides continuously rushed in with more reports of absolute chaos from around the city. And the country. And the world. They were inundated with paper and deep concern.

Dear Leader's wrinkled brow was also sweating. And he was also inundated. He was inundated by piles of fast-food hamburgers, chicken strips, "freedom" fries, and milkshakes. His tortured heart beat rapidly as he unwrapped another salt and grease sandwich and shoved it into his gluttonous mouth. Chunks of "beef", mustard, and ketchup dribbled out of his purple lips, down his triple chin, and onto his golden sports suit. He grunted at his soon-to-be eighteen-year-old "personal assistant" (Well, if three years can be considered "soon-to-be"). The young blonde girl immediately nodded her head with understanding and opened her youthful mouth to speak.

"Attention everyone! Attention! Dear Leader is demanding that our meeting begin. Please proceed with your praise and tributes to our most glorious Dear Leader." The various secretaries' eyes darted at one another before one finally spoke. "Ah yes, it truly is an honor to once again be in the presence of your glory, Dear Leader. And, as a tribute, I have the heart of a three-year-old immigrant boy. I have had it painted gold and placed on this wooden plaque. Do you see what it says? It says 'BEST DEPORTER EVER!' Isn't that nice? Do you like it, Dear Leader? Do you?"

Dear Leader farted and grunted with dismissiveness as he tossed the plaque into the corner. His eyes then gleamed as he picked up a packet of ranch dipping sauce. His wonderment quickly turned to intense frustration as the ranch packet kept slipping through his greasy fingers while trying to open it. He let out a loud whine and his teenage assistant used her brightly painted fingernails to open the slippery packet. Dear Leader squealed with glee and clapped causing grease to fly off of his pudgy little swollen fingers. The secretaries seated closest to him sat with pasted-on smiles while grease droplets pelted their faces. Dear Leader grunted again before plunging a chicken strip into the ranch packet.

"Yes, yes," another secretary began. "It is my highest honor to be in the presence of such greatness. Such strength. Such fortitude. And as my tribute, oh great one, I have brought you this pretty, little twelve-year-old girl. Isn't she just delightful? I know that your current assistant is getting a bit old for you, and I thought I would offer this little one to be her replacement. Is she to your liking, my liege?"

Dear Leader looked at the frightened blue eyes of the little blonde girl, then into the similar eyes of the secretary. He grunted at his current, nearly retired assistant who immediately said, "Um, Dear Leader would like to know who she is. Where did you get her?" The secretary's thin lips curled up in a wicked little smile as he said with pride, "Why, she is my youngest daughter, Dear Leader. She is of my flesh and blood. She is my pride and joy. And she is now yours. Have I pleased you, Dear Leader?"

Dear Leader began cackling and clapping. His grease and condiment covered lips smiled widely as he grunted at the secretary seated to his right and beckoned for the father and daughter to join him. "Y-yes, Dear Leader," the demoted secretary said sorrowfully. "I'll just find another seat." The secretary of the sacrifice took his place directly to the right of Dear Leader. He beamed with pride as he placed his daughter's smooth hand over the groin of Dear Leader. Dear Leader excitedly grunted at his current assistant. "Yes, Dear Leader," she responded in a nearly robotic voice. "Of course I will show her the ropes. And the whips. And the chains. I will train her for you, my lord. Here, little girl. It is really quite simple. Just take your fingers and pull down his zipper. Yes. Just like that. Now, place your hand inside of his pants. Yes. Good. Be careful now. It's a bit, um, slippery in there. Now firmly grasp his penis. I know. It can be difficult to find. Just keep groping around until you find a slight bump. There. Now just move your hand back and forth. Back and forth. Back and..."

The innocent girl drew her hand back off of Dear Leader's sweaty, pungent mushroom and recoiled in disgust. She looked at her father with pleading blue eyes and began crying. Dear Leader exploded into a rage of non-sensical guttural sounds. His bloated face turned beat red as he slapped the secretary's embarrassed face. "I'm, I'm so sorry Dear Leader!" the secretary blurted out. "I'm so sorry to have caused you this indignity. Don't worry. I shall take care of it this instant! And, and I have another! She just turned seventeen, but she is quite youthful looking! Especially if you put her in pretty pink dresses! You may have her! Please allow me to make this up to you!" The secretary reached into his suit coat, pulled out a revolver, pointed it at his whimpering daughter's head, and pulled the trigger.

The girl's brains splattered across the cheap gold trinkets that adorned the walls. Her blood and brain matter dripped off of the grandiose portraits of Dear Leader. There was a second shot, and the secretary's blood and brain matter joined that of his daughter upon the walls of this bastardized room of horrors. The guard placed his revolver back into his shoulder harness, grabbed the two deceased bodies and dragged them out of the room by their stiffening legs. Dear Leader grunted once again, and the department's under-secretary gleefully wiped blood from the seat and took his place at the prestigious table.

"Well, that was quite the pity," another secretary began. "Yes, quite the pity indeed. But I never did trust him, Dear Leader. I knew that he did not have our great nation's best interest at heart. I knew that he did not have *your* best interest at heart. I knew that he would disappoint you. Because he never realized just how glorious you truly are. He never realized that you are divinity upon our earth. As a Christian man of God, I have seen the pious and I have seen the pretenders. And nobody that I have encountered glows with divinity the way that you do, Dear Leader. You are truly a God amongst men. And a God must be given a proper tribute. Like this."

The Secretary of Faithful Submission pulled out his phone and pushed play on a previously recorded video. "Do you see, Dear Leader? Do you see all of the cute little school girls? Why, *anyone* can pay tribute with a single twelve-year-old. *This* is truly a tribute worthy of a God. This is my wife's third-grade class at a local Christian school. She has been grooming them all for this moment, Dear Leader. There are thirty of them. Thirty submissive little girls who are prepared to do your bidding. They are all yours. Just look at their tender little bodies in their little plaid skirts and ties. They are *yours*, Dear Leader. I can have them here tonight, if you wish."

Dear Leader lustfully stared at the small screen. He grabbed his assistant's arm and forced her hand into his pants. She began frantically tugging at his unfortunate growth while he stared on with his lascivious dark eyes and shoved fries into his mouth. After sixteen seconds of thrusts, Dear Leader let out an orgasmic wail and settled back into his chair. "Oh my," his assistant flatly replied. "That was your best one yet, Dear Leader. You truly have the stamina of a God." She returned to her rightful place while wiping Dear Leader's vile seed on the back of her short skirt.

"Listen! I don't mean to be an alarmist, and I mean no disrespect, Dear Leader!" the Secretary of Oppression yelled out. "But just what the fuck are we doing here? The entire city, hell the entire *world* is burning! People are attacking each other for no apparent reason! One minute they're docile, the next they're tearing each other apart! We have piles and piles of reports of extreme violence! It is happening everywhere! And we have no idea why! The Secretary of National Discipline is supposed to be bringing in a report as to the cause, but until he sobers up and we get his report, we have no idea what is causing this! And they have no fear of our troops! They are being overrun and...and...eaten! We don't have enough firepower to kill every fucking person in the country! We have to get to the root cause!"

The Secretary of Pestilence then spoke up in his deep, froggy voice. "I know *exactly* what is happening here, Dear Leader. It's very simple. It's the vaccines. My quack, um, I mean crack team at the National Institute of Anti-Science has concluded that vaccines, especially in combination, can cause autism. And just what are we seeing happen? Is this normal behavior? No, of course not. These are a bunch of people who have become suddenly violently autistic. And it's because of the vaccines. Some of them may have also been turned into drag queens but the science is speculative on that. Oh, to hell with it. The science is sound. Every drag queen or trans person we have brought in and experimented on have one thing in common. They are different races and come from different cultures and socio-economic situations. They are different in every way. But one. Each and every tranny that we have dissected have been vaccinated. All of them. Sure, they never got measles or polio or rubella. But at what cost? To be turned into a violent, autistic drag queen cannibal?"

"Oh, for fuck sakes," the Secretary of Oppression stated while slapping his forehead in frustration. "*This* again? Jesus Christ, man. You think that vaccines are the root of *everything* bad. You get some pseudo-scientist whispering in your ear about some fucking tin-foil hat conspiracy about vaccines and you buy it! Hook, line, and sinker! Listen, I understand what our regime has done all along. I understand the takeover of public education, universities, and museums so that we could indoctrinate the masses into our White Nationalist idolatry of Dear Leader. I understand purposefully bankrupting the farmers and other small businesses so that the oligarchs could swoop in and buy the land and shops for pennies on the dollar. I certainly understand the military on our cities' streets so that people would cower in fear and be submissive to Dear Leader. So that voices of dissent would be drowned out, and elections could be rigged through intimidation.

"And I get taking over all of the news networks and journalistic institutions so that people would only be exposed to the grandeur of Dear Leader. Half of this country was already indoctrinated by basically just one cable news network and a handful of radio programs and podcasts. All we needed was for that same information to be spread on *every* network and platform to indoctrinate most others. And I get rounding up the non-believers and sending them to our re-education camps. Plus, as a bonus, we finally had the labor force for the agriculture oligarchs that we had lost once we got rid of all the non-Whites. And, of course, I *totally* understand forcing the judicial and legislative branches of government into submission so that all of Dear Leader's whims would be enacted without a fight. Or consequence. Hell, I even understand tanking the world's economy so that Dear Leader could immediately reverse his economic policies and look like a hero on the world stage. I get it. I get everything that we've done. And we have succeeded. Or at least, we had. Until now.

"Because the one thing that I will *never* fucking understand is why we put this dipshit, moron, drug addled, conspiracy-theorist motherfucker in charge of this nation's health. There *is* no national health care! There are no scientists researching emerging viruses! Nobody researching cures for diseases! How has that furthered our White Christian Nationalist cause to take over the country, then the world? How does spreading disease and knowingly killing off our own supporters help the regime? And now, we have an *actual* health crisis on our hands! This is probably a *virus* that is causing people to descend into madness! A virus that we could have detected if we had any *actual* scientists around! A virus that could have been prevented or at least cured. And yes! Prevented or cured by fucking *vaccines* that have been proven to work and have eradicated diseases for decades! This is a disaster of our own making! And instead of trying to find solutions, we're sitting around wasting time singing the praises of Dear Leader while the city burns around him!"

An uncomfortable silence fell over the room. Dear Leader took another bite of a greasy cheeseburger, began laughing, and mimicked playing a small violin. There was the 'pop' of a gunshot, and the protests of the Secretary of Oppression were forever silenced.

The meeting room door then burst open. The haggard-looking Secretary of National Discipline staggered into the room holding his cell phone. "So sorry, I'm late," he slurred while attempting to tuck in his stained white shirt. "Oh fuck, you guys. My underlings at the National Institute of Psychiatric Health have fucked up. Here. I'll send you a text. Just read this shit." He leaned against the wall as his bleary eyes tried to focus on his cellular phone. He used his hairy thumbs to feverishly type a message of warning. He did not notice that he was sending the message on an unsecure application. Nor did he notice that he had included a broadcast anchor in the group. But worst of all, he did not think about drawing people's attention to the very instrument of death that he was warning them about. He hit 'SEND' and everybody's cell phones began buzzing. Everybody in the room shivered as they read his foreboding message.

Stay off of your fucking cell phones! All cellular networks have been corrupted! Anybody who views anything on their cellphone will turn into a zombie! I'll be home around five! And just in case anybody needs it, I'm attaching the nuclear codes for the Western Hemisphere. Don't share this with anyone! It's a secret!

Dear Leader grunted with confusion as he watched every person in the room become fixated by their phones. He opened his mouth to reveal stained teeth that were clogged by chewed animal flesh and grunted again. He grunted more emphatically and looked up at his nonattentive assistant. She looked down at him with whitened eyes and began growling. He grunted again and was greeted by his three-dozen white-eyed and drooling sycophants. His deteriorated mind struggled to contemplate the danger he was in. He grunted louder and his cabinet began snarling while rising from their seats. His greasy hand slipped off the arm of the chair as he tried to get up, and he fell back onto his flabby ass. He was then attacked.

Everyone in the room descended upon his saggy flesh. They tore off his ears and blood squirted from both sides of his head. It was the first time that either of his ears had ever been harmed. They gouged out his eyes and popped them into their mouths. They grasped his stinky, slimy, fat torso and began pulling. They pulled and pulled as he screamed in agony. His stretched flesh looked like pulled taffy until it finally gave way and all of his internal organs spilled upon the tacky gold carpet. His cabinet and their staff howled with delight as they chewed upon his flesh. One of the vicious marauders ripped Dear Leader's penis from his body. The zombie looked at the unsubstantial morsel of flesh with a confused look, tossed it aside, and plunged its gnashing teeth into his sagging scrotum. The room was awash with the blood, entrails, bile, and excrement of Dear Leader. This room that had once held some of the most patriotic and brilliant minds in the history of the world was now being ravaged by brainless, hate-filled, gluttonous zombies. Just as Dear Leader had desired.

And within a few moments, Dear Leader was no more. He had wanted to burn it all down and rebuild it in his own image. And he was successful. He burned it all down and humanity was reduced to its most basic, hate-filled, and violent form. There would be no grand military parades to celebrate his accomplishments. There would be no solemn funeral to commemorate his life. His huge banners depicting his intimidating face would be burned to nothingness. His outrageously exaggerated portraits would fall off of every wall and rot. He would never be remembered. He would be an absolute nobody and his time on the earth would be deemed completely insignificant. His lasting legacy would, however, be felt throughout the land. The destruction and extinction of humankind would be felt by every bird that could now fly in clear skies. By every fish who could swim in non-toxic waters. By every majestic beast who could forage without the fear of being shot and beheaded. By every reptile, and fish, and mammal that could now live their lives beyond the reach of the cruelty of man. Yes, his legacy would be felt. The legacy of one cruel man would be felt by every living species on the planet. And absolutely no one would ever acknowledge his unwitting contributions to their miraculous lives on the planet. At best, some might just think, "It's about fucking time. Now hand me that banana."

CHAPTER 10

TRANSITION

"Okay, Mom. Just hold tight. Now that I know what we're dealing with, I think I know what to do. The cellular transmissions are embedded with toxic subliminal messages. Messages that penetrate deep into the limbic system. I know what to do. Change the algorithm. Change the message. Round these zombie motherfuckers up and make them watch it. Maybe put them into camps or...fuck." Payekha chuckled to herself for a moment before continuing. "Yeah, round them up and put them in re-education camps. Jesus fucking Christ. Just like Dear Leader.

"But I'll be indoctrinating people for good, right? I have to try. I'm at least partially responsible for this. I'm the expert on subliminal messaging. I know how to construct messages that penetrate people's subconscious to adapt their behavior. It's why I was the only Black person and one of the few women remaining at the National Institute of Psychiatric Health. They purged pretty much everybody else who wasn't a pasty-faced White dude and replaced us with, um, a bunch of unqualified pasty-faced white dudes. The only qualifications? Be a pasty-faced White dude and have undying loyalty to Dear Leader. That's it. To say they're unqualified is putting it mildly. Hell, a lot of these assholes were barely out of high school. They had no experience and, based on my interactions with most of them, were swimming in the shallow end of the gene pool. Oh, hell, let's just call it what it is. Let's call a spade a spade. I sure as hell have been called one enough times.

"They knew that my skills couldn't be replaced by a fucking moron. And they're a bunch of fucking morons. That's what's so frustrating. A bunch of fucking morons succeeded in tearing down the pillars of democracy and replaced it with their unholy tyranny. The indoctrination had been happening for years. It started with fanatical radio hosts preaching the virtues and supposed trials of the White man while villainizing women and people of color and LGBTQ folks. Day after day, week after week, month after month, and year after year there was the constant drip, drip, drip of hateful messaging. Then, it became amplified by radical television networks. And the amplification and lethality of the messaging increased further as people became addicted to their fucking phones. All of them walking around like zombies drinking the xenophobic kool-aid. The seeds had been planted. All they had to do was find someone to be the fertilizer to feed all of their unwarranted hatred. Someone made of shit who shared their bullshit worldview of a White male dominant society. Someone who would be a champion for their little whiney asses. And Dear Leader was born. He spread his shitty self all over the seeds and the hatred and violence grew like wildflowers."

Payekha's bound mother violently gnashed her teeth at her daughter as Payekha continued. "Yeah, yeah, yeah, I know," Payekha said as she lifted her mother onto a dolly. "I know you get tired of me talking about this shit, mom. You always tell me not to be consumed by the negative. To stop and enjoy the nice breeze. Savor my food. Take time to delight in watching giggling children playing. Don't let this consume you. It will turn you into the very thing that you are fighting against.

"But fuck, Mom! You know, after spending years being beaten and raped, you kinda look at the dark side of life, y'know? Goddamit Mom! Work with me here! I just gotta get you strapped onto the dolly. Jesus, just look at your beautiful face. All twisted with blind rage. I'll get you back to normal, Mom. I can't wait to see your beautiful smile again. Lord knows you tried so hard when I returned home. You tried to expel the demons that those vile bastards had planted inside of me through their cruelty. You tried to give me a normal upbringing in what was remaining of my childhood. Birthday parties. Picnics at the lake. Laughing together. I cherished those moments so much. Still do. But you couldn't be with me all the time. You couldn't provide constant reassurance of my safety. You couldn't hold my demons at bay every moment of every day. Sometimes I was left alone with them. Especially at night.

"Yeah, when I'd fall asleep was when it was the worst. My wonderful dreams of being a princess or some shit would grow darker and then I would once again see their devilish faces. I could hear their demonic laughter. I could feel them putting things in me. I could smell their putrid breath as they sweat on me. I relived that living hell every single night. People don't understand the scars we survivors carry with us. They don't understand that being raped isn't just a violent violation of our bodies. It is a violent violation of our psyches. It is a violent violation of our very souls that we carry with us always.

"And it only became worse when Dear Leader ascended to power. Society had never exactly been supportive of victims. And under *his* brutal rule, abuse of women and children actually became accepted. We were, after all, inferior to the White man, now, weren't we? We were less than human. We were nothing more than playthings for the powerful and were put upon this earth to satisfy their every twisted whim, right?

"It was because of my abuse that I took an interest in human behavior. I needed to understand. What in the fuck could drive somebody to rape *anybody*, especially a *child*? What goes on in the recesses of their minds to think that that's okay? Hell, what the fuck goes on in their minds to even have a *passing thought* about it? To even have a passing thought of taking pleasure from someone else's excruciating pain. Especially a child's. What the fuck is wrong with them?

"So, I studied it. I thought that by understanding it I could maybe relieve myself of some of my own demons. My own thoughts of violent retribution. I had already murdered several people. But that was out of self-defense. I had no other option. I'm not a believer in vigilante justice. I truly am not. But I *am* a believer in *justice*. And there are times when there is a threat that is so great that it poses a danger to your very existence. And there are times when these existential threats are beyond the reach of society's justice systems. For whatever reason, the threats can't be touched. So, when faced with an existential threat that is beyond the reach of the justice system, what are we to do? As I see it, we have two options. Die or defend ourselves. It's as simple as that. It is survival of the fittest. You want to take my life from me? Well, you'd better be a good fucking shot, because you're not going to get a second chance. I repeat, I do *not* believe in vigilante justice. I do, however, believe in justice and our right to defend ourselves against tyranny. There's a big difference. And I'm sure as hell not going to be brought down by some dullard, knuckle-dragging motherfucker. Just like that dude that tried to rape me in college. Yeah, *that* motherfucker picked on the wrong chick. He threw me on the bed and pounced on top of me. I didn't scream. I didn't make a sound.

"I transported myself to a happier place just like I did when I was a sex slave. I went to a place that was filled with brilliant light and color and singing birds and light, cool breezes. A place where I wasn't a victim, but a valiant warrior. In my mind, I wasn't wearing a skirt and T-shirt. In that moment, in my mind I was wearing impenetrable armor. In my mind, I wasn't reaching for a letter opener on his nightstand. I was reaching for my sword. I remember smiling as I plunged my sword into his neck. In my mind, a soggy sapling had just collapsed upon me. I crawled out from under it and looked down at this would-be date rapist who was choking on his own blood. And I knew then where my studies would take me.

"I left that party out a side entrance of the house and went right back to my dorm room. I didn't even bother to change my clothes or shower. I left that boy's blood on my computer as a constant reminder of what I had just learned." Payekha grunted as she wheeled her mother's dolly through the kitchen toward the entrance to the attached garage. She rested her mother's struggling body in front of the refrigerator. "Fuck, my ankle hurts. Let's see what's in the freezer," she said as she opened the freezer door. "Sweet!" she exclaimed. "You must have just went to the store! Look at all the hot pockets! And frozen pizzas! Alright, let's just bag this shit up and…um…hey, Mom. I need your help. I can't push you and carry this shit at the same time. Here, just open your mouth and…yeah! That's it. Just bite down real hard on this bag's handle until we get to the car. No! Dammit Mom! I said bite down! Don't open your mouth again! Shit, now there's hot pockets all over the fuckin' floor. Fuck it. I'll come back for them. Let's get you loaded up."

Payekha navigated her mother's black SUV through the carnage on the city streets. Her screaming mother lay in the back as Payekha slalomed her way past burning cars, grasping zombies, and abandoned military hardware. "Okay, Mom, where were we?" Payekha stated as the front end of the SUV plowed through three jaywalking zombies causing their heads and torsos to explode onto the windshield. "Fuck, Mom. You need new wipers. And would it kill you to get your cleaning fluid filled up? Shit, how many times have I told you? Fuck. I can barely see through these red streaks. Oh, well. We'll be back at my place soon. Anyway, where was I?

"Oh, yeah. I had just killed another person. A person who was about to rape me. Perhaps kill me. He posed an existential threat to my survival. And I knew that he wouldn't be brought to justice, even if I survived to report it. Hell, in this fucked up society, it would probably get him selected to be a member of Dear Leader's cabinet! So, I did what I had to do to survive. I plunged my sword into his throat and left him to die. It was kinda poetic justice. He wanted to kill *me* by penetrating *me* with something. And that shit boomeranged on his ass. He died by having something penetrate *him*. Right through his fucking neck. And I didn't shed one tear for his pathetic ass.

"So, I went back to my dorm room and started going through my research. Everything that I had studied suddenly made sense. My studies and everything that I had experienced began merging in my mind. It was all coming together. The proverbial lightbulb came on, and I felt like the smartest fucking person in the world. I now understood why the oppressors were oppressors. I understood how they could take delight in another person's misery. And it was so simple. It was because they were pure fucking evil. The parts of their brain that allowed for empathy weren't developed. Which made them nothing more than narcissistic cavemen. 'I want eat! Eat now! I want fuck! Fuck now! I want kill! Kill now!' They were nothing but soulless sharks with dead eyes who just swam around eating and fucking anything and everything that they could.

"And it *also* hit me that even those with developed brains could be indoctrinated into twisted, evil shit. These were people who had the ability to empathize, but their fear response overrode any feelings of empathy. Precise messaging designed to stoke their fears could be used to suppress their empathy. Then turn their fear into anger. And their anger into violence. And voila! You have yourself the makings of a new recruit into the regime! He comes complete with brutality and cruelty, so no assembly required!

"So, I realized that because of people's brain structure, some are completely self-absorbed evil motherfuckers who will do anything to satiate their lust or greed or boost their tiny fucking egos. And I realized that *other* people could be indoctrinated into being evil fucks by the right messaging that was repeated over and over and over until they believe anything that they are told by the regime. The blue sky is red. The summer is cold. Vaccines are a threat to humankind. You know, stupid shit like that. And it becomes even *easier* when you take over the educational system so that you can indoctrinate children into the regime while stripping away their ability to process information and critically think.

"So now you have a whole bunch of these motherfuckers running around all indoctrinated and shit. But what of the others? What about the people who are truly empathetic? What about the people who have fully developed brains and are incapable of being indoctrinated into mindless hate? What do we do with *them*? Oh sure, the re-education camps were a start. But they're really fucking expensive. Plus, no matter how much those people were tortured, they never did turn into loyal subjects. They just cowered. Or died. Plus, there were so many of them! And many were smart enough to be able to assimilate into the culture without being detected. So, how to make them loyal, thoughtless subjects as well? Well, there was one thing that all of these people had in common. Yes, no matter how intelligent or emotionally evolved their brains were, they all had become addicted to one thing. Fucking cell phones."

Payekha turned the corner onto her street and roared onto the sidewalk. She heard a loud POP as she stopped abruptly on the sidewalk in front of her brownstone apartment. "Fuck, what was that?" she said as she opened the door and looked under her front driver's side tire. "Oh, shit, sorry Mister Peterman," she said as she looked at the crushed skull of her neighbor. "Fuck, that popped your eyes right out. Oh, well. Serves you right. I got really fucking tired of having to make sure all of my curtains were closed you old fucking perv. Okay, Mom. Let's get you in the house. But before I unload you, I gotta take care of this herd of zombies that have noticed us. Just give me a minute, Mom. I've got some *GROOMING* to do."

Payekha pulled her mother up the steps to her apartment, unlocked the door, and entered. She wheeled her snarling, drooling mother into the center of the living room and turned on the television set. "Here. Just watch this," she said as she began flipping through the channels. "Fuck. Everything's static. Well, not this one. This channel has an old zombie movie on. Oh, wait. That's the evening news. Okay, never mind. You're just gonna have to be stuck listening to me for a bit longer. Now, where was I?

"Oh yeah. People addicted to their fucking cell phones. And that's where my final epiphone from that evening came in. The final thing that I realized was that, although we are all susceptible to herd mentalities, we are herds made up of individuals. And yes, we are products of our nature. Our brains have developed in a way that is uniquely ours. Some people are good at math; some suck at it. This kid over here can play Gershwin on the piano at the age of five while this other kid couldn't play 'Chopsticks' after thirty years of lessons.

And some people are naturally kind while others are naturally cruel. Like Dear Leader. And his true believers. We are all unique in our brain development.

"Which makes our reaction to how we are *nurtured* unique as well. Nature is only half the equation. We are also impacted by external stimuli. It is both nature *and* nurture that determines our actions. The sounds that we hear. One person can hear a song and think it's the greatest thing ever, while someone else can't turn it off fast enough. The images that we see. One person can be delighted at the sights of a horror movie while another person is repulsed by those very same images. The tastes on our tongue. One person loves ketchup on hot dogs and another person, who would be absolutely correct, prefers mustard. And on and on. Our talents, our ideologies, our reaction to world events are determined by both our brain development *and* every experience that we have had leading up to the current situation. And every time we react, our behaviors get increasingly hard-wired. Here, Mom. Chew on this pillow for a minute. I need to get my computer out.

"For each of us, our brain development is unique and our reaction to external stimuli is equally unique. We are all islands of one surrounded by an ocean of confusion. But we are all islands of one living amongst other people. And our true drive, beyond eating and sleeping and fucking, is to have our uniqueness accepted by others. Yes, it's ironic, but we are all islands of one who are yearning for our uniqueness to be embraced by others. And not out of narcissism, but out of survival. In order to survive, we must depend upon other people. And in order to be supported by other people, we must be accepted by other people. We're all unique and we all know that we're kinda fucked up in one way or another. So, we hide our fuckedupishness as best we can so that we can be accepted and supported by the tribe. This is why like-minded people gravitate toward one another. It is why the truly evil amongst us cower in their closets of bigotry when society frowns upon their beliefs. It is why basically good people are nodding and smiling along right now while under the yoke of oppression. It is out of survival. And it is why people became addicted to those fucking cell phones. It was out of their drive for continuous approval from their tribe."

Payekha retrieved her flash drive from her purse and placed it into her computer as her bound mother wailed in the background. "And the evil ones know that pursuits of greed, lust, and power can be used to deceive people away from our more altruistic callings. They understood people's natural instinct to be accepted, and they understood that they could use humankind's most basic instincts to control them. And eureka! Propaganda was born!

"As you know, Mom, I graduated from university with honors. I was really lucky. I graduated just a year before the Great Academic Purge which greatly restricted anybody that wasn't a White male from attending university. I'm sure I wouldn't have been allowed in today. No dick and waaaay too fuckin' Black. So, I understood how our brain development and our reaction to external stimuli impacted our actions. And I understood how each individual was driven to be accepted by the larger herd. And I understood how precise messaging could impact different portions of the brain, especially the limbic system. And it was for that reason that I joined the National Institute for Psychiatric Health.

Payekha's eyes darted over the reams of numbers that had been downloaded off of her flash drive. "I was interested in using my own ability of being able to disassociate to help other survivors' healing process. I wanted to bottle it up somehow and share it. Was it possible to develop an algorithm that contained subliminal stimuli that could allow the victim of abuse to disassociate from their trauma while continuing to interact with the real world? Could I develop messaging that allowed them to be stripped of their fear so that they would have the fortitude to fight back against future attackers? Could I plant something in their brains that would be triggered when their flight or fight response became activated? That would allow them to shed the skin of helpless victim and emerge as a powerful warrior who could beat back anyone who sought them harm? Could I give them my gift of disassociation and strength? Could I do that systemically so that it would not matter what their brain development was or their natural response to external stimuli? The effect would be the same with everyone. Could I create a subliminal message that could swim across each of their individual oceans and reach every island of one?"

Payekha smiled as she looked down at the bloody, rust-colored fingerprints that she had left on her laptop's keyboard over ten years ago. Her smile broadened as she looked at the final analysis of her data. "The answer, Mom, is yes. It *is* possible. All of the data checks out. But it's never been used on a human subject. Everything is ready to go. I have the videos where I have buried the subliminal imagery and messages. I have them set to the exact correct frequencies needed to penetrate the viewer's limbic system. Hell, I even have the algorithms that could be used to distribute it throughout the world using cellular systems. But it's never been tested. I went to my superiors at the Institute and told them of my findings. And that's where I fucked up.

"Why in the fuck did I think I could trust them? I told Dawson and Hugo about my project and within two hours my request for a human trial was denied. But what *was* green-lit was a *new* project. A project to create an algorithm which would attach itself to every piece of information that was carried and viewed over the cell phone networks. A project to create subliminal messages of Dear Leader which would penetrate the limbic system. But, instead of reducing fear and promoting strength, this new messaging would do the opposite. It would *increase* the fear people had toward Dear Leader and the regime and make people subservient to him. And not just here. Throughout the entire world. My discovery would be used to dominate every person in every nation in the world.

"It turned my stomach when I figured out what they were wanting to use my work for. What I had created to try to help victims of abuse would be bastardized into a weapon. It would be used to create more victims of oppression throughout the world. I thought about quitting. I was the only expert in this, and those dumbass frat boys would never be able to figure it out. But I thought I might become a target for re-education. Plus, as an expert, I knew how to manipulate the data so that their desired result would never be achieved. The last grouping of algorithms and subliminal messages that I provided would have the effect of turning normal people into raging homicidal maniacs. I thought that *that* might frighten them and get them to abandon the project altogether. I thought they would think that mind control was just too dangerous, and I could go back to my tiny office and quietly continue my real work. I knew they would run the numbers. That should have been enough to dissuade them. I never thought they might actually test this shit on real people. But then again, who the fuck am I kidding? We're nothing but walking mind control experiments for these twisted fucks.

"But I was absolutely *sure* that they wouldn't be stupid enough to unleash this dangerous shit on the world. But again, we're not exactly dealing with the cream at the top, now, are we? More like the spoiled sludge in the bottom of the cup. After it's been left out in the sun. And now it's all gross and smelly and…fuck. I'm getting hungry. I need a hot pocket. And I really need to elevate my ankle. Hauling your old ass in and out of the car hasn't done it any favors. I'm sorry, Mom. I shouldn't have said that. This isn't your fault.

"It's mine. I may not have released this toxin, but I created it. I created it knowing what impact it would have on the world. I'm responsible for this fucking carnage. So now, it's my responsibility to end it." Payekha got up from her desk in the living room, picked up her computer, and limped toward her mother who was struggling against the straps fastening her to the metal dolly.

"Okay, Mom," Payekha said softly as her heart began beating more rapidly and sweat dripped off her brown brow. "Let's give this a shot. Fuck I hope this works. Please, Mom. Just look at the screen. Look at the bright colors. Look at the beautiful princess sitting on her powerful steed. Look at her glistening armor. Look at her mighty sword. And listen to the message that is buried in it. Listen with your subconscious. Listen to the message of hope. Of strength. Of freedom. Allow that message in. Allow that message to purge your mind of Dear Leader's hateful voice and grotesque image. Let my message of kindness, and acceptance, and fearless resistance against evil cleanse your mind. Let it cleanse your mind and soul from the bigotry, and hatred, and lust for violence. Listen to it, and come back to me, Mom. Please. Please just come back to me. I don't want to be alone in this world anymore. I need you on my island."

Fifty-eight-year-old Ezinne Popoola turned her head away from the computer screen. Her deep brown eyes looked upon her beloved daughter's hung head as she said in her slow drawl, "Yeeeeeesss? I'm here darlin'. Now why in dear lord's heaven am I strapped to this thing? And why am I so hungry? Untie me, dear. I'll go warm up some hot pockets. Oh, but I do want to catch up on my notifications first. Dear, where's my cell phone?"

CHAPTER 11

DREAMSCAPE

"Fuck your cell phone, Mom!" Payekha yelled out before embracing her mother. "I'm just so happy to see you!" "There, there," Ezinne Popoola said in her comforting, motherly tone. "Yeeesss, I'm just fine. But I had the strangest dream. Now, would you please untie me and fetch me my phone? I really need to check on my notifications. Why, I posted the funniest cat meme that I just know my followers will love. I need to see how many 'Likes' I've received. And then, I really must catch up on what is happening with all of my friends. Why, I have a friend in Argentina who just got a new job. I surely hope it's going well for her. And another couple who are friends were going to post pictures from their trip to Italy. Oh, how I've always wanted to visit there. But of course international travel is restricted to only White citizens who are certified members of the regime. That's the wonder of my phone. I can have my adventures through other people. Oh, and cat memes. I do so enjoy my cat memes."

Payekha was untying her mother as she began explaining the situation. "Um, Mom? Listen, I know this is going to come as a shock to you, but, um, you can't use your cell phone right now. Or maybe, ever."

"What are you talking about?" Ezinne screamed. "But, but I *have* to have my cell phone! I never know when someone might message me or when somebody has posted a new picture or, or there are always new cat memes! I must have my cell phone, Payekha! I must have it *right now!*"

Ezinne's enraged face suddenly began smiling broadly as she was transported to a magical place. She was floating on billowy, bright pink clouds as brilliant yellow rays of sunshine warmed her ebony face. Red, yellow, and orange tulips began blossoming around her as she walked through the pink clouds. She reached down and picked one. It immediately turned into a red lollipop. She began laughing and placed the lollipop into her mouth and began sucking. Her tongue was immersed in the intensely sweet flavors of cherry, then strawberry, then watermelon. From a distance, she could hear her daughter's concerned voice say, "Um, Mom, why are you sucking on the remote?"

Ezinne ignored her daughter and focused on the dazzling silver and gold glitter waterfall in the distance. The pink clouds massaged her weary feet as she walked towards the waterfall. She cupped her hands under the flowing glitter and splashed it onto her face. Her glittered face looked angelic as she turned around and looked to where her daughter's voice was coming from. "Dammit, Mom! What are you doing? You're soaked and you're getting water all over the floor! Why the fuck did stupid Chad leave the kitchen faucet on, anyway? Whatta dumbass."

Ezinne could feel something tugging at her arm. It was a majestic oak tree with smooth, rich brown bark. Its branches had extended and had delicately wrapped themselves around her arm. The tree then said, "Okay, Mom. Looks like I need to tweak the message or algorithm or something. I think that it's too intense. I think you're in some sort of weird disassociation. I wanted people to be able to disassociate from trauma but retain their courage and fortitude to fight back. But it's supposed to work on *real* trauma! Not some stupid bullshit like you can't use your stupid fucking phone. Although, for most of these lemmings, I suppose that *is* real trauma. Come on, Mom. I don't know where your mind is, but let's go over to this nice, comfy couch that has, um, tons of fucking potato chip crumbs all over it because Chad was too fucking lazy to clean up after himself and…okay. Not important right now. Let's just get you over to the couch and get you calmed down, okay?"

Ezinne smiled at the oak tree and allowed herself to be led through the pink clouds toward a majestic, brilliant white crystal. She sat on the crystal and felt like a queen sitting on her throne. She also felt strong, determined, and perfectly calm. She was happier than she had ever been in her life. And then, her happiness exploded as did an array of vibrant colors. Streaks of colored light whizzed throughout her world of pink clouds. They twisted and turned as they snaked their way around a large object. Ezinne squealed with delight as she got off of her crystal throne and stood in front of a large, glowing cell phone. Her smile continued to broaden as cats emerged from the phone and began dancing around her. There were dozens of balls of fur and whiskers gyrating to unheard music. Some wore hats. Some wore sunglasses. Some wore shiny gold and silver chains. And all were adorable.

She heard her daughter's voice once again. "Mom, now what the hell are you doing in front of the TV? The fucking thing's not even on. What are you watching?" Ezinne's only response was to pick up one of the animated kittens and begin twirling around the room with it while joyously laughing. "Mom, you wanna put down the vase? That thing was fuckin' expensive."

Ezinne put the kitten down and began pressing on the illuminated cell phone screen. Her mind was whirring as she looked at the bright green letters on the screen and guessed at the answer. "GROOM!" She yelled out. "The word is GROOM! I got it in only three guesses!" The pink clouds tickled her brown skin as she began swiping her phone. She opened app after app revealing all new vibrant images of wonder while continuing to ignore her daughter's voice. "Goddamit, Mom. You're getting fingerprints all over the TV screen. Would you please stop doing that?"

Ezinne's awestruck mind was immersed by bright pink clouds, gorgeous tulips, streaks of vibrant colors, floating, random green letters, and dancing cats. She laughed and smiled while looking at the incredible world of her own creation. Her heartbeat slowed and she felt tranquility envelope her. Her smile then faded and was replaced by a look of confusion.

"Payekha?" she said while looking around her daughter's living room. She was holding a soggy remote control while standing in front of a streaked TV screen. Water dripped off of her floral house dress and onto a blue vase that was resting at her feet. "Payekha? What is happening to me? I think that I might be going mad. I just had a dream. But it felt so real."

"Come on Mom," Payekha said as she once again took her mother's arm and led her to the couch. "Let's just sit down and talk, okay? First, how do you feel?" "Weeeell," Ezinne answered. "I feel just fine. Very calm. And I feel very strong. But I'm concerned about my mind, Payekha. I do believe that I'm seeing things."

"Uh,huh, you fuckin' think so?" Payekha responded while rolling her eyes. "So, what's the last thing that you remember?" "Weeeell," Ezinne responded. "I remember you telling me some fool thing about not being able to have my cell phone. And that made me quite cross, dear. You know just how I love my cell phone. Don't you ever try to tell me I can't have it. I know you hate those things, but to each their own dear."

"Yeah, yeah, yeah, okay," Payekha replied. "Okay, you got upset with me about your stupid fucking phone, then what?" "Weeeell," Ezinne answered. "The world suddenly changed. It was the most wonderful world, Payekha. There were beautiful pink clouds and sunshine and glitter waterfalls and beams of colored light. There were gorgeous tulips that turned into delicious lollipops when you picked them. And then, there was this huge cell phone, and all these dancing cats came out of it. It was the most wonderful world I have ever seen. It was the most beautiful dream that I've ever had. So much better than my *other* dream."

"Yeah, let's talk about *that* dream for a second," Payekha said. "Tell me everything that you remember from today." "Alright, dear," Ezinne answered. "Weeeell, it was a day just like most others. I got up and showered. I put on my goin' out jeans and top. I really do hate step-ping foot outside of my home and into this messed up world. But I was nearly out of Hot Pockets and frozen pizzas, so I got up my courage, got in my SUV, and drove down to the store. I must admit I cried all the way there. I cry every time I leave my home. I cry because I always see those masked thugs rounding up yet another family. And we both know where those poor people are going, don't we dear? We've talked about it enough. The White adults will go to a re-educa-tion camp. The ones who look like us? Who the hell knows. We're being systematically exterminated. I just know that we are. They just disappear us. And the children? Oh, my lord, I don't even want to think about those poor souls. The regime picks them up and sells them to an oligarch. Or uses them as barter for a new trade deal. And all the proceeds go to Dear Leader. He has become wealthy from traf-ficking children. Innocent children. Just like you were, Payekha. I've cried countless nights over the hell you lived through. And I now cry countless nights thinking about what these poor children are going through. It's so disgusting. No, disgusting isn't the word for it. It is pure evil. All of these White devils who bang their Bibles and wrap themselves in this country's flag are bastardizing everything that those two things stand for. They have no morality. And they have no patriotism. They are just a bunch of power-hungry, racist, sexist opportunists who are enriching themselves off of greed, lust, and power.

"I'm sorry, dear. I get this way every time I have to leave my home. Anyway, I went to the grocery store and thought maybe I'd treat you to a nice dinner of eggs and bacon. Doesn't that sound wonderful? It's been so long. But the few eggs they had were $24.00 and the bacon? Oh, child, don't even ask. So, it was right back to the $12.99 hot pockets and $15.99 frozen pizzas. It's the only thing that anybody can afford now. Well, except for members of the regime, of course. They can afford the eggs and the $89.99 bag of chocolate candy and the $129.99 pot roast. But not us simple folk. We live on Hot Pockets. But I did manage to get the last two egg and bacon ones.

"Anyway, I left the store, and it took me forever to get back home.

They had set up two more checkpoints, and I had to provide my papers. You know, my license, and my regime-issued ID. That's always good enough for the White folks. But folks like us? We also have to present our birth certificate, most recent blood and DNA results, and retina scan. Took me over an hour to get home. I was worried that my Hot Pockets might spoil. That's why I always keep a cooler in the car. Just in case there's a checkpoint.

"I came home, put my groceries away, and sat with my cell phone. I didn't do anything special. I posted my cat meme and played my games. I guess I was doin' that for nearly three hours when I started hearing something strange. I started hearing Dear Leader's voice. But it wasn't coming from the phone or the TV or from one of his announcements over the city-wide emergency system. No, his voice was inside of me. It was inside of my head. And then, I saw his face. His pudgy, made-up face. Now, child, I'm *always* repulsed by that man's face. And his turkey-neck. And every time I hear or see him, I get angry,

"But this time was different. This was a repulsion like I've never experienced before. And a hatred like I've never felt. And all I wanted to do was kill people. I've never had such strong feelings of violence. I wanted to rip people apart. I actually wanted to eat them. That's how messed up this dream was. I dreamed that I just sat there staring at my phone, praying that somebody would come through my door so that I could kill them. Then, some stuff happened. It was all dark red and black and hazy. I remember dreaming that I bit somebody. I remember trying to keep biting them, but I couldn't because my arms were tied down. I remember…oh, dear lord. I remember waking up from my dream and I was tied to that there dolly. I remember seeing a bite wound on your shoulder. Oh please, Payekha, please don't tell me that wasn't a dream."

Payekha watched her mother's face grow increasingly despondent as she explained the current state of the world. She explained how the regime was working on an indoctrination program designed to make people subservient to Dear Leader. She explained how the subliminal messages were planted into everything on the internet and broadcast through cellular phone systems by manipulating algorithms. And she explained her role in this madness. She explained how she had manipulated data at the National Institute of Psychiatric Health so that they could never create a useable product. She explained how her most recent data submission would have the result of creating mindless, violent zombies. She explained how she believed that that would have been enough to have them abandon the insane project.

She explained that it was her belief that the NIPH had somehow released the subliminal messaging using her data and, as a result, every single person in the world who had looked at their cell phones had become a hate-filled, violent zombie. Meaning, nearly every person in the world had now become a hate-filled, violent zombie. And she explained that she had the cure. That she had subliminal messages that used her actual data that could deprogram people. No matter how far a person had gone down their detestable zombie rabbit-hole of rage, they could be brought back. They could be redeemed. But that constructed message had one other effect. It would plant a subliminal response of disassociation anytime the person was under duress. They would disassociate into a dream-like state while strengthening their fortitude to fight back against the threat that confronted them. And she finally explained that it seemed as though her messages needed a bit more tweaking.

"So, that's why you went into pink cloud, dancing cats, lollipop land, Mom," Payekha concluded. "There's something not quite right. You shouldn't have disassociated just because you were upset about your phone. And the disassociation shouldn't have been that strong. You were barely able to interact with the real world. There's supposed to be a balance between the real world and the dream world so that the person can interact with both. I gotta turn the volume down a bit. But I can't figure it out from here. All I have on my flash drive are my current conclusions. I need the underlying research so that I can figure out what I did wrong and change it. It really shouldn't be a big deal. I think I know where I made my error. But I need to look at my research to be sure. And that means that I've gotta get back into the NIPH.

"All of my research is stored there on a private server that I had installed. Those fucking morons had no idea that I was stashing all of my *real* work on a separate server. All my fake shit was done on the office computer and stored on the NIPH server. My *real* shit was done on a laptop and stored on a small server that I hid in the ceiling in my office. After I got fired, um, oh, yeah. I got fired today, by the way. Not that it fucking matters *now*. Anyway, after I got fired all I had time to do was download my conclusions from that computer onto this flash drive. I didn't keep any of my research on that computer. It was just on the server. And I didn't have time to get to the server. Which is a mistake I'm going to correct right fucking now.

"All I need to do is dodge zombies, get into the building, get into my office, grab the computer and server from the ceiling, get out of the building, dodge *more* zombies, come home, review the research, adjust my messaging and algorithm, and voila! We're ready for mass deprogramming! Then, back to NIPH, load the updated messages and algorithm into their server, and send it out into the world. I haven't figured out how to get millions of zombies to look at their cell phones yet, but one step at a time. Which reminds me. I really need to get this done and get some ice on this fucking ankle. So, I'm going to have to take off for a bit, Mom. And I'm going to need your car."

"That's fine, dear," Ezinne replied as she shook off her bewilderment. "But just where is *your* car?" "Stupid fucking Chad lost the keys," Payekha answered in a disgruntled tone. "I never did understand what you saw in him. Or in any of your other involvements," Ezinne stated in a lecturing tone. "I mean, my lord, child. You must be a magnet for the laziest sons a bitches on the planet."

"Yeah, I know," Payekha answered through light snickers. "But that was kind of the point. Yeah, they were all lazy. And selfish. And sponged off of me. And they were all pretty stupid. But they were harmless. None of them had enough ambition to get off the fuckin' couch, let alone try to hurt me. Plus, they were easy to order around and were usually pretty good lays. They were nothing but distractions while I was waiting for Mister Right. You know, somebody who wasn't indoctrinated into the regime. And wasn't a misogynist. And wasn't a pedophile. And had an actual job. I know, pretty low fucking bars to hit, but hell, ninety percent of the asshole men in this society can't even hit *those* fucking targets. Anyway, they were all slobs, but harmless slobs. I never had to worry about them hurting me and I got my natural urges served once in a while. So, win, win, I guess. But, yeah, stupid fucking Chad lost my stupid fucking keys, so I need to use your car."

"That's fine. But I have just one more question before you go," Ezinne countered. "Why on God's green Earth do you have so many bottles of that vile man's scent? Dear lord, I passed someone who was wearing it once and it was absolutely putrid. I nearly vomited." "Yeah, well, that's kinda why I have all that shit. And the squirt guns," a chuckling Payekha answered.

Payekha limped towards the door carrying her purse, a large bag for the computer and server, and a large water cannon filled with *GROOMING*. She cautiously opened the door and was immediately greeted by the sounds of explosions and people being eaten alive. "Well, I guess they're still at it. I wonder if they ever get tired and sleep? Another question for another day. Alright Mom. I should be back in a couple hours. Keep the door locked. If anybody breaks in, look into their eyes. If their eyes are normal, shoot the motherfucker with the gun. If their eyes are white, shoot the motherfucker with *GROOMING*. Then clean up the vomit. And blood. And bile. And internal organs. Got it? Oh, and one last thing. For the love of God, stay off your fucking cell phone, Mom!"

Chapter 12

The Blame Game

"Aw, fuck, Mom! Sorry about your car!" Payekha yelled to herself as she mowed down three more jaywalking zombies. "Your front end is so totally fucked up. And I'm not too sure about your undercarriage. I've been dragging one if these assholes for five blocks now. He sure is resilient though. Still screaming under there. I wonder if he has any skin left? Fuck it. Not my problem. What *is* my problem is how I'm going to explain this damage to Mom. She saved for years to get a decent car. It's only got 5,000 miles on it. It was her dream car. And now..."

Payekha instinctively ducked as a female zombie splattered across her windshield. "Oh fuck! I didn't even see that bitch! Damn, they're fast. Anyway, now her nice big, black SUV is royally fucked up. I hope her insurance is paid up. Shit, what am I saying? Like there's insurance anymore. Who in the hell am I going to call to report this shit? And even if an insurance adjustor comes out, he'll be more interested in eating me out than...um...I think I'll rephrase that. My point is there's no way to get recouped for this shit. Not like there was ever any insurance anyway. It's always just been a big fucking scam.

"Health insurance. Car insurance. Home insurance. Name it. Just a big fucking scam. You pay thousands of dollars in and then, when you have an actual claim, they deny you the coverage that you've paid thousands of fucking dollars for! Or, at best, they make you go through all sorts of arduous paperwork and at the end of it? Yep, you get covered. Minus your huge deductible or co-pay. And then, because you filed a claim that wasn't even your fucking fault, you get to pay even more in premiums! So, they collect thousands upon thousands of dollars into this shit, pay themselves really fucking well, just so they can fuck you over. And over. And over. I've always said this. There's no such thing as insurance. Just a big fucking scam so asshole agents and CEO's and middle-management dicks can have themselves a nice second home in Vale. Makes me fuckin' sick. But not sick enough to see a doctor. I can't afford the co-pay. Okay Payekha, hold on. We're here and we're coming in for a hard landing."

Payekha heard a loud crunch under her front tires as the SUV screeched to a halt. "Fuck, *that* didn't sound good," she said to herself as she reached for her leg crutch and water cannon filled with *GROOMING*. She flung open the now dented and blood-spattered door of the SUV and looked down at her tires. "Ooooh, fuck. Sorry Mister Daniels. Jesus H., your whole fuckin' head kind of exploded, didn't it? Popped your eyes right out of their sockets. Ah, well. Serves you right. Even though you were one of the most racist mother-fuckers in this place, it didn't stop you from staring at my tits every time I walked into the room, now did it? And how many times did I have to put up with your hands on my Black ass? Well, those days are over, because those are some mangled motherfuckin' meat hooks you got there. What comes around, goes around, asshole. Now, how in the hell am I going to get into this building."

Payekha looked up at the towering stone thirty-story building that housed the National Institute of Psychiatric Health. The top three floors were consumed by flames as the final ashen remnants of Dear Leader's glowering banner floated harmlessly to the ground. Payekha picked up a burning piece of the banner and said, "Shit, I can use this. Hey, Mister Daniels, you got your smokes on you?" She hobbled over to the SUV, bent down, and reached into the breast pocket of the deci-mated man's shirt. "Fuck, it's been too long," she said as she placed a bent cigarette between her dry lips and used the piece of flaming portrait to light it. She heavily inhaled, then let out a plume of smoke along with a satisfied sigh. She then began coughing uncontrollably.

"Yep, fuck! That's why I quit that shit!" she exclaimed as she threw the cigarette to the ground and used the sole of the sneaker on her leg crutch to extinguish it. "It was fun while it lasted though. Now, back to business. How the fuck am I going to get in he…oh. The asshole zombies crashed right through the glass in the front door. Well, *that* was convenient. Alright. Let's limp our ass up to my office on the twenty-third floor. Before this whole fucking building goes up like a witch at a Salem Barbeque."

Payekha began laughing as she entered the building and looked around at the carnage of her prior workplace. In every corner of the vast, gold lobby screaming men were being eaten alive by carnivorous zombies. One man was having his skull bashed on the marble tile until it cracked open. The gluttonous zombie squealed with delight and buried his face into the wailing man's grey matter. Another group of zombies were battling over a shrieking rotund man. Several zombies stood on either side of the tortured man and were pulling on his arms. "Hey! That's not gonna work!" Payekha yelled out to the grunting zombies. "You're just gonna end up…yep. Thought so. You're just going to end up pulling his arms off. Ah shit. And now he's loose! You dumbass zombies! Look at this fat fucker running around the lobby with blood spurting out of his arm holes. Now somebody's gonna slip on the…yep. Toldja. Somebody's gonna slip in the blood."

Payekha laughed harder as she played announcer to the hilariously morbid scene. "And bald zombie almost has him, but noooooo! Fat fuck turns to the left and bald zombie goes sliding on the blood and crashes into the wall! Now hipster zombie has an angle on him. He's stretching out his arms and….noooo! denied! Fat fuck ducks under his arms and runs past him. Fat fuck is in the lead here folks, but I don't know how much he has left in him. He's losing an awful lot of blood from his arm holes. But he's resilient! He headbutts mid-life crisis zombie knocking him on his ass! Uh, oh. He's cornered folks. Pedo vibe zombie and comb-over zombie have him trapped. Does fat fuck have enough energy left to escape once again? The suspense is killing me! Here they come. They're walking slowly towards him. Oh, just listen to fat fuck wail as he contemplates his next move. And there it is! A head fake, then a move to his right and…oh shit. Fat fuck slipped in the blood. And there goes comb-over and pedo vibe in for the kill! Oh wow. They certainly are enjoying their victory. There goes his spleen. And there goes his intestines. And more intestines. And more intestines. And…oh fuck this. I need to get upstairs. Thanks for the show, fellas!"

Payekha limped towards the elevators and pushed the 'Up' button. "No fuckin' way I'm climbing twenty-three flights," she said as she waited for her elevator. The elevator door opened, and she was greeted by three pairs of zombie eyes looking up at her from their latest meal, who happened to be Herb from accounting. "Uh, this one seems a bit full. That's alright. I'll take the next one," she said as she pressed the button to close the door. She heard a 'Ping' from behind her as another elevator door opened. "Alrightythen, here we go," she said as she limped into the blood-soaked chamber. "Fuck, I really need to watch my step. Entrails everywhere. And the fuckin' stench! I almost prefer the scent of *GROOMING*. Almost."

Payekha tapped the foot of her leg crutch to the rhythm of *Don't Worry, Be Happy* that was playing on the overhead speaker as the elevator slowly ascended to the twenty-third floor. By the fifth floor she was also whistling. By the twelfth floor she was singing along at the top of her lungs. The door opened and her high-pitched melodious voice immediately attracted the attention of five zombies who were growling at each other around the water cooler. She emerged from the elevator, lifted her water cannon and nonchalantly said "Fuck off, assholes." She couldn't help but smile as she limped down the hallway toward her former office to the sounds of violent retching.

She approached her office door and paused. She leaned against the wooden entryway and listened intently. From inside, she could hear the sounds of things being thrown about. She took a deep breath, turned the knob, and yanked. "Fuck. Locked. I wonder if they turned my key card off yet. Nope," she concluded as a green light glowed above the door handle. She once again turned the knob, flung open the door, and began spraying the entire office with *GROOMING*.

"Jesus Christ! What the fuck are you doing?" Hugo yelled out as he covered his mouth in an attempt to decrease Dear Leader's stench. "What the fuck am *I* doing?" Payekha yelled back. "What the fuck are *you two* doing in *my* office?"

"Um, it's actually not your office anymore," Dawson sheepishly replied while wiping thick globs of *GROOMING* from his splattered face. "What are *you* doing here, Payekha?"

"What the fuck do you think?" she shot back. "The entire population of the world has been turned into mindless, violent zombies, and I think I have the cure. You two want to tell me how this happened? You want to tell me how the subliminal messages got released out to the general public?"

"Um, well, you see," Dawson began stammering while looking down at his shuffling feet. "We had just completed a test on live subjects using the latest data that you had provided. And, um, well, after our two test subjects watched the video with the subliminal messages, their eyes turned white, and they just began beating the hell out of one another. The subjects were, um, put down and we realized that your data was way off. We realized that this particular test message and associated algorithm was way too dangerous to have around. So, we deleted it. Except, instead of hitting the 'Delete' button, um, well, we kinda hit the 'Transmit' button. So, um, you know. The message went out into the world through all of the cellular networks, and the algorithm attached it to everything that was being viewed by cell phones. Everything. Emails. Videos. Games. Everything was corrupted by the subliminal messages and within a few hours the entire world had descended into chaos. People who used their cell phones for anything at all became these mindless, violent, um, I'm not sure what to call them."

"Zombies?" Payekha contributed. "Yeah, okay," Dawson agreed. "I guess zombies is as good a word as anything for them. They *are* mindless. And completely inhumane."

"Yeah, not unlike Dear Leader's followers, right boys? Completely mindless and completely inhumane." Payekha playfully retorted. "Oh, fuck you!" Hugo screamed. "What is up with you overly sensitive snowflakes, anyway? Why are you always pointing fingers? Why are you always politicizing everything? This is a crisis! This is no time for finger pointing and name calling! Besides, it hurts our feelings when your kind says that stuff about us. We aren't mindless *or* inhumane! We just followed Dear Leader's orders to ensure that our country was controlled by White men who are predestined for dominion. That's all. And inhumane? It was *you* fucking snowflake terrorists who protested in the streets wearing your fucking frog and unicorn costumes! We had no choice but to round you up and send you to concentration camps to be deprogrammed and work in the fields. You snowflake terrorists started this shit by not accepting your lot in White man's society and bending to Dear Leader's glorious vision! You started this shit!"

Payekha stood in silence for a moment as she processed the inane drivel that she had just heard. It was the same inane drivel that she had heard from countless former friends over the years. People who were once kind, decent, and accepting of each other's differences had been twisted by the hateful rhetoric of Dear Leader and his sycophants. Their acceptance had turned to hatred. Their decency had turned to oppression. Their kindness had turned to malicious cruelty. They had turned into the Walking Red. They had become merciless zombies who thoughtlessly acted upon every barbaric utterance of Dear Leader. They were no longer human because their humanity had been stripped from them. They had become nothing more than appendages for this inhumane, anti-Christian movement.

Payekha took a deep breath, looked Hugo in the eyes, and said, "Do you fucking hear yourself? Okay, I have a few points to make here, Ace. First, what exactly are we? Are we simpering, sensitive little snowflakes? Or are we horrifically violent domestic terrorists? Because we can't be both. So, get your fucking lie straight and pick one. Oh, and they are *both* lies. We are *not* being overly sensitive when we protest and speak out against the brutality being waged against ourselves or our fellow people. We are not being overly sensitive when we protest and speak out against our rights being stripped from us. When we see masked agents of the government kidnapping people and sending them to concentration camps. When we see innocent people, including children, being beaten and bound. We are not being overly sensitive when we protest and speak out against our Constitutional Democracy being bastardized into an Authoritarian Oligarchy. That is not being overly sensitive and protesting and speaking out sure as fuck isn't terrorism. *You* are the fucking terrorists who sanction this shit! You are the ones who have allowed this brutal takeover of our nation! *We* are the fucking patriots who are trying to maintain equality for all in this fucked up country! And speaking truth to power and placing blame at the feet of the root cause of a problem is *not* being political! It's being factual! You can't solve a problem until you diagnose the cause! And you motherfuckers have been the cause of a whole lot of problems for decades! You stupid, piece of shit asshole!

"Oh, I'm sorry. I called you a name, didn't I? Oh, did that hurt your feelings? Does it hurt your feelings when I hold a mirror up to you so that you are forced to confront the fact that you are *indeed* a fascist, neo-Nazi, bigoted, misogynistic, piece of shit? Listen, sweetheart. I'm not calling you names. I'm pointing out facts based upon your own fucking actions. And truth fucking hurts, now, doesn't it? Now, you can take your hurt feelings and shove them straight up your arrogant ass… you little goosestepping pussy snowflake."

"You fucking bitch!" Hugo yelled out as he lunged at Payekha. He immediately stopped and began gagging as Payekha squirted another wad of *GROOMING* on his face and said, "Bad Hugo. Bad.

"Now, boys, just calm yourselves. I may have a bum ankle, but I can still easily kick your fucking pasty-white asses. Or slit your fucking throats. I've done it before, and I can sure as hell do it again. Now, I have a question for you both. Whose brilliant idea was it to put the 'Delete' button next to the 'Transmit' button? What fucking Einstein came up with *that* brilliant design?"

"Um, well," Dawson awkwardly responded. "You see, the console was originally designed by a Korean-American woman. And, um, since she was, um, you know, um, Korean and um, a woman, she was fired for being a DEI hire and the console was redesigned. And *that* guy changed everything and kind of put the buttons next to each other, um, I guess."

"Uh, huh. Uh, huh," an exasperated Payekha replied as she tapped the foot of her leg crutch. "I see. There's *no way* somebody of Korean descent could *possibly* be qualified to design a big, scary, science thingy. And *especially* if she is a woman. No, those two random demographic factors *obviously* make her unqualified. So, it took a big, strong, White man to come up with the brilliant design of putting the 'Delete' and 'Transmit' buttons next to each other. And probably both red, right? Yep, thought so. Sure, sure. That tracks. And do you know what? They were right. A woman of Korean descent had no place designing that console. She was incapable of designing it to fulfill the final outcome. Yep, it took some White, male dullard motherfucker to design it so that it could end the fucking world! Nice job, boys. Really nice job."

"Well, what about you, huh?" Hugo answered while wiping *GROOMING* off of his face. "It was *your* data that provided the construction of the subliminal messaging. It was *your* data that provided the linking algorithm. *You* are just as responsible for this! How the fuck did you get this so wrong?"

Payekha looked down for a moment at the shuffling foot of her leg crutch then proudly lifted her head. "Oh, you stupid motherfuckers. I *didn't* get it wrong. I got it *right*. I knew *exactly* what I was doing because I knew *exactly* what you were using my data for. I knew why I was the only Black person here. And one of the few women. Because you couldn't do your warped mind control bullshit without me. Yeah, I knew. Because, despite my being a so-called 'DEI hire,' I actually have a fucking brain. And I used my DEI brain to figure out that you were using my data to construct subliminal messages that would be connected to an infectious algorithm and spread through the cellular networks. And I knew that the end result would be a completely docile populace that could then be easily dominated by Dear Leader. I knew. And *that* shit just wasn't going to happen on my watch. So, I manipulated the data. I constructed the data to make people who viewed the message increasingly violent. I never in a million years thought you dumbfucks would look at the data and actually use it on human subjects. It should have been obvious to you what the result would be, and it should have been obvious at how dangerous it was.

"I manipulated the data hoping that the project would eventually be deemed a failure and scrapped. But nooooo! *You* two fucking geniuses had to not only use it on human test subjects but then release it into the world! Nice fucking job! Yes, I manipulated the data, and I did it purposefully. And I'm fucking proud of myself for doing it. Uh, uh, Hugo. Don't you take one fucking step towards me. I told you that I'd slit your throat, and I will. And besides, you dumb motherfuckers need me. Yes, even though you two assholes just fired me for absolutely zero cause, um, until *now* I guess, I am here to help you.

"I see that you're rummaging through my office. Trying to find my notes and shit? Trying to see if I have figured out a way out of this? Well, let me save you some trouble. Yes. Yes, I have. As I said, I manipulated the data and stored all of that on the server here at the institute. But my *real* data is stored on a server that is just above you. Hugo, make yourself useful, get on that chair and pull the black box and laptop from above the ceiling tiles. That's it. Steady yourself. We wouldn't want big, strong, White snowflake warrior to fall down and go boom. Yes, there they are. Hand them to me Hugo. It's of no use to you. Everything on there is encrypted and I'm the only one who can access it. You see, *my* security passwords are a bit more complicated than '1,2,3,4.' I bet you didn't think I knew your passwords, didja? You two are a couple of creative motherfuckers, gotta hand you that. And *you* hand me that server and computer.

"With the data that is stored on this, I can construct an alternate message. One that can de-program these zombies. I've already done it with my mother. One minute she's trying to eat my brains, then, after watching a cute little cat video with my message implanted in it, she's my mother again. But it's not quite right. The message I constructed is supposed to increase people's fortitude by projecting them into a dream-like state when confronted with danger. When they are threatened, they go to a place of calm and security where their empowerment is fortified. But they are also able to interact with the real world as well. They are living in two realities simultaneously so that they can remain calm and strong while vanquishing the real-world threat. Pretty cool huh?

"But it's not quite right. The dream-like element is too strong. My mother was barely in touch with reality, and she was going around sucking on remote controls and shit because she thought they were lollipops. Don't get any weird thoughts there, Hugo. That's my mom you're thinking about, you fucking perv. Let me just plug this into my computer. And now the flash drive. I'll take all this data, reconfigure the message, and we can transmit the new message through the cellular networks. Anybody who isn't yet infected will be protected because if they look at their cell phones, they will now be seeing *my* message. And we can deprogram the others if we can get them rounded up in front of some big fucking video screens. We can stop this madness and turn the world into a better place all in one fell swoop. I just need to take this home, make the adjustments that I need, and I'll come back here to transmit. Easy, peasy."

"Huh, uh," Hugo firmly stated. "You'll do it *now*." Payekha turned around to confront a pistol-wielding Hugo. "Come on, Hugo, this isn't necessary," Dawson pleaded. "Yeah, it is," Hugo answered while staring at Payekha. "She fucked us over before. How do we know that this (derogatory term omitted) bitch won't fuck us over again? Just use the data to construct a message that she'll just show to *her* kind? Leave the rest of us White patriots in this burning hellhole while she builds an army of DEI motherfuckers. I don't trust (derogatory term omitted) and I don't trust bitches. So, Poopala, you're going to analyze your data and construct your message right here. And we'll all go up to the transmission room together. And as long as you play nice and do exactly as I say, I promise I won't put a bullet through your (derogatory term omitted) brain. Got it? Now get to work. You (derogatory term omitted) bitch."

Chapter 13

Gratuitously Disgusting

She was tired of being called that word. That word that was used by knuckle dragging White people that was intended to dehumanize her. Animalize her. Put her people back into chains on the plantation. That word that had become commonplace in this tyrannical society. She used to hear it in quiet whispers. For the last several years, she would hear it quite loudly as people yelled it into her pretty, ebony face. Or it would be painted on her car or the door of her home. Accompanied by the obligatory swastika, of course.

She seethed as the cruel impact of that word crashed into her psyche. She understood how she was expected to respond. She was supposed to immediately feel inferior to this simpleton White man. She was supposed to cower reverentially at his feet and do his bidding. She was supposed to shred herself of her dignity and become his dutiful slave. But on this day, this dullard bigot had chosen to use this word on the wrong woman.

Payekha Popoola allowed that word to seep into her consciousness. Then her subconscious. She closed her eyes for a moment and connected with her emotions. This word that was supposed to instill terrorizing fear was instilling strength. This word that was supposed to strip her of her dignity was instilling pride. This deplorable word that was supposed to make her wilt reinforced her fortitude. She suddenly felt no pain as a wave of calm washed over her. Her bitten ear no longer hurt. Her bitten shoulder no longer ached. Her twisted ankle no longer throbbed.

She could feel her steel armor growing around her tone body. She could feel the handle of her mighty sword. She smiled and opened her eyes. Standing in front of her was a court jester pointing a harmless wand at her. His ridiculous face was painted in white with a big, red nose and his feet were comically large. Her office had transformed into a majestic rainforest complete with colorfully animated chirping birds, croaking frogs, and laughing monkeys. A cable that hung from the ceiling tile transformed into a scaly bright green serpent. Her red stapler became a fluorescent crimson flower. Her computer screen became the entryway into a magnificently lighted cave. And this simple man who was threatening her with a gun had become nothing more than a harmless object of ridicule.

She understood the threat that was standing in front of her. She knew where she was. She knew that the snake was a cable, the flower was her stapler, and the cave was her computer screen. She knew this petty man was holding a gun and not a wand. She was living in two realities simultaneously. She was in her office being threatened by a man with a gun. *And* she was enveloped in a glorious, safe, warm rainforest of her own creation. This was *her* rainforest, and it was *her* domain. She, and she alone, was the ultimate power here. He was nothing more than an unwelcome interloper who did not belong. He was powerless here. He was impotent.

Strength and fortitude surged through Payekha's muscular body as she clenched her sword / leg crutch. She stared at the court jester / Hugo with determination. She wickedly smiled at him. And then it hit her. "Holy fuck, this it!" she cried out as the rainforest evaporated leaving only her dingy office. "This is fucking it! This is *exactly* the effect that I'm trying to achieve for everybody! Don't you see? No, of course you don't. You didn't have the experience that I just had. You aren't able to disassociate yourself into a safe space when confronted with danger in the real world. But I *can*, and this is it! I was living in the real threatening world, but I was simultaneously living in a lush, safe rainforest of my own creation. Instead of being frightened, I was empowered. Instead of cowering, I was inspired to fight back. I felt safe and strong in my rainforest while being completely aware of the threats in my real surroundings! So, thanks fucknut for pissing me off. This is just what I needed. I needed to experience this for myself one more time. It hasn't happened for a while. But you calling me that dipshit name has given me the final piece of the puzzle and this is fucking it! I think I know exactly what I did wrong. It's not in the algorithm. It's in the messaging. I've gotta check my data."

Dawson stood with his jaw agape as Payekha opened her laptop and furiously typed in her twenty-three-character password. "Hey, hey, no funny stuff (derogatory term omitted)," Hugo demanded while continuing to point his gun at Payekha's back. "Oh, fuck off, Hugo," Payekha dismissively answered while opening her files of data. "I'm serious, bitch," Hugo replied in an attempt to sound threatening.

Payekha let out an exasperated sigh, looked up at her ceiling and said, "Lord, really? These are the dumb motherfuckers that you instilled feelings of superiority into? What the fuck are they superior over? A cupcake maybe? I've seen them conquer enough of those; I guess. Jesus, I don't have time for this. The entire population of the world is eating each other out, um, I *really* need to start rephrasing that, and I'm stuck here babysitting these two dumbasses. Fuckin' whatever."

Payekha got up from her chair and walked over to a trembling Hugo. "Hey, I said no funny business. Just…just get back to your computer and get back to work, bitch," he said while the gun shook in his hand. "Oh, shut the fuck up," Payekha calmly responded before swinging her leg crutch at Hugo. The sole of the bloody sneaker slammed into Hugo's wrist and the revolver flew against the wall. There was a loud BANG and Hugo grasped his now-bloody ear.

"Oh shit! I've been shot!" He wailed. "Oh, let me look at it," Payekha calmly said as she removed his bloody hand from his wounded ear. "Ah shit, it's just a little nick, you big fucking baby. But see? *This* is how an ear that's been shot looks like. There's actually a piece missing from it. Here, I'll get a tampon from my purse. Put this on it. That'll make you look really cool. Quite the fashion statement, there dumbass. Now, are you done with your pussy-ass, macho man bullshit? Can I get back to work now?

"And Dawson, you really are a fucking little spineless worm, aren't you? You just stand in the corner and shiver while waiting for somebody to tell you what to do. Who the fuck *are* you, man? Are you the seemingly decent, polite, respectful, ethical guy that I trained with? Or was that just an act to try to get into my pants while you were *actually* just another one of these White Nationalist, fascist cumwads? Or are you neither? Maybe you have no real personality at all and are just the product of whoever the dominant force in your life is at any given moment. Whatever. Don't know and don't fucking care. Just stand there and shiver and stay the fuck out of my way. And keep this other pussy piece of shit out of my way too."

At that moment, there was a loud crash and the office door exploded into flying, wooden shrapnel. "Oh goddammit, they must have heard the gunshot." an unflinching Payekha said while reaching for her water cannon of *GROOMING*. A horde of fast-moving zombies rushed into the room and lunged at their nearest target. Hugo squealed like a child as a carnivorous zombie bit two fingers off of his right hand. Another zombie began gnawing his left eye and sucked it out of its socket. Blood sprayed throughout the room while the trembling Dawson stood in the corner and watched impotently.

"Ah, Fuck!" Payekha yelled out before saturating the mindless mob with the putrid scent of Dear Leader. The zombies halted their onslaught, sniffed the air, and began convulsing. "Oh shit! Oh shit! Oh shit!" Payekha screamed just before being blasted by projectile vomit. Her face and afro were covered in tan, chunky sludge, causing her to begin vomiting as well.

Impacted by the horrific smell and disgusting imagery, Dawson keeled over and vomited on the laptop. Hugo tried to cover his missing eye with his three-digited, bloody hand while covering his mouth with the other. It didn't work. The entirety of his partially digested lunch erupted through his fingers and onto the anguished face of a violently ill zombie. Four zombies, Hugo, Dawson, and Payekha were all heaving up whatever remained in their intestinal tracts. The vomit-covered, cheap linoleum tile became as slick as an ice-skating rink causing Dawson to slip onto his backside. His plunge onto the floor sent a wave of thick, sticky, tan, brown and green human refuse splashing upon the walls. Then Hugo slipped, sending him cannonballing into the lake of hurl. Payekha watched the insanely grotesque scene with glee and began to laugh until she mistakenly breathed in from her nose. The repugnant aroma of vomit mixed with the scent of Dear Leader caused her to resume her violent retching. Her ribs ached from the continuous violent upheaval, and she slipped and fell face first into five inches of chunky vomit, zombie internal organs, intestines, and spent corpses. She grunted as she placed her hands on the floor and pressed herself up. Her right hand slipped, and her face and body were once again submerged in the revolting goo.

She lifted her head out of the sludge and saw her leg crutch floating nearby. She reached for it, stood it on its foot, and used it to steady herself as she pulled herself out of this ocean of intestinal carnage. She carefully sloshed over to the weeping Dawson, extended her leg crutch and helped him out of the slimy refuse. "Now, go help your asshole friend," she ordered. Dawson slipped and fell three times while trying to get to his partially submerged colleague. Each time he fell, Payekha was splattered with yet another wave of chunky, grotesque sickness.

As was the glowering portrait of Dear Leader. Putrid vomit of his scent's own creation slowly oozed down his tyrannical image. Payekha dripped globs of refuse while looking around at her decimated office. "FUUUUUUCK THIIIIIIIS!" She screamed out. "Oh fuck. That was the most gratuitously disgusting thing that I've ever experienced. Jesus Christ, it wasn't enough to just have the zombies vomit everywhere? Why the fuck did *we* have to vomit? And *slip* in this shit? And get *submerged* in it? This is fucked up. I don't know who's writing this shit, but this is fucked up. I don't even *want* to be in this book anymore. Fuck this. I quit. Find another heroine, asshole. And good luck with that, because pretty much every other bitch in this book was addicted to cell phones and are now zombies. Or dead. Which means, oh goddammit. Which means, I *can't* quit. I've got to go on. I'm this world's only hope. Fine. I'll stay in the fucking book. But listen, you twisted motherfucker. You'd better write that I get a fucking shower and some clean fucking clothes. Right fucking now. And this shit had better *not* happen again. Got it?"

Payekha gingerly slid her feet past the tortured Hugo and despondent Dawson towards her desk. She picked up her laptop and wiped three inches of vomit from it. "I *said* I wanted a shower, motherfucker. But I guess I'd better get *this* shit first because there's no fucking way I'm coming back in here again. And just fucking great. The computer's fucked. The whole plan is fucked. Fuck it. I'm getting cleaned up."

Three trails of pungent refuse led to the nearby lavatories. "Where the fuck do you two think *you're* going?" Payekha inquired of the closely following and submissive Hugo and Dawson. "You're not coming in here with me. Go to the little boy's room and do your shit. We'll meet back out here when we're done. Huh. I'm kinda surprised there's still a ladies' room in this place. It sure as hell hasn't been used much." She entered the restroom and opened a stall door. "Nope not used much at all. So why in the fuck is there a glory hole in here? Jesus fucking Christ! You perverted motherfuckers!"

She began the arduous cleaning process by washing off her purse, crutch leg, and water cannon in the sink. She then entered the stall. There was a loud SLAPPING sound on the cold tile each time she removed a vomit-logged article of clothing and threw it over the side of the metal stall. She submerged her sopping hair and face into the toilet, swished it around, and flushed. And flushed. And flushed until her afro and face had been cleansed of the vile spew. Her naked frame limped back towards the sink. She filled her hands with soap and scrubbed her entire body. She then rinsed herself leaving a pool of water, soap, and hurl on the restroom floor.

"Now, what the fuck am I going to wear?" she said to herself while her exhausted eyes looked around the room. Use paper towels as pasties? Toilet paper panties? Yeah those two pervs would love that shit. Wait a minute. Those lockers. They keep extra lab coats in those lockers. Yeah, that'll work. And I should be able to wash off my shoes." Payekha began dry heaving once again as she poured thick vomit out of her shoes and rinsed them clean. "This so fucking gross," she said as she put on the lab coat and shoes. "Good. Extra-large. Covers me down to my knees and bulky enough to keep me from exposing my niblets too much. Those two assholes do not deserve a thing. Especially a peep show."

Payekha carefully stepped over the vomit trail and sat her weary body upon a bench in the hallway as she waited for Hugo and Dawson to emerge from their restroom. "What the fuck is taking them so long? They don't have *nearly* as many crevasses to clean out that I do. Oh fuck. What are we going to do? I have so much on my computer at home, but it's worthless without the data that's on my other computer. I was so close and now I just feel…I just feel…so fucking helpless. I'm not going to cry. I'm not going to cry. I'm not going to…"

Her self-dialogue ended as she heard the men's restroom door open. She instinctively raised her *GROOMING* cannon and waited. Hugo emerged first. His right hand was wrapped in bloody gauze as was his left eye socket. He somberly limped toward the bench and sat next to Payekha. "I'm really fucking hurt," he said to her while staring blankly up at the ceiling with his remaining eye. "I've lost two fingers and an eye. I need a doctor."

"Yeah, well," Payekha replied. "I don't know if that's in the cards there, champ. Listen. I have some first aide shit back at my house and some aspirin and shit. That's the best we'll be able to do until we can cure this shit. Hopefully there's a doctor out there somewhere that we can deprogram and he can help you. Of course, it would be *helpful* if all the hospitals and clinics and medical schools weren't purged of every female doctor. That would've increased our odds at finding one. Nope, if you're a woman and want to work in the medical field under Dear Leader's regime, the best you can do is be a nurse. And that's only if you're under thirty-five and can fit into those skimpy fucking uniforms. Plus, the medical profession in this country has taken quite a few steps back since the tinfoil hat brigade took over. But hopefully we can find you a doctor that can provide you with the best care from 1939."

Dawson then emerged from the restroom. Payekha looked at him, shook her head in disbelief, and said, "Do ya think you might wanna get a larger lab coat?" "What?" Dawson asked before looking down at the head of his member peaking from the coat's hem. "Oh, God! Sorry! Be right back!"

Dawson re-emerged into the hallway wearing a lab coat that reached his ankles to hear Payekha saying, "Yeah, I don't know what we're going to do. I have a bunch of shit on my computer at home, but I've got to have the underlying data that's on the computer here. Without it, I won't be able to safely manipulate the subliminal messaging. Hell, I might just create a world of assholes *worse* than this. And that computer is obviously filled with vomit and is useless now. I don't know what to do." Payekha hung her head in defeat for a moment before she heard Dawson's voice.

"Um, what about the server?" he inquired. "Didn't you say all of the data was stored on the server? And it's completely sealed. So, all we have to do is get it and clean it off. But, um, in order to get it, you're going to have to go back into your office and wade through the vomit."

Payekha lifted her seething face and stared at the adjacent wall. She squinted her mahogany eyes and her stare intensified until her author's mischievous blue eyes came into focus within the wall. She opened her full lips and growled at him, "You sadistic motherfucker."

CHAPTER 14

––––––––––

FORTITUDE

"This is getting really fucking old," Payekha grumbled to herself while rinsing vomit off of her leg crutch...again. "But I have the server. I have all of the data and underlying research. I can turn this around. But I can't do it here. This place is going up like a whore's skirt. The cellular transmission network here is unusable. There must be another one. Somewhere."

She limped out of the restroom to find the forlorn Dawson and beaten and bloodied Hugo sitting on a bench waiting for her. "We gotta get outta here fellas," she said while clutching her purse which contained the server and her flash drive. "The smoke is penetrating this floor. The fire's expanding. This whole fucking thing is about to go down like a sorority pledge at a frat party. Let's get to my car."

"No!" Hugo yelled out. "We'll take *my* car! I'm not leaving my brand-new car in the parking garage! I worked my ass off for that thing! Come on, we'll take the elevator."

Payekha and Dawson ignored Hugo and began walking towards the staircase. "The elevators are fried, dumbass," Payekha stated bluntly. "And I don't know how long it's going to take, but this whole fucking building is going to collapse right on top of the parking garage *and* your precious swasticar. It's an ugly piece of shit anyway. I knew you were an asshole the minute you bought that hideous thing. Only assholes drive swasticars. We're going to get our asses down these twenty-three flights as fast as we can, get to my mom's SUV, and get the fuck out of here. You do what you want."

Hugo fumed as he watched Payekha and Dawson disappear behind the door of the stairwell. "Fuck that (derogatory term omitted) bitch, I *will* do what I want," he said to himself as the elevator dinged. The door opened and plumes of black, sooty smoke flowed from the chamber. Hugo began coughing from the onslaught of soot into his lungs and onto his face. He heard a loud creaking sound as the elevator cables strained against the intense heat from several floors above him. The cables gave way, and the elevator car plummeted to the basement of the building. White-hot flames shot into the hallway and Hugo yelled out, "Hey guys! Hey! Wait up! Wait for me!"

The trio were united on the bottom floor. Payekha looked at Hugo as he emerged from the stairwell and shook her head. "Really? You really gotta emphasize your racist bullshit by wearing black face? Christ, you're an asshole."

"Wait, what?" a confused Hugo replied. "What are you talking about? I, oh! No! I didn't do this on purpose, um, this time. I mean, I did go as a lawn jockey last Halloween, but, um, never mind. Hey! Squirt those zombies!"

Payekha pivoted and saturated a horde of approaching blood-thirsty zombies with *GROOMING*. She then said, "Let's get out of here. I can't see any more vomit right now."

They ran from the building as quickly as their battered bodies allowed and jumped into the SUV. "Um, is that Mister Daniels under your front tire?" Dawson meekly inquired. "Not anymore," Payekha answered as she started the car. "Now hang on. We gotta get the fuck out of here." Payekha put the car into 'Drive', slammed her foot on the accelerator and immediately flew into a street filled with embattled zombies. Blood and bones exploded around the SUV as Payekha mowed them down like a combine through a corn field. Wails and screams could be heard from the dying zombies as the SUV thumped its way through the carnivorous crowd. The wails and screams were then drowned out by a much more violent sound.

"Jesus Christ!" Dawson yelled out as the entire building that housed the National Institute of Psychiatric Health collapsed in a heap of fiery rubble. Payekha stopped the car at a nearby underpass and watched her former workplace burn in a pile of twisted metal and concrete. Severed arms, legs, heads, and torsos were intermingled with the flames and contorted rubble. She closed her eyes and was briefly transported to a scene from a few years earlier.

"We are so very excited to have you with us, Ms. Popoola," her Hispanic, female supervisor said to her while wearing a wide grin. "We know that you had so many other opportunities in the private sector. More lucrative opportunities. We are just thrilled that you chose to use your expertise in subliminal messaging to lift up humankind rather than finding ways to brainwash people to buy more soda and sneakers. We have been following your work very closely, and it is an honor to have you on our team."

"Thank you so much, I'm excited to be here," Payekha sincerely answered. "And I'm excited to get to work. If I'm right, I think that I can come up with a way to safely have people drop their insecurities and fears so that they can stand up against threats. So that they can stand up to abusers and bullies. Throughout all my research on bullies, I have found that they are nothing but little pussies. They are insecure. They are weak. And they have to project dominant strength in order to obtain any sense of self-worth. That's why they rape. That's why they beat children and animals. That's why they join militant organizations. That's why they have to surround themselves with guns and wear silly little camo costumes while camping in the woods with their boyfriends. And it's why they always have a scapegoat to terrorize. They succeed in beating down one group of people? They'll move onto another, then another, then another. They will eventually turn on and cannibalize their own supporters. Why? Because they are soulless sharks who are never satiated. They must *always* have somebody to oppress and terrorize to get over their daddy issues or whatever pussy melodrama they have stuck in their underdeveloped psyches.

"I started my research thinking that we could make the world a better place by learning about oppressive bullies. Figuring out what makes them so unsatisfied with life that it causes them to commit evil atrocities against others. Finding a way to instill a sense of self-worth and use their self-esteem for altruistic ends rather than abusive ones. The theory was very basic. Subliminally infuse them with a strong sense of self-worth. Then, turn fighters into lovers. Turn bullies into protectors. But I abandoned that line of research.

"What I discovered was that these people, who are mostly men by the way, were so damaged that they had become inherently evil. They were unreachable. The only thing that could satiate them for a brief period of time was committing acts of cruelty upon others. They are sadists who are beyond redemption. And there are so many others who can easily be indoctrinated into this sadistic ideology. People who feel slighted by society and who are more than happy to abandon their self-professed faith and replace it with cruel scapegoating of 'the other.' I don't believe that those people can ever be changed, and I don't believe that there will ever be a shortage of them in our society.

"But what I believe *can* be changed is how we *react* to the oppressors and sadistic bullies. As the saying goes, it takes two to tango. The sadists feed off of oppression. But what if nobody plays along? What if nobody succumbs to their torment? The problem is that most decent people are non-confrontational. They don't want to make waves. They just want to live their lives in peace and be left alone. And most decent people try to be understanding. They try to empathize with the damaged person. They try to help them in some way. But the sadist is *incapable* of empathy, and they view it as a weakness. They view empathy as something that they can exploit for their personal gain. The more they exploit someone's empathy, the stronger and more aggressive they become. And they will keep pushing the envelope. The boldness increases. The cruelty of the act increases. With every victory they have over an empathetic person, their sadism increases. So, our empathy, when applied to a sadist, is a detriment. It is a detriment to us personally and to our society at large because our empathy isn't helping them. It is emboldening them to commit more deplorable and more frequent acts of cruelty.

"No, I believe that in order to stop the sadists of the world, we must abandon empathy and understanding for them. We must abandon cowering to them. We must abandon looking the other way. And what we must adopt is fortitude. We must strengthen our own beliefs in humanity by extinguishing our fears and insecurities so that we have the fortitude to stand up against the bullies. To call out their racist or homophobic jokes. To shun them from our social circles. To publicly mock and ridicule their knuckle-dragging bullshit. And if we must, to defend ourselves by any means necessary when they present an existential threat to us. Gone must be the days of compliance. Gone must be the days of compromise. And instead, we must usher in a new age of unconditional fortitude against all forms of tyranny. And to do *that*, we must relieve ourselves of our reservations so that our humanity is free to fight back. Because when we fight back, the bullies always cave. Always. As I said, they are big pussies and they cannot handle being confronted by true strength. They back down and go searching for a weaker target to terrorize. But if we, as a society, are filled with strong, resolute people, then they never find their next victim. They are castrated. All doors to their sadism are closed and they just sit alone while fuming about their miserable lives without anybody to take it out on. Or they commit suicide. Whatever. Either way is a win."

"So," Payekha's new supervisor began inquired in a concerned tone. "You are saying that we must abandon our empathy? But doesn't that make all of *us* just like *them*? Aren't we being just as cruel and sadistic as *they* are?"

"Well," Payekha replied through a light chuckle. "Yes and no. I am not going to create something that eliminates our empathy. It is our *empathy* that makes us *humane*. And it is our *humanity* that makes us *truly human* as opposed to just being a neanderthal homo-sapien whose sole purpose is self-gratification. *We* are human. The *sadists* are neanderthals. So, I would never create something that strips us of our empathy. What I *am* going to create is something that alters our *definition* of empathy based upon who we are interacting with. If you see a starving child, your empathy will still guide you in helping to feed them. If you see a motorist broken down on the road, your empathy will still guide you in pulling over. If someone loses a loved one, your empathy will still guide you to say kind, comforting words.

"But if you date someone who begins abusing you, your empathy will not be for the abuser. It will be for yourself and for society at large. Your inhibitions and fears are stripped away and your empathy for yourself and other potential victims of this sadist will cause you to stand up and fight back. Your empathy for the abuser will be gone. Your empathy for peaceful society will not only be present but strengthened. And the bullies will no longer have a tango partner to feed off of. See the difference?"

"I do, indeed," Payekha's supervisor answered while wearing a sly smile. "I *do* understand the difference. And I hope that your research bears fruit. And soon. I fear what is beginning to happen in our world. I fear the sadistic bullies, as you refer to them as, are gaining more of a foothold in our nation's psyche by the day. And I fear what will happen if they are ever to assume power. Yes, this is quite exciting. And I have the perfect person for you to partner with. His name is Dawson, and he is a new hire as well. Come on, I'll take you to his office."

Payekha looked at her former friend's defeated face as the NIPH building burned in the background. "Jesus, Dawson, what the fuck happened to you? We were such good friends. Hell, I actually thought that we had a shot at being something more than friends. You were the one man in my life that I had met that I respected and didn't fear. You were so kind. And smart. And then, you just turned into one of *them.* Ignored me. Called me those awful names behind my back. Fired me. What the fuck, man?"

Dawson continued to look down at the floorboard of the SUV. Tears welled up in his blue eyes as he said, "I'm so sorry, Payekha. I thought I was a better person. But I'm not. I'm weak. I threw you and so many others under the bus for my own self-preservation. I told myself that if I blended in, I could maybe use my position for good later on. But that was all just self-rationalization bullshit. I blended in, alright. I blended in, and you are right. I became one of them. I started fearing and hating people that I was told to by Dear Leader. People who had done me no harm had become my sworn enemies because this fucking self-appointed messiah said so. I went down that rabbit hole, and I never came out. Until today.

"When we conducted that test today and we turned human beings into savages, I knew that I was wrong. And when we fired you today. When I participated in firing my friend, I knew that I had become someone that I didn't even recognize. Take this for what it's worth. I know I've participated in some cruel shit, and I don't expect you to forgive me. But do you know what I was doing before we realized that we had hit the 'Transmit' button? Before we realized that we had unleashed this unholy technological virus upon the world? I was packing my shit. I wasn't even going to submit my resignation. I was just going to walk out the door and never look back. I was disgusted with myself. And I was done with it all. The testing on human subjects. The hatred. The undying loyalty to Dear Leader. I was done with it like a snake shedding its worthless skin. I was going to go to your house and see if maybe you wanted to run away with me. Some-where. Anywhere. Just jump in a car a drive. I wanted to be redeemed in your eyes. That was the plan. And now, it's fucked because I've destroyed the world. There is no redemption for me. And I'm so sorry. Come on. We'd better get going. We've attracted another group."

Payekha sat motionless for a moment. Her introspection was interrupted by Hugo. "Hey, you (derogatory term omitted) bitch! You gonna drive or what?" Hugo was immediately struck in his good eye by Dawson's clenched fist. "Don't you *ever* call her that ever again. Do you understand? If you ever do or say anything to harm her ever again, I swear, I'll kill you."

"Huh," Payekha stated as she started the car. "Maybe everything's *not* fucked, Dawson. And yeah, we might not have a choice but to run away together. Oh, and my mom needs to come with us. Because we need to find a new cellular transmission center. And fast. Oh, and fuck Hugo. He isn't coming along."

"Fuck Hugo, huh?" Hugo snapped while rubbing his swelling eye. "Well, you two may want to think twice about that. Because there *is* another cellular transmission center. And *only* one. And *I* know just where it is. In fact, I've been there a couple times. So, I'll cut you two a deal. I'll play nice. And you're going to take me along with you. Otherwise, good luck finding this needle in a haystack. Once we do what we need to do, we can part ways. We got a deal?"

Payekha and Dawson looked at each other for a moment and shrugged. "Yeah, fuckin' whatever," Payekha said as she put the SUV into gear. "Just don't fuck with us. You wouldn't be the *first* man that I've sliced from dick to sternum."

Payekha came to a screeching halt in front of her apartment. Dawson got out, looked down at the front passenger tire and said, "Holy shit! You just crushed that guy's skull so hard his eyes popped out!"

"Yeah, that's been happening a lot lately. And that's just the crazy-ass Bible-banger from 3C. I'm not shedding any tears over him." She began banging on her apartment door while yelling, "Hey Mom! Open up! It's me! And I've got a couple dudes with me so don't freak out and spray *GROOMING* all over us! We're not infected!"

"Yeeeeessss? I'm coming, dear," Ezinne Popoola answered. Payekha calmly tapped the foot of her well-worn leg crutch and whistled while listening to her mother ever so slowly unlock the deadbolt. Then the other deadbolt. Then the doorknob. And finally, the chain. "There you are, dear. Welcome home. Oh, you three must be starving. Would you like for me to warm you up some Hot Pockets? And...And...oh dear lord. Payekha! What have you done to my car?"

CHAPTER 15

MAGIC 8 BALL

"Ummmm," Payekha cautiously replied as she, Dawson, and Hugo entered her apartment. "Yeah, I'm sorry about that, Mom. But the streets are just crazy. There are zombies everywhere attacking each other in the middle of the streets. There are buildings on fire and collapsing. The whole fucking world is burning and is a complete shit-show. So, yeah, I might have put a few, um, dents in your ride. But not to worry. There are tons of new cars sitting in car lots that we can just take. Who in the hell is going to stop us? Once we get out of the city, we'll look for some small-town car dealership and, um, y'know. Trade yours in. It'll be fine."

"What do you mean 'get out of the city', dear?" Ezinne inquired. "Why would we leave the city? We are safe here. Lord knows what the rest of the world looks like and what dangers there might be. Why would we leave a place where we are safe? Besides, this city is my home. I have friends here."

"Yeah, well, I think it's a pretty safe bet that your friends are eating each other out right now. Damn. I *really* need to rephrase that. Listen, Mom. We need to go. I know it might be dangerous, but we can load up with water and Hot Pockets. We have some real guns, water guns, and a shit-ton of *GROOMING*. We don't have a choice. I got my server from my office that had all my research and data on it. I just need to reanalyze and tweak my subliminal messaging. My current message sends viewers into too deep of a dream-state. They have to live in the dream-state just enough to shed their fears and build their self-confidence while confronting the dangers of the real world. They have to interact with two realities simultaneously. Otherwise, they'll just be all hippie-dippy and shit and wander around like they've just OD'd on mushrooms. I think I know what I did wrong and I think it'll be easy to fix.

"So, while I'm working on that, I need you three to load up the car and get ready to go. We need to get to a new cellular transmission center that Hugo knows about. Just where are we going, Hugo?"

"Huh-uh, not a chance," Hugo replied as he applied fresh bandages to his empty eye socket. "I'm not telling you. You'll betray me and leave me behind. Let's just say we're heading West. And it's going to be a long drive. I'll navigate. You'll drive. That's the deal."

"Yeah, well, I just was asking because we need to know how long of a drive it will be so that we bring enough supplies, that's all," Payekha replied with an unassuming, innocent tone. "We have a deal. Just keep your bigoted comments to yourself and don't be a dick and you can come along. No worries, there Champ. But we do need to know how long of a journey it will be. You know. For supplies and driving rotations and shit like that."

"Fine," Hugo grumbled back while unwrapping his right hand and staring at the two bloody nubs where his fingers once were. "It's going to be about one-thousand miles. So, plan accordingly. You three do what you need to do. I'm going to raid your medicine cabinet for antibiotics and pain killers. The shock of the day is wearing off, and this shit is really starting to hurt."

"That's a good idea," Dawson said. "Yeah, we should pack up as much medicine as we can. I mean, whatever medicine that's available. Most of it was banned two years ago by the Healthy Americans Against Autism Act. Or HAAAA. Ha, indeed. Yeah, the laugh was on all of us. Man, what a bunch of crazy bullshit. The Regime took over and suddenly everything under the sun caused autism. Literally! Even sunscreen was banned. And the funny thing? No reduction in the occurrence of autism. None whatsoever. Oh, but we were greeted with a *huge* spike in measles and deadly flus and mutations of viruses that people were once protected from. The hospitals have been overwhelmed by hundreds of thousands of sick people. Most of them have died because they were turned away from medical care because of no health care coverage. Nope, The Regime took that away from normal folks too and allowed hospitals and clinics to send people away to die. Hell, people couldn't even wear masks in public to try to protect themselves from the multiple pandemics because anyone wearing a mask could be picked up and be designated a 'domestic terrorist.' While the *real* domestic terrorists, The Regime's thugs, could wear masks all they wanted as they kidnapped innocent people off the streets. Jesus Christ, how did I not see just how evil this shit is?"

"Yeah, yeah, yeah," Payekha replied dismissively while plugging the server into her home laptop. "This fuckin' shit's been crazy as fuck, and you were brainwashed into believing it was normal. I'm glad you're finally deprogrammed. Welcome back to the right side of history. Of course, there's hardly anyone around to know about it, but hey! Better late than never, right? And I've got a little surprise for you. Pull the medicine cabinet from the wall. I've got all kinds of contraband medicine that I had a visiting friend from Canada smuggle in for me. It's been nice having a close friend who lives in a civilized country as opposed to this Banana Republic on steroids. She was a girl that I saved from, um, never mind. You two don't need to know about that.

"Use what you need, Hugo, and pack the rest of it up. I've got duffle bags in my bedroom closet. The heavy one has guns and ammo in it. Real ones. Hugo, don't you even *dare* to look at it. I'll give *you* a little yellow water pistol filled with *GROOMING*. I can't trust you with anything more. Now, get going you two. And Mom, load the cooler up with water and Hot Pockets. And everybody be quiet about it! I need to concentrate on this shit."

"But what then, dear?" Ezinne inquired. "What happens when you perfect the subliminal messaging?"

"Well, Mom," Payekha answered as her eyes began scanning rows of data points. "Then we go on a little road trip. To wherever the hell Hugo is taking us. We need to find a cellular transmission station because the one at NIPH is, um, well because that building collapsed in a burning heap of rubble. Oh, fuck. I just thought of something. I forgot to take my little metal spinny stress relief thingy off of my desk. Oh well. It's covered in several inches of vomit, anyway. So, we go to the transmission station, break in, fire it up, and I insert my handy dandy flash drive. We replace the violent Dear Leader message with my Fantasy World empowerment message and we transmit it. Everywhere. So, anybody who has yet to be infected won't be. If they happen to look at anything on a cell phone, they will have *my* sublim- inal messaging implanted into their limbic systems and won't turn into violent zombies."

"But what of the ones who have *already* been turned, dear?" Ezinne continued to inquire. "We will still be living in a world that is filled with mindless, violent zombies. Billions of them. What do we do for them?"

"Good fuckin' question, Mom," Payekha shot back. "Really good fuckin' question. Listen, this plan is far from perfect. The reality is that these zombies are going to rip each other apart until there's nobody left standing. If we were to just crouch down and hide for a few months, this whole thing will probably play itself out to a final, grisly conclusion. The vast majority of the human population is doomed. But maybe not all. We might be able to lure herds of them someplace. Like a big stadium or something. We lure them in, hook a cellphone to the jumbotron, and deprogram them. Then, those depro- grammed folks can go around and do the same thing. We could build an army of deprogrammed, now-decent people, to go from town to town and get zombies to view the messaging. The more people that get deprogrammed, the larger our army grows. The larger our army grows, the more people get deprogrammed. Make sense?"

"Yes, I suppose it does dear," Ezinne responded. "And that might work for *our* continent, but what about Europe? Asia? Africa? South America? Australia? How will we ever reach *them*?"

"Oh fuck, Mom!" a frustrated Payekha roared back. "I don't know!

I'm trying to save the human race one step at a time so get off my ass and let me get to work!"

"Fine, dear," Ezinne said in a hurt voice. "I'm sorry to have bothered you with my silly questions. I just thought that it would be wise to have a plan before we go driving half-way across this decimated country. But if having a plan bothers you, then I'll just keep to myself and go pack the Hot Pockets."

"Ah, fuck," Payekha muttered to herself before spinning around in her office chair to address her mother. "Mom, I'm sorry. I shouldn't have said that. It's just been a real shit day. I mean, *every* day I wake up under the oppression of Dear Leader's Regime is a shit day, but *this* one takes the cake. Dipshit Chad locked my keys in my car, so I had to take the bus. I had to deal with racist and sexist bullshit at my job, *again*, before getting fired by these assholes. Then I'm attacked by fucking zombies on a bus. I sprain my ankle. Discover Dear Leader's putrid scent kills the zombies. Got squirt guns from a toy store. Came back here and killed my kinda-boyfriend. Fought my zombie mother and dragged her ass back here. Deprogrammed her and watched her suck on my remote, splash water around, and dance with my vase. Went back to my office and had to deal with *these* two motherfuckers again. Then, this fucking author made me deal with an explosion of vomit. Don't you *dare* recap that in detail, motherfucker. I don't want to *ever* think about that again. I then survive a collapsing building, drive through hordes of zombies, and get back home so that I can use my brilliance to save humanity. So, I'm sorry, Mom. It's now five in the morning. I'm tired. I'm hungry. I have to deal with dumbass Hugo. And the entire fate of the human race is falling on my shoulders. Plus, my fucking ankle hurts. So please excuse me for being a little short with you, Mom. I didn't mean to take it out on you. But please. Everybody. I need to get this fixed. I need to concentrate. I need quiet with no interruptions. Then, we'll all take a powernap and get on the road. Okay?"

"Of course, dear," Ezinne lovingly stated as she bent down and embraced her daughter. "I understand. Dawson, Hugo, and I will pack up and load the car and will leave you be. You just perform your magic, my most brilliant daughter. Perform your magic and deliver us all from the pure evil that is Dear Leader's message."

"Oh fuck, *now* what?" Payekha yelled out an hour later after hearing yet another crash from her bedroom. "Sorry!" Dawson yelled back. "Hugo's depth perception is off, and he ran into a shelf and knocked a bunch of porcelain cats on the floor. Oh, and I think he knocked himself out!"

"Oh, shit! My porcelain cats?" Payekha lamented. "I've been collecting those for years. Please tell me the large, white one isn't damaged." There was an awkward silence from the bedroom before Dawson's voice emerged. "Um, yeah. It's pretty much smashed. Well, all of them are, actually. Sorry. But, hey! Good news! Hugo's waking up and not dead!"

"How in the fuck is that good news?" Payekha grumbled to herself. "Just please keep the fucking noise down! This reanalysis is taking me way longer than I expected and the numbers are just starting to run together. I need sleep. But I have to finish this first. So please! Keep it down!"

"Will do!" Dawson said as he brought another large duffle of *GROOMING* from the bedroom. "Just one more bag and we'll have all the *GROOMING* ready to load." Dawson scurried back to the bedroom and there was another loud crash. "Oh, fuck," Payekha said as she rubbed her weary eyes. "Sorry!" Dawson yelled out. "Hugo fell face-first into your mirror! I'm gonna have to take a break and take these shards of glass out of his face! Damn, buddy. These are going to leave some scars."

Another hour passed. The SUV was loaded. Payekha could hear the loud snoring of Dawson and Hugo coming from her bedroom. Her mother was asleep in the recliner. And Payekha's blood-shot eyes were staring blankly at a screen filled with numbers. "I don't understand. Why can't I figure this out? I'm so close. My original message was so close to what it needed to be. It should just be a little tweak. Just turn the volume down on the fantasy part of the message. But every test I run using slightly adjusted data comes out worse.

"Trial One would have destroyed the positive messaging

completely and left us with what's happening outside. So, *that's* no fucking help. Trial Two would leave people barking and chasing cars. Seriously. I could turn them into fucking dogs. Who knew? Trial Three? Um, well, they go from *being* dogs to fucking everything *doggy-style*. That one would completely strip away their inhibitions and turn their sex-drive up by a million. They would literally just keep fucking until they died. I guess you could say that they'd fuck themselves over. Better than eating each other out, I guess. I really need to rephrase that. Trial Four. Zombies again. Better, less aggressive zombies who just sit and stare and drool, sure. But zombies, nonetheless. Nice windfall for nursing homes though.

"Trial Five. Shit, now I'm getting desperate. I've totally turned all the numbers on their heads. Doing everything in complete reverse. And the brilliant result? Everybody who watched this would be fearful of everything. They would cower at the slightest sound. They would hide in their homes under their covers and be too afraid to come out so they would piss and shit all over themselves then eventually die of starvation. So, Payekha. What now? What now, genius?"

Payekha could feel tears of hopelessness welling up in her eyes. She shook her full afro and said, "never again. I'm never going to cry again. I'm never going to..." Her self-talk was interrupted by her psyche's defense system overriding her consciousness. The numbers on the screen turned various colors and began dancing. And singing. And winking at her. She was especially taken by an overly flirtatious number '8'. Payekha began laughing and said to the curvaceous numeral, "Yeah, I'm flattered there 8. But I don't swing that way. Maybe you should hook up with a '6' and a '9'."

The vibrantly colored numbers began giggling and the overly friendly '8' winked and waved for Payekha to follow her. Payekha's disassociation sent her into a swirling kaleidoscope of numbers and equations. She stared at her computer screen while mentally falling into the brilliant, rapidly rotating numerical vortex. She landed with a thud on a computer chip and looked up. Standing over her was the beautiful '8'. She batted her lush eyelashes and was holding a bright red laser pointer. Payekha's eyes drifted to the equation where the laser was pointing. The equation began pulsing in bright green and Payekha's brown eyes widened with understanding.

"Oh fuck, that's it!" she exclaimed as the bright numbers immediately retreated into their drab, black rows. "This equation right here! I forgot to carry the one! I'm such a dumbass! Okay, let's try *this* then. Trial Six." Payekha's smile grew as the new trial data calculated the impact the subliminal message would have on a human subject. "Uh, huh. Uh, huh. Straight to the limbic system, like all the others. Good. Enter into a dream world. Someplace of each person's creation where they feel safe. Perfect. Then, the fear diminishes. The inhibitions diminish. Their strength and fortitude are increased. They feel safe and strong and are not held back by their fear. Yes. Fucking perfect. And, while they are in their sanctuary dream world, they are equally conscious of the real world and can interact with it. This is it. It's perfect. It's my personal experience. My experience of drawing strength through disassociation. I can give it to others. I've done it. I've fucking done it. I can turn this thing around. I can save lives. I can save humanity. Man, I've always loved numbers, but this is the first time I've ever thought about fucking one. Thanks '8'. I owe you one."

CHAPTER 16

HOW THE TABLES HAVE TURNED

"Oh shit, how long did I sleep?" Payekha wearily asked as she rubbed her eyes and exited her bedroom. "Weeeeelll, dear," her mother answered. "Around ten hours. It's okay, dear. You needed the rest. We all did. We need to be well rested for our journey. Did you get everything done that you needed to?"

"Yeah, I did, Mom," Payekha replied. "I did it. I figured out my error in the subliminal formula. I've now constructed the perfect subliminal message that will attach itself to everything transmitted over cellular networks and allow the viewer to disassociate into a world of strength while simultaneously engaging with whatever threatening shit is happening in the real world. It's perfect. I've stored everything on my computer, backed it up on my server, and have it on my flash drive. There's no fucking way I'm taking any chances with this. Hell, I'd tattoo it on my ass if I thought it would help.

"All we need to do is have dipshit Hugo take us to the transmission station, plug the flash drive in, and we'll be ready to deprogram folks all over the world. And I've been thinking about how we can do that. As we round up people and deprogram them, we'll build an army of volunteers who can call people all over the world. We'll set up phone banks. We know that it's impossible that every single person has been indoctrinated or, um, eaten. There must be some survivors out there. We just have to keep calling and calling until somebody answers. We'll instruct them to watch anything on their phones so that they are exposed to my empowering subliminal messaging. Then, we'll have them to start calling and calling until we can build an army of volunteers in every nation. I think it will work over time. Unless there's nobody left to answer their phones. What are you two watching?"

Payekha sat on the couch between her mother and Dawson and looked at her TV screen. The images were split into eight boxes that rotated fiery scenes from around the world. In the upper left quadrant was a disheveled, unkempt anchor who was continuing to broadcast his apocalyptic updates.

"It's now three in the afternoon here on the east coast," the anchor said in his worn-down voice. His face was covered with unshaven stubble. His tie was off, and his coffee-stained shirt was half-unbuttoned. And his forlorn thirty-three-year-old White face looked to have aged by at least twenty years.

"I've now been on the air continuously for nearly twenty-four hours. And quite frankly, folks, I'm not sure how much longer I can go. I'm going to give one final report to anybody that might still be listening. To anybody that might still be alive. Then I'm signing off. I can't bear to watch this travesty any longer. I've said it a million times in the past twenty-four hours. Stay off your phones. I don't know why, but there's something about cell phones that turns people into monsters. I've seen it first-hand.

"Yesterday's broadcast started out like all the others for the past several years. Story after story about Dear Leader's successes. His eighteen hole-in-ones. Again. His sexual prowess with a Middle Eastern princess. In front of his wife. Again. How he works tirelessly for his people to improve their lives. Even though most people now work eighty hours a week and live in squalor. Story after story that was nothing more than bullshit. I can say that now, without fear. He's dead. Everybody in the government is dead. There is no government. There is no Dear Leader. And, quite frankly, that is the only silver-lining in this shitstorm. We may all die, but we will all die a free people. We're no longer under the thumb of this tyrannical regime. We don't have anybody to lord over us. We are all on our own to make our own choices. We are all on our individual islands, surrounded by an ocean of chaos. It's all on *us* now as to what type of person we will be.

"Anyway, we had just reported a story on Dear Leader's gold leafing his ballroom, again, and thrown it to break. My co-host looked at her phone. Hell, everybody in the studio immediately looked at their phones. We've all been indoctrinated to stare at those fucking things every free, waking moment. I would have too, but I left mine in the dressing room. Otherwise, I would have been right there with them. Watching stupid videos. Playing a game. Anything to distract me from the atrocities that Dear Leader was inflicting upon us. Anything to divert my attention and drift mindlessly into an alternate reality, if just for a moment. I would have been with them. But yesterday, I wasn't.

"Everybody looked at their phones. Then they all started muttering something about the grotesqueness of Dear Leader. They started frothing at the mouth. They started growling. Their eyes turned pure white. And then, they began viciously attacking each other. I pulled out my gun and began blowing them all away. I murdered my friends and colleagues out of fear and self-preservation. Of course, I'm used to that. I'm used to turning on people I once cared about. The Regime has numbed us all to it. But still, I had never personally killed anyone, and it was quite shocking to see their contorted bodies lying in the studio in pools of their own blood. And at that moment, I knew.

"I knew there was something imbedded in their phones that had caused this. I don't know what. Are aliens responsible? Or is this something that we have done to ourselves. Probably the latter. That dipshit Director of National Discipline, or whatever stupid title he's given himself this week, probably released some experimental bullshit throughout the planet. It's not like he was the brightest bulb. Or the most sober. He was known for transmitting all kinds of stupid shit when he was drunk. Which was pretty much every day. It got to where other nations could cut way back on their national intelligence because all they had to do was check this asshole's posts and they would know what we were planning. Fuck, how many of our soldiers did he get killed? Oh, I know the number. But it was never reported. Not by me. Not by anybody. No, our reports would be about yet another perfect strike of glory against the evildoers in some foreign land. You know. Like Portland. Oh well. I guess it doesn't matter anymore. All I know is that something in the cell phones is turning people into enraged monsters. And not just here. Everywhere. Reports began coming in about it from all over the world.

"It didn't matter if you were in a city or in the country. Every place in the world was being overrun by these…these…zombies, I guess you'd call them. The world's cities are in flames. Small towns are decimated. And everything in-between. Humanity is lost, folks. Pretty much everybody has either been turned into a zombie or has been eaten by a zombie. I'm praying that there are still a few pockets of people left out there. Maybe in extremely rural areas of the world where there are no cell phones. But who knows how long *they* will last either. It's all lost. The human experiment is over. Pretty soon, everybody will be dead, and nature is going to reclaim our concrete fortresses. Our buildings. Our shopping centers. Our homes. It's all going to be covered in bushes and trees and flowers. Wildlife will use our shopping malls as caves. Birds will nest in our gutters. It will be like we never existed. And maybe that's not such a bad thing.

"Anyway, as I said, this is my final broadcast. I'm going to leave you with the images on your screen. These other seven boxes are live video feeds from cities throughout our nation and the world and are running on a constant loop. At least, for as long as the power stays on. You can sit there and watch as city after city collapses upon itself. You can sit and watch people rip apart their fellow man. You can sit and watch the death throes of humankind. Good luck to you with that. I can't watch it anymore. So, for the final time, I'm Jake Jackhoff and praise, um, I mean…*fuck* Dear Leader."

The anchor grimly stared into the camera, took a revolver from his desktop, placed the barrel into his mouth, and pulled the trigger.

"Huh," Payekha said while watching the anchor's exploded head fragments drip down the studio's cityscape back drop. "He had more brains than I thought. I mean, that's a lot of fuckin' brains that just got blown onto that wall. I never did like him anyway. I mean, I didn't like *anybody* in the media. I knew that they were just the broadcast arm of The Regime. They weren't real reporters. Just regurgitators of Dear Leader's propaganda. But this Jackoff guy always got on my nerves. His voice was whiney, and his hair was just a little too perfect, y'know? Anyway, we'd better get going. Is the SUV loaded? And where in the fuck is Hugo?"

"I'm right here," Hugo answered from behind the couch. Payekha, Dawson, and Ezinne turned around to find Hugo holding a gun in one hand and another object in his other. "What the fuck are you doing *now*, Hugo?" an exasperated Payekha asked. "And be careful you don't drop that gun. You've lost two fingers on that hand, dumbass."

"I'll tell you what I'm doing," Hugo replied. "I'm protecting myself. I know we had a deal, but I'm making sure you live up to your end of the bargain. I'm making sure you don't back stab me. I know your kind. Once you got your Black assess off of the plantation you just kept wanting more, didn't you? Economic stability. The right to vote for representatives that looked just like you. Equality in employment and housing and owning businesses. Yeah, you wanted it all. Just like Dear Leader told us. You wanted it all and it came at *our* expense. You didn't want equality. You wanted to take everything from *us*. The White man! All of your so-called gains were at the expense of a White man losing out. Your nice house? A White man could have owned it! Your fancy car? A White man should be driving it! Your new restaurant? You shouldn't own it! You should be waiting tables for the White owner! Your six-figure job? Should have gone to a qualified White man and not some (derogatory term omitted) free loader. You took it *all* from us. But Dear Leader set things right.

"He put White men back in charge of everything and put you back in your place. Waiting tables. Serving us. Picking our crops. It was how Dear Leader intended it to be. It was how *God* intended it to be. But now, I can see you taking advantage of what's happening. You people are trying to take everything over again. Including me. You're going to take over and take my life. But I'm not an idiot. I know what you're doing and I'm not going to let you. You're going to follow my instructions. We're going to travel to the transmission station. And I'm going to make sure you don't fuck it up. I'm holding the flash drive until we get there. Then, if you're good, maybe I'll let you get on your way. Got it, bitch?"

"Oh Jesus Christ," Payekha mumbled while shaking her afro in disbelief. "Okay, just a few things I need to point out to you there, Champ. First, my people, or anybody *else* for that matter, did not take one goddamned thing from any pasty-faced cracker motherfucker. There had come a time in our society where the playing field was being leveled and people from every walk of life had the same *opportunities* to *compete* for better education and good paying jobs and businesses so that they *too* could afford a nice house and car and higher education for their kids. We didn't take anything from *you*. We were finally allowed to *compete*, and the most qualified person was rewarded so that we could *all* share in the wealth of the most prosperous nation in the history of the world. That's it. I know you can't wrap your ignorant head around that, because you believe you're so much fucking smarter than everybody else. But you're not. Let me clue you into a few examples of just how fucking stupid you are.

"For starters, you're pointing a squirt gun filled with *GROOMING* at us. I know it *looks* real and is heavy as fuck, but it's not a real gun. It's from the Junior Patriotic Armament collection. You can pull the trigger if you want. You're just going to make us smell like Dear Leader's shitty ass. And then you're going to have to ride in the car with us. And I'm not going to roll down the fucking windows!

"Secondly, I have the new messaging not only on my flash drive but also on my computer and server. And there's no fucking way you're going to be able to hold onto all three. And my flash drive is password protected and everything on there is encrypted. So good luck hacking that shit, Mister '1-2-3-4'. Oh, and another small point. You're not holding my flash drive. That's my lipstick, dumbass. Jesus just how hard did you hit your head? And man, is your face fucked up from the broken mirror. You look like you've just gone ten rounds with a fucking bear! So, just calm the fuck down, dipshit. We're all going to look at my computer screen and watch the new subliminal message. We'll then be protected. And maybe you'll end up learning something, asshole."

The defeated Hugo stared down at the floor and placed the gun on the table next to the laptop. Payekha sauntered over to her desk and cued up the video with the implanted message. "Now, you three. Just watch this."

It was a video of a black cat chasing a laser pointer. The frantic feline scurried around a living room trying to catch its elusive prey. He jumped on furniture, slid on a round yellow rug, and crashed into a wall before climbing a set of unsuspecting blue curtains. The curtain rod gave way, and the curtains plummeted onto the floor. The cat shook his head, looked at the crumpled curtains with disdain, and strutted into another room.

The foursome were laughing at the impossibly cute video. They then became eerily quiet as a warmth began to fill their psyches. Their eyes widened as their feelings of fear, mistrust, and worthlessness melted away. Payekha shook her head and exclaimed, "Wow! Kind of a trip, huh? How does everybody feel? A bit stronger? A bit more self-confident? And *that* shit only intensifies if we're put under duress. Let's give it a test run, shall we?"

Payekha picked the gun up from her desk and placed the barrel against Hugo's temple. "What are you doing, Payekha?" a chuckling Hugo asked. "Are you going to squirt me in the head?"

"Nope," Payekha answered in a determined voice. "I'm going to blow your cracker fucking brains out. You're so fucking stupid, Hugo. I lied to you. This *is* a real gun. With real bullets. One of which is about to go through your balding fucking head."

Hugo began hyperventilating and sweating while the curious Dawson and Ezinne looked on. His body began shaking and he closed his eyes while waiting for his grisly demise. He was suddenly enveloped in a swirl of colors. He opened his eyes, and the room was filled with bright streaks of multi-colored lights. The plants were animated and laughing while their eyes rolled around in their impossibly large sockets. The remote controls were dancing on the coffee table while the curtains swayed to music that only he could hear. He smiled as he could feel his body growing armor around it. He reached for a sword. He confidently looked his marauder directly into her deep mahogany eyes and smiled. She was no longer a threat to him because of her skin color. Or her gender. Or for any other inconsequential reason that he had been indoctrinated to believe by his parents, and church, and regime. She was a threat to him because she was holding a gun to his head. And he now experienced a strength and sense of self-worth that enabled him to fight back against this existential threat. His smile widened and he swung his sword at her.

Payekha laughed as she grabbed the end of the cane that he had just swung and said, "Alright then! Good boy, Hugo!" She laughed louder as she squirted him between the eyes with *GROOMING*. "Man, you really are a gullible sonofabitch, aren'tcha? I wasn't going to shoot you, man. This really is just a squirt gun. Now let's finish packing up and get our asses on the road. But Hugo. Take a quick shower first. You smell like shit."

The squeaky clean and freshly bandaged Hugo stepped back into the living room just as Dawson was opening the front door. "I want to try another test before we go," he said to Payekha and Ezinne. "I want to see just how much trust and empowerment this messaging can implant in a bigoted nazi like Hugo. So, tell me Hugo. Tell us all. Just where the hell are we going?"

Hugo looked up and saw three pairs of eyes staring back at him. He searched his soul for a moment. His mistrust of this trio was nowhere to be found. He searched deeper. He felt confident in his own capabilities. Confident in his intellect, his physical abilities, his humane convictions towards his new-found colleagues. He held no fear as he clearly said, "Colorado. Pueblo, Colorado. That is the only transmission station that is powerful enough to send our message everywhere. It's the only place that we can upload the message, then implant it into the cellular network's algorithms. It's the only place where we have a shot at saving humanity. But we'd better go. It's about fifteen hundred miles away. If we switch off drivers, it will take us twenty hours. Well, twenty-one or so, depending on how often we have to piss, so let's watch our fluid intake. But every minute we wait, another innocent person is being indoctrinated by the evil messaging of Dear Leader. Or being murdered by one of his creations. Every minute we stand here, is another life lost."

Payekha cocked her head in disbelief at what she had just heard. This vile, small man was exhibiting caring for others. This once groveling sycophant was now a confident, humane person. Payekha decided to try one more test on her subject. "Um, Hugo, listen. Before we go, I need to tell you something. I don't think you heard the news report, and I know how much you idolized him, but, um, well, Dear Leader is dead."

Hugo did not hesitate to respond. "Who gives a fuck. He was a soulless piece of shit. Are we ready to get going now, or what? Oh, and Payekha. Here, give me that bag with the computer and server. You shouldn't be putting that much weight on your bum ankle."

Dawson stared at Hugo in disbelief as he watched him shoulder this Black woman's burden. He, having lost two fingers and an eye and had sustained a concussion and face lacerations, was now sacrificing his own well-being for another. And not just *any* other person. He was doing it for *Payekha*. A Black woman who he had always been envious of. A Black woman who he had always loathed in the deepest fiber of his being because of her intellect. A Black woman who he called the vilest of names both behind her back and to her face. And a Black woman who Dawson had secretly loved. "Um, that's okay, buddy. Here. Let me get that for her. You just get in the back and relax. I wouldn't want you to reinjure yourself."

Payekha looked at the pair of White men with a perplexed expression before saying, "Um, okay. Thanks, boys. Fuck, I should have invented this shit a long time ago. I kinda like a pair of White boys waiting on my Black ass, heh, heh, heh. But just hand that bag over. That shit stays with *me*."

CHAPTER 17

JUST SHUT UP AND GET IN THE CAR

"Well, shit, we can't go *that* way either," a frustrated Payekha stated while being confronted with yet another blocked entry ramp to the interstate. "How in the fuck are we going to get out of this town? In just over twenty-four hours, most of the side streets have been blocked by burned out cars, collapsed buildings, trees, and…and…"

"And zombies, dear," Ezinne thoughtfully contributed from the front passenger seat of the dented black SUV. "Don't forget about the zombies. Still thousands of them out in the streets attacking anything that moves. Including each other."

"Uh, yeah, I know, Mom," Payekha retorted as she made a U-Turn to try to find another entrance ramp. "The side streets being blocked make sense. They are tearing the fuck out of everything and it's all ending up in the street. But the entrance ramps? They're being blocked by cars. Carefully parked cars with no drivers in them. It's almost as though they're doing this intentionally. Like, they're purposefully preventing anybody from leaving the city. But how is that possible? How can a bunch of mindless zombies who are acting on pure impulse also be that calculating? It doesn't make sense."

"Actually, it kinda does," Hugo answered from the back seat. "I'm not sure about this, but maybe the Dear Leader virus doesn't wipe everything away. I mean, sure, it turns people into violent, impulsive zombies hell-bent on destroying everything. Just like Dear Leader, as it turns out. But as brain-dead as they are, maybe they are also still able to plan. If they are running out of food, meaning people to eat, maybe the hunter-gatherer portion of their brains kick in. Maybe they are able to set a trap to ensnare more prey. Just think about it. They have ravenous appetites. If they aren't eating, then they're *thinking* about eating. And thinking about how to obtain more food. And all those base instincts and skills that have allowed humankind to survive up to this point are still hard-wired in their brains. So, they set traps. With cars or whatever else they can find. I dunno, what do you think of my theory, Dawson?"

"Um, yeah, I suppose," Dawson meekly answered while staring at Payekha's mahogony eyes reflected in the rear-view mirror. "Yeah, I suppose their most primitive drives could still be active. And our primitive drives certainly can motivate us to perform all *sorts* of acts, now, can't they? There are all sorts of things humans are capable of doing out of greed. Or self-preservation. Or lust. Um, I guess. We would need to analyze the data, Hugo, but yeah. I think we need to just go on the assumption that these zombies not only act spontaneously but can plot and plan and calculate as well. Which makes them a helluva lot more dangerous than we thought. Hey, Payekha. Why don't you hand me your flash drive and laptop. I'll see if I can't come to a more definitive answer."

"Nope, not gonna happen," Payekha defiantly countered. "My little black server, my little black laptop, and my little black flash drive are *all* staying on *my* little Black ass in this duffle strapped around *my* little Black tits. I'm not taking any chances with this shit. Sorry. No exceptions. Maybe we can look at it together later on when we stop for a break. In the meantime, I gotta find a way out of this fucking hellhole of a city. And now, I apparently have to watch out for zombie traps."

"Like that one!" Hugo yelled out. The SUV came to a screeching halt immediately after turning a corner. Standing between their vehicle and the entrance to I-270 was a fleet of abused cars, trucks, and vans that were being driven and methodically moved into position by white-eyed, sneering zombies. "Holy shit!" Hugo exclaimed. "They're not acting independently! They're working together somehow! Fuck, Payekha! Turn around!"

"Uh, yeah, I think that maybe I'd better," Payekha answered in a quivering voice as several pairs of white eyes glared at her from behind their respective steering wheels. She placed the SUV in reverse and began backing out of the one-way ramp. The growling zombies put their cars into 'Drive' and turned their vehicles to face them.

"Weeeelll, we'd better get out of here, dear," Ezinne stated. She was interrupted by the roar of four engines as the zombies trounced on the accelerators. "Fuck!" Payekha shouted as she did the same. The tires of the SUV made loud screeching sounds as she whipped the large van around and floored the accelerator. One of the zombie vehicles just missed their rear bumper and went careening into the ramp's concrete support. The car exploded and the driver's crispy, smoking head crashed through the windshield of the SUV and onto Ezinne's lap. "Hot, hot, hot!" Ezinne yelled as she rolled down her window and tossed the smoldering head out of the car.

Payekha darted down a side street and frantically steered the SUV in order to dodge the neighborhood's scattered ruins. And hordes of warring zombies. The SUV once again became soaked with blood and covered in dismembered body parts as it thumped its way through the crowd of insane carnivores. She turned right onto a street that was relatively clear and breathed a sigh of relief. Her relief did not last long as a pair of zombie pick-up trucks maneuvered onto either side of her. They snarled at her from their frothing mouths while ramming their trucks into the side of the SUV. Then everybody's heads jerked back when they felt a large cargo van ram them from behind.

"Ah, shit!" She exclaimed. "We're boxed in! These motherfuckers have boxed us in! They aren't mindless! They know *exactly* what the hell they're doing! And they're coordinating their attack on us! This shit is waaaaay worse than we thought! They aren't just hate-filled imbeciles acting on their impulses! They're hate-filled imbeciles who have enough brains left that they can strategize!"

"Just like the members of the fucking regime," Hugo muttered under his breath as the SUV was battered once again by the three attacking vehicles. "Oh, fuck this!" Payekha screamed as her mind began disassociating from her feelings of impending doom. The mangled streetlights began glowing bright red and emanating fluorescent streaks of color. She was no longer driving the SUV. She was driving a heavily fortified bus that could mow down anything in its path. She was now the hero in the middle of a car chase scene in an action movie. Her eyes darted while searching for a sign. And she saw one. Several blocks away were glowing arches that were beckoning to her. *Over here, Payekha,* they were saying in childish voices. *Bring them over here. We want to play with them.*

She guided the SUV to the left until it was grinding against one of the pickups. The zombie gnashed his teeth and snarled while trying to maneuver his pick-up back to the center of the road. Payekha's black knuckles turned white as she guided the SUV/fortified bus further and further to the left. There was a loud explosion as the pick-up careened through the base of a fast-food sign. A pair of yellow arches collapsed on the cargo van that was behind them while the pick-up rolled three times until the twisted metal came to a rest in the drive-through.

"Two down, one to go, then we can roll the credits," Payekha said with determination. She slammed on her brakes, and the smoking SUV/fortified bus came to a screeching halt in the middle of the avenue. A kaleidoscope of colors streaked by as the final truck flew by her at seventy miles an hour. Its large tires squealed as the zombie driver turned it around and came flying back towards them. Payekha could see what it was. It was a white, heavily dented metal cargo van. And it was also nothing more than a soft, chewy marshmallow that could do her no harm that was being driven by a harmless clown.

Payekha calmly retrieved her super-duper water cannon from the passenger floorboard and stepped out of the SUV. "No, dear, don't," Ezinne pleaded while Payekha jogged away from her car and onto a sidewalk that was littered with decaying corpses. Payekha looked down at the carnage and saw a beautiful, calming field of green clover.

The zombie instinctively turned the pickup toward her. Just as she was about to be run down by the marshmallow/cargo van, Payekha rolled to her right. The pick-up crashed into the closed garage door of an oil change business and the zombie began wailing in pain.

Payekha sauntered up to the broken driver's side window and looked inside at the tortured zombie that was pinned by his steering wheel. He was no longer a clown, and he was no longer the creamy center of a marshmallow. He was a suffering human being trapped in a metal tomb. She stared into his pained, white eyes, and for a moment, she thought that she might take out her laptop. She thought that she might show him a better way. A better life. A life where he was no longer ruled by unnecessary fear and hatred. A life where his interpersonal strength could lead him to empathy and acts of kindness towards his fellow human beings. The moment was fleeting. She looked at his greasy, blonde mullet under his stained gold ball-cap that professed his admiration to his Dear Leader.

She shook her head in anger, lifted the water cannon, and said, "Fuck you. You're the root cause of all this shit motherfucker. I have empathy for my fellow people. But I have *none* for *you*. If it weren't for bigoted, self-absorbed motherfuckers like you, none of this would have happened. None of it. You supported this. You cheered when people were rounded up in the streets and sent away to so-called re-education camps. You cheered when children were left starving. You even cheered when your health care was taken away. And your education. And your basic services. You cheered while society was being torn down and you cheered when all that money was given to the rich and powerful. You supported this shit. You cheered on this shit. You and people like you doomed us all. And the world will be a better place without you in it. You thought you'd been groomed by Dear Leader? Well, motherfucker, you haven't seen *anything* yet."

Payekha could not help but laugh as she listened to the final revolting convulsions of the zombie while approaching her SUV. "Everybody, okay?" she said as she opened her mother's door. The door creaked open, then immediately crashed onto the pavement. "Oh, my poor car, Payekha," Ezinne lamented as she walked around her decimated vehicle. "And who is this that you ran over? You've popped his eyes out of his head."

"Fuck if I know," Payekha answered while scanning the area. "He was probably an asshole. But one thing's for certain. This van is completely fucking shot. We need a new vehicle. Okay, I have a plan, folks. Dawson, look up there. There's a ramp to the interstate about a mile away. And, conveniently enough, they're doing some construction near it. How about this. You jog up there, hot wire that bulldozer and clear that ramp. Hugo, you stay here and guard our shit. If any zombies come around, *GROOM* the fuck out of them. Mom and I are going over to that car dealership and get ourselves a new ride. Are we cool?"

"Um, sure Payekha," Dawson answered. "But why don't you put your bag down and leave it with us? It's gotta be pretty heavy, especially on your bum ankle." "What the fuck did I say to you?" Payekha shot back. "Why is it that White boys can never take 'no' for an answer? My shit stays with me. End of discussion. And my ankle feels fine. Just needed a few hours off of it. I am gonna kinda miss my leg crutch though. Oh well. It was starting to rot and smell anyway. Now, go get that ramp cleared. We'll be back soon with our new ride. Oh, and Hugo. Get your credit card out. You're paying for the gas."

"Okay, Mom, how about this one? Plenty of room in the back to store our shit. And it has the dual temperature settings that you like," Payekha stated to her mother as the pair surveyed their options at the new car dealership. "Plus, no dents. The ones parked near the street are dented as fuck, but the ones back here are still untouched. Yes? We got a winner? Cool. I'll break into the dealership and find the keys and off we go."

"Weeeelll, I don't know about *this* one, Payekha," Ezinne responded while stroking her chin. "The interior looks like a cheap vinyl. And it doesn't have a CD player. You know how I enjoy listening to my music and now that I can't use my cell phone I'm going to need some CDs. And yes, it has plenty of storage, but it is just so damned long. This will be quite difficult to park in a crowded parking lot. I'll have to park quite a ways from the entrance of the shopping center in this.

Plus, it is red. You know what they say about red cars, dear. They are cop magnets. You go just one mile over the speed limit in this thing, and I can guarantee you will be met with flashing lights. Plus, the insurance on this thing must be just astronomical. No, I don't think so, dear. Let's find something a bit more economical. And easier to park. And not red."

"Are you fucking kidding me?" an astonished Payekha asked. "You are joking, right? Okay, let me take your concerns one by one. First, I'm thinking cheap vinyl is a plus. I'm certainly not hoping for it, but odds are that we're going to be tracking blood and vomit and lord knows what else into this SUV and cheap vinyl will be easier to clean. Point number two. They don't make cars with CD players in them anymore, Mom. Yes, I know yours had one. But that's because we had it put in special, remember? And I'm pretty sure that there's nobody alive who can do that for us, so we'll just have to deal with the radio. If there's anything being broadcast. Next point. There's nobody at the shopping centers, so parking won't be an issue. Everybody's fucking dead. And the color? Oh, fuck, Mom. A red car isn't going to attract anybody's attention because there's nobody around. Except zombies and they don't give a fuck about the color of the car. If you're driving a car, they want to eat you. It doesn't matter if it's red, green, blue, or that puke tan. If you're breathing, you're on their fucking menu. Car insurance? I'll tell you what. If the world ever gets back to the point where car insurance is a thing again and if it's too expensive, we'll trade it in on a cheaper model. Okay? Now it's got decent gas mileage and is big. That's all I fucking care about. This is the one. We don't have time to fuck around. I'm getting the keys."

The sun's final fuchsia rays were setting behind a bank of wispy clouds when Payekha and Ezinne pulled up in their brand-new, bright red SUV which was blaring eighties hip-hop out of its open windows. "What in the hell took you two so long?" Hugo asked as he and Dawson began transferring heavy bags of *GROOMING*, weapons, food, and water from one vehicle to another.

Payekha let out a deep sigh and rolled her eyes before saying. "Yeah, well, you want to explain that, Mom? No? You gonna make me do it? Fine. So, we finally found this car after explaining to Mom that the color of the car makes no fucking difference. It took me a while to break into the car dealership and find the keys. We started it up and guess what? Almost out of gas. So, we went to the gas station, and I had to fight my way into the place through vomiting zombies so I could turn on the pump. And how the fuck do you do *that*? Fuck if *I* know. *I've* never worked at a gas station. I found a manual though and got the pump turned on. And I cleaned them out of chips and dip and meat sticks and shit. So be careful loading that shit. Don't crush the chips.

"Anyway, while I'm gassing up the car, Mom's sitting there fucking with the radio. But the one station that she likes is static. Everything else comes in fine. But does she want to listen to that? Fuck no. Golden oldies? Nope. Classic rock? Naw. Country? 'Oh please, dear, be serious,' she says to me. So, realizing that she would bitch all the way from here to Colorado if we didn't find her some music to keep her occupied, we went to that big box store at the end of the shopping center. Do you know how hard it is to find a portable CD player nowadays? Pretty fucking hard. Do you want to know how hard it is to find one while dodging vomiting zombies? *Really* fucking hard.

"But we found one. Seriously. They had exactly one. And a bin full of discount CDs that we had to go through. One by one. And if it was an artist that she liked, she had to read the track list to make sure she wanted it. 'Oh, no dear. I don't care for his later work. Oh no, dear. They became too commercial on this album.' And on and on like that until we came up with twenty-three discs that will keep this old lady satisfied for at least half the trip. So, keep that in mind, boys. When we stop for gas, check to see if they have any old CDs and load up on those fuckers. I love my mother, but I swear if I hear her bitch about one more thing today, I'm leaving her by the side of the fucking road. So, Hugo, does that answer your goddamned question? Are we loaded? Can we *finally* get the fuck out of this town?"

The very long, very red SUV was accelerating off the entrance ramp and onto I-270. Abandoned, wrecked cars from people who had become zombified while texting and driving were strewn along the corridor. Payekha could hear light snoring coming from Dawson and Hugo in the rear seat. Her mother quietly looked for a CD to play. She was lapping up this moment of tranquil silence like a dehydrated dog drinking from a cool pond. She looked into her rearview mirror and smiled as she witnessed black plumes of smoke consuming this once-great capital of this once-great nation. Centuries of persistent struggle for equality for all people had been decimated by the sadistic regime of Dear Leader. But he had ultimately failed in his vision of elevating his so-called master race to dominance. Everybody was now truly equal. Gender did not matter any longer. Nor did race. Or culture. Or sexual orientation. Or religion. Every remaining person left on Earth was now completely equal and free to become a carnivorous zombie. Or one of their meals.

Payekha let out a satisfied sigh as her eyes returned to the illuminated road. The SUV's brilliant headlights shone on mangled vehicles, twisted road signs, and buzzards eating the remains of this fallen human race. She swerved to miss the various corpses and other debris, looked at her mother and smiled. Her smile turned to an exasperated grimace when Ezinne opened her mouth and said, "I know you did your best dear, but I really do not like this car. No, the bass on the stereo is off. It needs to be a bit more, um, thumpy. And I don't care for that whirring sound the tires make on the road. It is quite annoying. And this seat is so hard on my aching back. I know I was put on this Earth to suffer, but my lord, child, this is like sitting on a brick. And one other thing that I don't care for is..."

CHAPTER 18

INTROSPECTIVE JOURNEY

"Could we *please* turn the music off for a while?" Dawson pleaded from the back seat. "I just can't listen to any more of these jungle rhythms. The same beats and thumping bass and I can't even understand what they are saying. Can't we just drive in silence for a bit?"

"Jungle rhythms, huh?" Payekha shot back. "Why would you refer to *this* music like *that*? Because the artist is Black? Because all Black people are nothing more than unsophisticated tribal tree swingers? Is that why? I'll have you know, Dawson, that some of these songs are as intricately constructed and complicated as a concerto written by a wig-wearing White dude. So, just shut the fuck up."

"Sorry," Dawson awkwardly backtracked. "I didn't mean it like that. I mean, that's what my parents always used to call it. Jungle music. I didn't mean any offense. I just would like to have a few moments of silence. I just want to live with my thoughts and try to process this insanity. Okay? Please?"

"Mom, are you alright with that?" Payekha inquired. "Yeeeessss, I suppose that would be alright," Ezinne replied in her slow drawl. "I suppose we've tortured these White boys enough with our *tribal beats*, right Dawson?"

"You know what's weird?" Hugo interrupted. "I used to hate this shit. I mean I *really* hated it. And not just because the music was culturally unfamiliar to me. I hated what it represented. I hated the freedom and empowerment it contained for Black people. In my opinion, if a Black person wanted to get up on stage and croon a song that was suitable to my White ears, that was okay. He could be my dancing monkey. He could entertain me. I would allow him that. As long as it was on *my* terms. But *this* music came from a different place. These weren't songs that were sanctioned by the White producers. These songs came from the human condition. It came from the struggles of the Black race in our society. Its DNA lies within the old slave hymns and delta blues that spoke about their oppression. It filled their hearts with fortitude and hope. This music scared me because it was empowering to Black people. And I hated Black people, so I hated their music. They were a threat to my kind, and their music was a source of their strength. But now?

"Now that Payekha's subliminal message has eliminated my need for petty hatred? Now that I understand that my achievement isn't dependent upon the persecution and subjugation of other groups of people? Now that my eyes have been opened and I can truly empathize with others' experiences? Well, hell. I kinda like it. I mean, it's never going to be my favorite style of music, but I have a better understanding and appreciation for it. I do, however, wish we could listen to something with some guitars at some point. Y'know. Just to break it up a bit."

Payekha and Ezinne looked at one another's faces that were bathed in the light of the evening's full moon and smiled. "Yeeeeesss, that would be fine, boys," Ezinne answered. "Next time we stop for gas at a truck stop we'll get you boys a few White CDs. Fair is fair, I suppose. Do either of you have any suggestions for what to look for?"

"Ummm," Dawson meekly answered. "Well, if you happen to see anything by Journey that would be cool. They're my favorite band. Um, I think. I really only know a few songs."

"Oh, Jesus fucking Christ," Payekha replied while shaking her afro in disgust. "*Journey*? Yeah, it doesn't get any whiter than *that* shit, does it? Show me a person whose favorite band is Journey, and I'll show you a person with no personality. No real conviction. No appreciation of true art. No curiosity. No desire to be intellectually challenged. Just let these waves of middle of the road, milk toast notes sweep over me in my comfy little cocoon. I'll eat my dry pot roast that my Stepford wife has made me again, drink my martini, pat my ugly fucking kids on the head, and listen to this mindless drivel until I have to get up and do it all over again tomorrow. Journey isn't art. It's just a way to pass the time. Just a way to peacefully drift a little closer to death. Jesus Christ. Journey. I swear Dawson, the more I get to know you, the less I really know you. I thought you were deeper than that."

"It was just a suggestion," Dawson replied while hanging his head. Ezinne looked in the back seat at the admonished Dawson then at her daughter. "Weeeelll, I for one don't see anything wrong with Journey. They have catchy pop hooks. Payekha, dear, I think you're reading far too much into who a person is based upon the music they like. I think you owe Dawson an apology."

"No, I'm not, and no I don't," Payekha snapped back. "You can tell a *lot* about a person by the music they listen to. Obviously, everybody has their own taste, and everybody has some guilty pleasures in their music collection. Hell, I'll even admit that *I* like some of Journey's stuff. But for *them* to be your *favorite* band? Or any *other* slickly produced, made for the masses bullshit whether it be pop, rock, country, or whatever? If your favorite band plays music that was produced *only* for indoctrination of the masses so you can sell overpriced T-shirts, then that says a lot about a person. I stand by my previous statement. Now everybody shut up. I'm with Hugo. I think we all need some peace and quiet."

The red SUV drifted along Interstate 68 with its passengers in contemplative silence. They were each on their own individual islands as they looked out the windows at the burned-out cars. And half-eaten corpses. And small towns that smoldered in the distance. They were each alone with their waves of thought that would crash upon their shores of consciousness.

Ezinne lamented the state of the world as it now existed. She struggled to understand how humankind could continue to be so hateful and cruel to one another. How could one person purposefully beat another person down just because of their ancestry or skin color or religion? How could they smile and laugh at the hardship experienced by another? She looked upon her daughter's determined face for a moment and shed a single tear. How could people take delight in confining, beating, and raping children? How could they have taken delight in performing these macabre, sinister acts upon her beloved daughter and many other innocents? What darkness dwells in the blackened souls of so many? Do they not understand how truly evil they are? Do they believe they are justified in inflicting such cruelty? Do they truly believe that every drop of blood that they cause to spill upon the ground, every tear they cause to roll down a helpless cheek, and every painful cry that they force an innocent person to emit will get them one step closer to their version of heaven? And does any of this even matter at this point? The human race was now nearly extinct. They had committed mass suicide against one another. Their greed, hatred, and lust for power caused it to all come crumbling down in one violent, fiery conclusion. The human race was letting out their final, tortured scream. And then, it would be silenced. For all time. Ezinne smiled at her reflection in the passenger window and said to herself, *Weeeeell, maybe there truly is a God.*

Hugo's shore was being beaten by a haunting montage of his past cruelties. His savagery against a much younger boy whose parents did not speak English. His ridiculing classmates based upon their ethnicity. His participation in college of hunting down members of the LGBTQ community on campus. Hitting them. Kicking them. Stomping them until they lay unconscious in a pool of their own blood and indignity. Hugo bowed his head and covered his eyes with his trembling hands to hide his tears of remorse. He was being visited by every person that he had committed atrocities against. Face after face after face came crashing upon the shore of his island. His heart ached with regret as the bloodied, tearful faces came into focus and their suffering was absorbed by his opening heart. He could not believe the monster that he had been just a few hours before. He could not bear the humility and disgust that he held for himself. *I have just one final task upon this Earth,* he thought. *Get Payekha to the transmission station. Help her stop this insanity. Then, pray to my maker for forgiveness before I draw my last breath.*

Dawson looked out the window in awe of the complete destruction that had befallen every town that they passed on the interstate. His jaw dropped every time he witnessed another horde of violent zombies mindlessly beating one another along the roadside. He wondered if this truly was the end of human civilization. Or would Payekha be successful in pulling the entire species away from the brink of extinction. Could she indeed build her army of awoken people, one region at a time. Could she round them up and show them her message of empowerment through kindness on stadium jumbotrons. Could those people then do the same by going from town to town, state to state, country to country. Would she be able to succeed in turning a once-warring species into an empathetic collaborative? Could she do to others what she had done to Hugo.

He is unrecognizable to me now, Dawson thought of his friend. *She is indeed brilliant. And quite beautiful. Although interracial relationships have been outlawed for several years, I could not help but be in absolute awe of her. She is much more intelligent than I am. More educated. More cultured. I know that she could never be interested in a dullard like myself. Especially one that likes Journey, I guess. No, she is too advanced for a person like me. The only way for a person like me to get a woman like that is for him to be the last man on this Earth. And I nearly am. As far as I know, there is also only Hugo.*

Hugo's smug face came crashing on the shore of Dawson's island. *Yes, my dear friend and partner in crime, Hugo. Hugo who now is everything that she seems to admire in a man. Since being indoctrinated by her subliminal message, he seems more intelligent. More empathetic. He seems to genuinely care about others, including her. He seems to be genuinely remorseful over what he has done to others. Including her. All the names he called her and the cruel jokes at her expense. He seems to be quite sorry for it all. He seems to have become the type of man that she deserves in her life. And I think that they sense it. They look at each other differently now. Before, they would look at one another with blind hatred. And now? Now their eyes are softer. Almost, dare I say it? Affectionate. Yes, they seem to suddenly have genuine affection for one another. Perhaps they are destined to be together. To have children together and rebuild the human race in their image. A White man and a Black woman become this century's proverbial Adam and Eve. Two days ago, I would have laughed at such a notion. But now? Now it seems much more like an eventuality than a possibility. Yes, their union seems inevitable to me now. Unless they are confronted by a snake in their little garden of Eden, that is.*

Payekha carefully navigated her space cruiser around the cosmic debris that littered the roadway. The brilliant, golden full moon reflected off of her mahogany eyes as she focused upon her mission. *I am Captain Payekha Popoola,* she thought to herself as glowing streams of colorful lights flew by her spacecraft. *I have been entrusted by the Overlords of the Galaxy to save all humankind in the universe. I have but one mission. Spread my message of love, caring, empowerment, and compassion throughout the cosmos. Spread it to every living being so that they may stop their wars. Their hatred. Their unspeakable violence. Spread it so that they can become what their creator had intended. Kind beings. Just navigate my spacecraft to the planet Transmission, fight off any remnants of this planet's evildoers, plug in my intergalactic flash drive 3000, and spread my message. Oh, and pick up a stupid fucking Journey CD too, I guess. Gotta keep the crew happy, I suppose.*

This is what I was trained to do. This is what the Overlords of the Galaxy has placed me here for. They knew that there would come a day when humanity needed to be saved. They knew there would come a day when humanity would need a champion. And I am it. I was spared from the toxic indoctrination for just this purpose. Everything that I studied at university and every project that I worked on at the NIPH has led me to this moment.

Her disassociation then grew darker as sadistic images pounded upon the shore of her island of one. "I'm never going to cry again," she muttered softly before merging her disassociation with the horrific memories from her past. *Every rope burn from being tied up. Every rash from the tape on my lips. Every pang of hunger. Every drop of blood from the merciless belts and whips. Every painful dagger that was plunged into me. Every harsh indignity that I was forced to endure. All of it was to prepare me.*

Train me. Make me cunning. Make me devious. Make me determined and strong and powerful. Each depraved act they committed upon my childhood flesh that was designed to break me down and destroy me created the exact opposite reaction.

Every lash upon my raw bottom strengthened me. Every object that was forced into me made me more determined. Every slap upon my tender face made me more empowered. Until I completed that portion of my training. I grew stronger and stronger until I had the fortitude to slice my tormenters up. All of them. One by one. I murdered them all and I freed the other victims. The Overlords of the Galaxy had to test me. They had to have someone with enough fortitude to triumph in this darkest hour. The abuse I experienced was a test. And a training ground. So that I could be promoted to be Captain Payekha Popoola, commanding officer of the USS Big-ass red SUV. Everything that I have experienced has been to prepare me for this moment. The Overlords had to have someone who had been the victim of human cruelty to be the savior of the human race. And I sure as fuck fit that bill. Almost out of space fuel. Better find a fueling asteroid around here soon, or we'll be spacewalking the rest of the way to Planet Transmission. Better pay attention to the space directional signs and...

Ezinne, Hugo, and Dawson were suddenly pulled from their islands and back into the SUV when they heard Payekha shout out, "Holy fuck! I just thought of something!" Her three passengers slid across their seats as the SUV took an abrupt right turn onto an exit.

"Payekha! Where in the hell are you going?" Hugo yelled out. "Why are you getting off the main road? Do you know how many horror movies start with people getting off the main road? And in case you haven't noticed, we're right in the middle of a fucking horror movie!"

"I know, I know," a nearly hyperventilating Payekha answered while the SUV's tires squealed around the sharp curve of the exit. "I know. Maybe this is nuts. But I just saw a sign that told me where we might find some survivors. Real survivors. There was a sign back there pointing to a community. An Amish community. Get it? The Amish don't use modern technology. Which means, they don't have cell phones. Which means they haven't been indoctrinated by Dear Leader's toxic messaging. I'm not sure if they can be of any help to us, but we can at least find out if they're alright and warn them about what's going on. Plus, we need fuel and they might have some or at least be able to tell us where we can get it. It's just a few miles down this road. We'll just go in and check it out. If they're dead or zombified, we'll get the hell back on the main road. And, if not…"

Payekha could feel her throat choking up before she finished. "And if not. If they're alive then, then…we'll actually have some fucking hope. And we can warn them so that they can protect themselves. We'll leave them with some *GROOMING* and shit. Alright?"

"Yes, I think this is a great idea, Payekha," Dawson stated. "Yes, we should check and see if there is any possibility of pockets of survivors. Just take it slow and be careful. We might end up facing something worse than zombies."

Payekha drove the SUV down a narrow, gravel lane. Under the bright moonlight she could see three houses surrounded by a large barn and several utility sheds. The structures were being backlit by what appeared to be a large bonfire behind them. The bright yellow moonshine and deep orange glow mixed with the blackness of the night to create an eerie aura around the community. Payekha stopped the car and turned off the ignition. The foursome could hear a chorus of horses whinnying in the barn, tree limbs creaking in the breeze, and the chirping of crickets as they quietly opened their doors and cautiously exited the SUV.

They then heard the tell-tale sound of a rifle being cocked. "Now just you four don't make any sudden moves," a man's stern voice came from behind them. "I don't know who you are or where you're from, but I do know this. I know that your kind has finally destroyed the world. I know that your kind has been coming onto our land and been trying to murder and eat us. And I know your kind ain't welcome here no more. So, we're just gonna go out to that barn down yonder. We're going to ask some questions. And, depending on the answers, we'll see if you four will get to drive off in your fancy car. Or if we're going to add you to the others on our bonfire."

Chapter 19

No Good Deed
Goes Unpunished

A chill ran down Payekha's spine as she stared at the determined, bearded face of the Amish man. The thick, ghastly scent of burning corpses tingled in her nose and throat and caused her eyes to water. She glanced at the frightened eyes of her mother, Hugo, and Dawson, raised her hands slowly, and said, "Hey, hey. No need to overreact here. I get it. It looks like you folks have been through quite a time protecting one another. Please listen. We aren't infected. We aren't zombies, or whatever you want to call them. In fact, we're on our way to Colorado. We think we can fix this. Put things back the way they were."

"You think you can fix this, huh?" the Amish man sternly replied. "With what? More of your fancy computers? With more of your damned technology? Naw, you can't fix this. You'll just make it worse somehow. Your kind always does. I know a lot of you people ridicule our way of life. They laugh at us for not embracing technological advances and continuing to live as we always have. You say your life is easier than ours. Easier how? It seems to me that the more advanced you became, the busier you were. Just a pack of rats running faster and faster on your little treadmills trying to capture more and more cheese. And destroying each other in the process.

"And what do you use your technology for that is so much better? Entertainment? We have books and stories and games and joyful time that we spend together. Heat? We have fireplaces. Light? We have candles and lanterns. Transportation? We have our horses and buggies and have no need to go much further than the nearest town. Health care? Seems to me that you folks can't even get access to it, so what use is it? And when it is our time to meet our maker, then it is our time. Personal protection? Well, we have our shotguns as you can see. And *our* weapons don't threaten the annihilation of the entire world, now do they?

"Our way of life doesn't pollute the waterways and the precious air that we breathe. Our way of life doesn't threaten the very existence of the human race. Our way of life may not be as comfortable as yours, but we take our comfort in knowing that every day of our back-breaking work is a day we have been blessed to be on God's green Earth. Every drop of sweat. Every sore muscle. Every problem that we figure out with our very own minds and hands. Everything that we do is comforting. We take comfort in the knowledge that we are truly free. We are free from dependence upon contraptions. We are free to achieve everything that our brains and brawn will allow. We are free to live our lives. And that, missy, is much more comforting than air conditioning or driving down the highway or wasting time watching trivial things on your little boxes.

"We are one with each other. We depend on each other and act in unison to live the best lives that we can. And that dependence gives us respect for one another. Unlike you. You are all isolated in your own little worlds. You not only do not depend on one another, you actively work against one another. Your kind is consumed by greed and lust for power. You want recognition. You want shiny, expensive things. And you are willing to do anything in order to get them. And that, missy, is what your technology is truly used for. You use it to one-up your fellow man and woman. Look at my new car. My new TV. My new phone. Look at my new kitchen. Look at my new virus that I can use to kill the population of this country. Look at my new poison that I can belch into the sky. Look at my new bomb that I can dominate the world with. Look at me, look at me. Your technology is used for self-absorption and personal gain. To make you feel superior to your neighbors. To keep you isolated from one another. To keep you resentful of one another. It strips you of your basic humanity.

"So, yes, we know that many of you laugh at us for our so-called backwards ways. But we laugh at you, too. We laugh at how delusional you are that you think you are living happy lives while staring at your phones instead of enjoying the wonder of nature. We laugh at you for thinking you are free while you get up every morning and drive an hour in congested traffic to a job that you despise. We laugh at you while you run on your treadmills chasing your cheese. All by yourself without any regard or respect for anyone else. But I suppose nobody is laughing now, are they? Nobody is laughing at the downfall of humankind. That I believe was somehow caused by your technology. I'm right, aren't I? One of your contraptions got a mind of its own, and is destroying everything isn't it?"

Payekha averted her mahogany eyes from the man's sullen gaze while thinking of a response to the wisdom she had just heard. "Yeah, you're right. Our technology has surpassed our humanity, and we've finally done it. We've finally created something that turns people into nothing more than violent animals. In less than a day, we have toppled everything that humankind had built for centuries. But not you. You and your way of life are safe from us. And I thank the stars for that. You are blessed. We're sorry to have bothered you. We just wanted to warn you about what was happening, but I see our warning isn't necessary. It was *your* warning that the rest of *us* should have been paying attention to. Not the other way around. Please just let us be on our way. We won't darken your peaceful community again."

The Amish man wiped a tear from his weathered eye and lowered his rifle. He looked at Payekha and forced a smile. "You aren't bad people. Misguided, sure. But not bad. And you look like you could use a nice meal and a bit of rest. Stay the night here and relax. Then tomorrow, you can get up and take care of whatever you need to. And you will carry my blessing along with you. Please stay the night. We have plenty of rooms. Yes, we have plenty of rooms now.

"There were a bunch of them that came from the highway. We had no idea what was happening. They stared right through us with their white eyes as they ripped us to shreds. They tore us apart and ate us. Men, women, children. My wife is gone. My three daughters are gone. Those of us that remained after the initial onslaught grabbed our rifles and defended ourselves. We were a community of three families. When the sun rose yesterday, there were twenty-three of us. By sunset, there are only ten. Three adult men, three young boys, and four young girls. Everybody else is gone. Our families are being burned on that pyre along with those that attacked us. Their ashes are floating up to heaven now. And I pray mercy upon all of their souls. My name is Joshua, and you are welcome to stay in my home tonight."

"Ooooooh my," Ezinne responded in her slow drawl. "Why, that is very kind of you sir. Especially after all that you've been through. Are you sure you want our, um, kind to stay here?"

"Yes, I'm sure," Joshua's weary voice replied. "We are all dependent upon one another, remember? In order for any of us to survive this, we must be kind and giving to one another. It is what my beloved wife would have done. And my precious daughters. Yes, please stay. It will be a tribute to our fallen loved ones."

Following dinner, Payekha sauntered onto the front porch and down the front steps. She marveled at the perfectly manicured flower gardens that lined the front walkway. She bent down, carefully lifted a yellow rose to her relaxed face, and breathed the sweet scent in. She smiled and looked up at the brilliant stars that sparkled against the unsullied backdrop of the pitch-black night. She continued her peaceful stroll until she heard a man's sobbing coming from behind a sturdy wooden shed. She quietly stepped around the shed and found Hugo sitting on a stump with his beleaguered face buried in his drenched hands.

"Hey there, buddy, what's going on?" Payekha asked as she tenderly placed her hand upon his heaving shoulders. "I just can't take it, Payekha," he answered in his choked-up voice. "I just can't stand what I was. All the terrible things that I did. All the terrible things that I said. All the needless hate that was in my soul. Once I saw your subliminal message, it opened my eyes. It allowed me to look into the mirror and truly see myself for who I truly was. And I was ugly, Payekha. Hideous. A hideous, petty little man willfully eating up all of Dear Leader's hate-filled bullshit. A horrible little man who persecuted others based upon the whims of another horrible little man. I look at the kindness that Joshua and the others have extended to us, and I know that I wouldn't have done the same. I wouldn't have shared my food or home with them. I would have considered them to be a threat. I would have sent them away. Or worse. I'm not a man, Payekha. I'm a soulless sponge. I'm a fucking weaponized pawn. I'm disgusting."

Payekha sat next to her beleaguered friend, lifted his head from his hands, and stared into his bloodshot, blue eyes. She was moved by his sincerity and his newfound humanity. She smiled at him. The smile communicated kindness. It communicated understanding. It communicated forgiveness. Hugo wiped his eyes and felt the warmth of Payekha's smile in his heart. Their heads slowly moved toward one another. They kissed.

An observing figure was shrouded under a nearby darkened tree. He looked upon the tender scene while clenching his fists. The longer they kissed, the tighter his fists became. His heart sank as he watched Payekha take Hugo's tear-soaked hand and lead him toward Joshua's house. He looked upon the two embracing silhouettes in an upstairs window. Their entangled bodies were illuminated by a single oil lantern. One of the silhouettes bent down for a moment. And the light went out.

"Thank you so much for the fuel," Hugo stated as he, Payekha, Ezinne, and Joshua emerged from a barn on the outskirts of the commune. "I'm sure there will be plenty of gas stations along the way but having a few extra gallons doesn't hurt. Thank you so much, Joshua. Thank you for welcoming us into your home and for the food and the…"

He was cut off by Payekha's playful voice. "And for the comfortable bed, right Hugo?" Ezinne looked at her daughter then at Hugo's blushing White face. "Weeeeell, I'll be," she said to her daughter who smiled broadly as she mouthed back, *Oh, shut up Mom*, before giggling.

"Um, yeah, the bed was, um, really nice," an embarrassed Hugo replied. "And, um the dinner last night was really good."

"Reeeeaaally good," Payekha stated through her giggles. "Yeah, that *white meat* tasted great. How was the *dark meat,* Hugo?" "Okay, Payekha, please just stop this. This is really embarrassing," Hugo stated. "Okay, listen you two. Um, Payekha and I kinda, um, well, we kinda did something last night that, um...well, you see, we, um, kinda..."

"We fucked," Payekha bluntly stated while slapping Hugo's ass. "No shit, huh?" Joshua replied. "I figured that out this morning as you two were serving each other breakfast. Well, good for you. It's nice to know that there can still be some happiness found in this cruel world that we find ourselves in."

"I figured it out last night when I kept being awoken by those creaky bedsprings," Ezinne contributed. "For a White boy, you have some stamina."

"Okay, can we just drop this please," the red-faced Hugo ordered. "I don't know what this means. It just kinda happened. And I really don't want Dawson to find out. At least not yet. I'm not sure, but I think he might have a thing for you, Payekha, and I don't want to rock our little boat until we complete our mission. Alright?"

"And *then* what?" Payekha asked as she stood in front of Hugo and halted his march. Hugo put the gas cans down, looked Payekha in her dancing eyes, smiled and yelled out, "Then I'm going to tell the entire world that I'm in love with you!" He picked up the squealing Payekha, spun her around and gave her a long, passionate kiss. "Oh fuck," Payekha said as Hugo placed her feet back onto the lush grass. "I've never had a White boy make my knees so wobbly. And yeah, okay. Let's just keep it cool until we get to Colorado. No sense upsetting Dawson and..." her thought trailed off as the foursome came over the ridge.

"And...and...what the fuck has happened?" she yelled out. The quartet stood in horrified silence as they saw all of the houses engulfed in white-hot flames. They dropped their gas cans and began sprinting towards the carnage. In the middle of the front yard were nine corpses lying in their own intestines. They reeked of vomit and *GROOMING*. Joshua let out a torrent of tears while Hugo and Ezinne ran to the well to retrieve buckets of water. Joshua fell to his knees and looked pleadingly up to the wistful clouds in the sky while letting out an anguished guttural scream. Payekha fell beside him and wrapped him in a strong, solemn embrace. She seethed with anger as her confused mind searched for a possible explanation of this horrific scene.

Her enraged eyes looked up when she heard Dawson's beleaguered voice approaching. "I-I'm so sorry. I don't know what happened. I mean, I thought my phone's battery was dead. It fell out of my pocket. The kids went over to pick it up and it had turned on somehow. They started laughing at a video that was playing. And then...and then...it happened. They changed. Their eyes turned white and they started to attack each other. The men tried to pull them apart, but the children went berserk. They tore out their eyes and ripped the skin off their faces and started eating them. Then, an oil lamp fell, and the house went up in flames. I ran out of the house, and they all followed me. I picked up my squirt gun and sprayed them all. Right here on the front lawn and they puked themselves to death. The fire spread to the next house, then the next. I'm so sorry. I swear, I didn't know."

"Why in the hell didn't you just try to contain them or something?" Payekha screamed. "We could have shown them my message on my laptop! Why did you spray them? Why did you kill them all?"

"Show them *how*, Payekha?" Dawson yelled back. "They don't have any fucking electricity and the computer's battery is dead!" "I could have plugged it into the car goddammit! Goddammit! *Goddammit!* What have we done to these innocent people!" Payekha painfully howled.

"Just leave now," Joshua quietly said as he watched Ezinne and Hugo futilely throwing buckets of water on the inferno. He pushed Payekha onto her back and stood up. His eyes reflected the unforgiving flames as he said in a dark voice, "Just leave. Leave us be. I was wrong about you. You are *not* good people. You are a plague. You are a dark cloud that spreads your pestilence everywhere you go. You have destroyed the environment. You have destroyed wildlife. You have destroyed each other. And now, you have destroyed everything that I have ever held dear. I was raised to love others. I was taught that every single person has kindness in their souls. But not you. I loathe you. I hate you. I hate everything that you represent, and I hate everything that you have done to my land and my home and my family. You are indeed a plague, and I pray for your extinction so that nature can reclaim this world from your selfish pillaging. Just go now. I am going to join my family. When it is our time, then it is our time. And it is now my time. And yours. Just die. All of you."

Payekha screamed out "Nooooo!" as her mortified eyes watched Joshua's defeated body enter the emblazoned house. The structure, along with this peaceful community that had persisted and thrived for well over a century, collapsed upon him in a blazing heap of sorrow.

C HAPTER 20

____

U RBAN D ECAY

Hours of silence passed along with a blur of trees, burned-out cars, and decomposing corpses that littered the sweltering interstate asphalt. Fuel stops were nothing more than a morbid ritual of spraying *GROOMING* on whatever warring "human" life had congregated at the filling station, then watching them retch themselves to death. The solemn quartet would then once again climb into their red SUV and proceed down the darkened road of unforgiving despair. Past more trees. And burned-out cars. And rotting corpses. They kept the windows rolled up to block the stench of humanity's decay, giving their dejected journey a new meaning to the phrase 'dead silence'. Their collective eyes scanned the roadway for obstructions while their collective thoughts were fixated on the gruesome image of a defeated man retreating into his enflamed, collapsing home.

The vast rural stretches of highway proved to be mostly uneventful. The occasional abandoned vehicle. The occasional, white-eyed zombie chewing on its latest victim. The frequent billowing smoke and brilliant flames seen from a distance of yet another extinguished small town. The urban areas proved to be a bit more challenging.

As they cautiously entered what had been Columbus, Ohio they encountered yet another blocked roadway. The hours-long silence was finally broken when Payekha said, "Ah, shit. Look alive folks. This doesn't look good. The interstate is jammed up with wrecked cars. I need to get off at the next exit and find a way back on. And don't anybody even fucking *dare* to pull out their phones to GPS this shit."

Payekha turned off the headlights and coasted down the exit ramp. Her path was illuminated by streetlamps and flickering infernos from nearby engulfed buildings. Her brown eyes darted as she carefully navigated her vehicle around the wreckage, refuse, and decaying, half-eaten corpses. "Well fuck!" she yelled out as the road was once again blocked by a large cargo van. "I hate to say this, but we gotta get out and get this thing out of our way." The SUV rolled to a stop. "Mom. Get in the driver's seat and keep this thing running. If we run into trouble we're going to jump back in, and we'll have to reverse course. Got it?"

"Yeeeeesss," Ezinne answered. "I understand dear. I *will* need to adjust the seat, though. You certainly did get your father's long legs. Why, my toes barely touch the pedals after you've been driving. And I don't care for how you adjust the mirrors and..."

"Mom, we really don't have time for this," an exasperated Payekha replied as Hugo and Dawson exited the SUV and began approaching the cargo van. Ezinne came around the car and placed herself in the driver's seat. Payekha looked her mother in her eyes and said sternly, "One other thing, Mom. I want you to hang onto this black duffle bag. This bag needs to be with one of us at all times, okay? I may have fucked Hugo, but I still don't trust him. Or Dawson either, for that matter. This is *our* emergency bag. I sewed the flash drive into its lining. It has some protein bars, bottled water, a pistol and ammo. Oh, and it's also got three squirt guns and three bottles of *GROOMING*. In case we have to abandon the car, we'll at least have something to protect ourselves. Okay?" "Yeeeeeesss, of course dear," Ezinne replied. "Now just get that thing out of our way."

"Well, that was easy," Dawson said as he and Hugo pushed the cargo van to the curb while Payekha steered. "Yeah," Hugo agreed. "Maybe everybody here is gone. Maybe all the infected have murdered the uninfected. And each other. Let's get back to the van. I need some painkillers. My eye is fucking killing me. And my hand. And my face. Yeah, I think this is just a ghost town now."

"Oh, yeah?" Payekha answered with trepidation as she began slowly backtracking toward the SUV. "I don't think that growling is coming from ghosts. In fact, I think…I think…Oh fuck! Run!"

Dozens of frothing zombies descended upon the trio from the fire escapes of the dilapidated, brick apartment buildings that lined the street. "Fuck! We're cut off from the van!" Dawson screamed. "And there's too many of them to squirt!"

"Mom!" Payekha ordered. "We're going to run like hell up this street! Back up, go around the block and pick us up at the corner!" The squeal of the reversing SUV's tires merged with that of several zombies who were being crushed under its weight. "Squirt the fuck out of the ones to our right so we can clear a path up the street!" Payekha, Hugo, and Dawson furiously pulled the triggers of their super-duper water rifles while the gnashing teeth of another horde approached them from behind. The threesome ran through the vomiting congregation like all-pro running backs and darted up the darkened side street.

"The ones from behind are gaining on us!" Hugo shouted. "We gotta take cover and regroup! Here! Let's go in here!" Hugo smashed through a glass door and tumbled onto the tile floor. He was immediately followed by Payekha and Dawson. And enraged, starving zombies. "Squirt 'em! Squirt 'em! Squirt 'em!" Dawson yelled. The trio saturated the zombies who were jamming themselves into the doorway in a feeding frenzy. The warm summer breeze picked up the repugnant scent and carried it into the street causing the trailing zombies to bend over and violently heave up their internal organs.

"Help me move this!" Payekha commanded. Dawson and Hugo immediately went over and assisted her in dragging a large, heavy, filing cabinet to the shattered, hurl-covered doorway. The filing cabinet was followed by a heavy desk. Then a work bench. "Whew. That should keep them out. For a while," Hugo stated as he wiped his forehead with his fully fingered left hand. "But we used most of our *GROOMING* up. And where's your mother?"

"Oh, shit, yeah. Where the fuck is she?" Payekha answered. "Hugo, stay here and guard the door. Dawson, let's go up to the roof and try to find her." Dawson and Payekha cautiously climbed the three flights of creaky wooden stairs until they reached the rooftop entrance. They opened the door, stepped onto the flat rooftop, and looked up at the brilliance of the night sky. The Milky Way glistened in a misty white while thousands of distant stars winked at them. The full moon bathed the entire city in a warm golden hue as a flock of geese serenely flew overhead.

"Wow," an awe-struck Payekha stated. "You know, we may not be successful in saving humankind. We may not be able to find any survivors. And even if we do, we may not be able to deprogram them. We truly may be witnessing the demise of humanity on this planet. But looking up at this sky, I'm beginning to wonder, so what? Humankind is literally tearing itself apart down here. And you know what? The universe doesn't give a fuck. Whatever is happening in those solar systems and those billions and billions of planets just keeps on happening. Right now, there's an alien baby being conceived. Or some squid-like creatures are enjoying dinner. Or taking in a play. Or maybe some two-headed motherfuckers are doing the exact same thing we are. Destroying themselves. We are dying and the universe doesn't even notice. It just keeps doing its thing.

"As does nature. You think those geese give a fuck about what we're doing to each other? You think they care about how cruel we are to one another? Well, actually, yeah. *They* might care. Because we aren't cruel to just each other. We're cruel to *everything* on this fucking planet. We're cruel to the plant life and the animals. We poison their air and water. Hell, we fucking murder them for *sport*. So, yeah, the geese probably care about what we're doing. And those cocky motherfuckers are rooting against us. Yeah, they're saying, 'Stupid fucking humans. Yeah, please kill each other off. You've fucked up our home enough. It's *our* turn. It's time for the rise of the Planet of the Geese!' Or something like that. Whatever. I'm just trying to find a little silver lining in case we fail."

"Oh, we won't fail, Payekha," Dawson replied with an uncharacteristic confidence. "This isn't the end of mankind. There *will* be survivors. Survivors who will evolve and take mankind to even *greater* heights of dominance over this planet. Don't worry about it. No matter what happens with us, mankind will survive. And thrive. Oh, look! There's the SUV!"

Payekha thought to herself, *How the fuck can he be so sure of that?* before looking down and seeing her mother's smiling face looking up at them from behind her blood-soaked windshield. Payekha put her finger to her lips then made the universal hand-push gesture of *just stay right there. We'll be right down.*

"Hey Dawson," she asked. "You think you could climb down there and join my mom? You know, to keep zombies away and shit while I go get Hugo?" "Yeah, I could do that," Dawson answered. "I've still got some *GROOMING* in my gun. Plus, there's more in the van. Go get Hugo. I'll meet you down there."

"Hey Hugo," Payekha said as she re-entered the ground floor. "Mom and Dawson are down in the van waiting for us. The street's clear at the moment and we can get to them by climbing down from the roof. So, grab your shit and let's go."

"In just a second," Hugo answered. "I need to do something first. I need to do something to *you* first. Now just sit in this chair and relax. I promise it won't hurt, um, much."

"You motherfucker," Payekha snarled. "You're still the same twisted, sexist, racist asshole you've *always* been. My subliminal messaging didn't change you at all. You've just been putting on an act. For what? So you could get into my pants? Jesus fucking Christ, I'm so fucking stupid! I actually allowed myself to care about a man! And a White motherfucker at that! And I actually let you fuck me! So, now what, Ace? You gonna tie me to that chair and torture me and shit? Because I've got news for you. I can kick your white, pasty ass from here back to fucking Washington. So, make your move, asshole. I'm ready to end this shit once and for all."

Hugo let out a mischievous chuckle before replying. "Okay, I guess I can see how you came to those conclusions. Communication was never my strong suit, and I guess I wasn't very clear. And I can see how you would believe all of that. Especially after I've been such an asshole all my life. But Payekha, it isn't like that at all. Your subliminal messages *did* work on me. I see the world and my fellow human beings completely differently now. And what I'm going to do to you is just going to hurt a *little* because, um, well…because we've landed in a tattoo parlor and I'm not sure if I'm going to make it to the end of this journey or not and I wanted to give you the coordinates to the transmission station in Pueblo and the entrance code. I thought that instead of writing it down and taking the chance on your losing it, I could tattoo it on your forearm. Then, you'll be able to complete our mission without me, and nobody will know what those numbers mean. Not even Dawson. So, could you please just sit in the chair? And again, I promise it will hurt just a little. Okay?"

"Payekha!" Ezinne cried out as her daughter and Hugo entered the SUV. "My dear, what happened to your arm? Why is it bandaged? Are you injured?"

"Naw, I'm okay Mom," Payekha answered while adjusting her seat and mirrors. "Just, um, scraped it against something. I'm fine. It only hurt a little. Now let's get the fuck out of this town."

Indianapolis, Indiana proved itself to be the speedway capital as a group of hooligan zombies in souped-up sports cars chased the red SUV around the town in a circular loop. Over. And over. And over. For two hours until all of the sports cars careened into an overpass or building and exploded. It was very boring and tedious. Except for the explosions. Those were cool. In St. Louis, Missouri, they arrived just in time to see the great archway to the west crumble and collapse into the neighboring hotels and baseball stadium. Payekha navigated the SUV around flying chunks of concrete and metal until the fiery cityscape was replaced by tranquil waves of green fields of corn.

They once again drove in an exhausted silence until Dawson said, "Hey Payekha. Could you maybe pull over at this gas station at the next exit?" "Why?" Payekha asked. "We've still got a half of a tank. We can make it to Kansas City and gas up there." "But I really need to take a piss," Dawson protested. "Then I'll just pull over here and you can piss," Payekha countered. "What's the big fucking deal?"

"Okay, I'll tell you what the big deal is!" Dawson yelled back. "It's not really something I enjoy talking about but that latest round of Hot Pockets didn't sit particularly well and I'd like to use an actual restroom with some privacy and toilet paper! Now can we please pull over?"

Payekha emerged from the gas station convenience store while shoving meat snacks into her black duffle. "These things are thin, lightweight and chock full of protein," she said to her accompanying mother. "Kinda like Hugo's dick."

"Did I hear my name?" Hugo asked as he exited the men's room. "Uh, no," a chuckling Payekha answered. "Just talking about meat snacks. Jesus, is Dawson still in there? Maybe we need to check the expiration dates on those Hot Pockets. He started gassing up the car, then made a beeline to the shitter. Oh well. This is one thing that I'm not going to rush. The car should be gassed up by now. And just look at it, Mom. As shiny and new as the day we drove it off the lot. Its fucking amazing. Getting barricaded and driving over zombies in Columbus. Zooming around and around and around Indianapolis. Nearly getting crushed by the St. Louis arch and not a scratch on it. Now, can Captain Payekha Popoola fly this spacecraft or..."

Payekha, Ezinne, and Hugo were thrown ten feet backwards through the convenience store windows and into a rack of potato chips as the pristine SUV was consumed by a violent explosion. "What the hell happened?" Dawson yelled out while zipping up his pants. "Is everybody okay?"

"Yeah, but what the fuck, Dawson? Our car just fucking exploded! How can that happen just by filling it up with gas?"

"How the fuck should I know?" Dawson roared back. "I just put the nozzle in the tank! Maybe there's something faulty with it! All I know is that we're damned lucky to not have been in that death trap!"

"Weeeell," Ezinne stated. "It surely was a lovely car. But we had all of our belongings there. All of our food. And weapons. And that horrid man's scent. It's all gone. We need to find another car. But where? We're in the middle of nowhere."

"Alright, don't panic," Dawson confidently answered. "We're going to be fine. Just fine. In fact, I don't know why I didn't think of this earlier. I don't just know where we can get a new car and weapons. I also know where we can find more survivors."

"And how the fuck do you know that?" a suspicious Hugo asked. "Because, my dear friend," Dawson answered. "I know *exactly* where we're at. Everything that we need is just about five miles down that road in Fulton. This is my hometown. And I just happen to know a group of guys who have a, um, retreat, I guess you'd call it. They're kind of survivalists and they didn't use any technology that was invented past 1985. They always said that anything invented after that date was unnecessary. So, I'm sure they haven't used any cell phones, and I know their retreat is fortified and protected. I know these guys. They're really nice and can hook us up with a car. A really *old* car like a Pinto or something, but still a car. We get wheels, a hot meal, and a good night's rest. Then, we're back on the road to Pueblo and off to save the human race. What's everybody doing just standing around and looking at me for? I mean, if our car was going to blow up, it's a damned good thing it happened here, right? Come on. We've got over an hour's walk."

Payekha looked at Hugo with concern in her eyes. He mirrored her expression and shrugged. He then nodded at her black duffle bag and began following Dawson down the cracked asphalt toward Fulton. Understanding Hugo's cue, Payekha reached into her duffle and retrieved her handgun. She checked the safety and placed the firearm into the back waistline of her jeans. She mentally put on her glistening suit of silver armor, sighed with heavy resignation, and began following the three shadowy figures down the lonely highway. Sweat was pouring off of her brow as she placed one heavy step in front of the other for what seemed to be an eternity. An owl could be heard hooting in the distance. Crickets chirped. Squirrels scurried through the dense brush on the side of the road. They were all preparing for an oncoming storm. Thick clouds began rolling in, blanketing the celestial lights of the universe in darkness. Her world turned black. She stopped for a moment to allow her mahogany eyes to adjust to the reduction in light. She opened her eyes and looked straight ahead. She saw that her three companions had stopped and were standing twenty yards away in front of a weathered sign that read, 'Welcome to Fulton.' The greeting sent an instinctive chill down her stiffened spine. As did the self-congratulatory grin on Dawson's face.

CHAPTER 21

WELCOME MAT

The weary quartet was being pelted by warm rainfall as they approached the ten-foot-high iron gates of a sprawling estate just north of Fulton. Jagged streaks of blinding lightning crashed into the nearby earth, illuminating a vast mansion sitting at the end of a long, well-manicured driveway.

"I don't feel good about this, Dawson!" Payekha shouted over the exploding thunder and pounding rainfall. "Let's just find shelter someplace else! Maybe check this place out in the morning!" "Hey, everybody!" Dawson yelled back while wearing a broad smile. "Just calm down! I'm telling you; these guys are really nice! They may be a bit quirky in their lifestyle, but they're really nice! They will help us! Don't worry about it!"

His smile broadened as he pressed the intercom button. "Uh, yeah? Who is it?" a surprised voice came through the crackling speaker. "Hey! It's Dawson! You know! From 4-H and a bunch of other stuff in high school! I'm here with three friends! Could you let us in please? We need your help!"

"Dawson, ol' bean!" the disembodied voice replied in a cheerier tone. "Oh, my lord! I can't believe you've made it through this insanity! Of course, my friend. Come in. Just make sure you get that gate locked behind you. Everybody's gone crazy out there."

The four colleagues sloshed up the lengthy driveway, climbed a set of marble steps that led to the vast mansion, and rang the doorbell. The twelve-foot solid oak door creaked open, and they were greeted by twenty-two smiling faces. Twenty-two male, White, smiling faces. They were all wearing pure white slacks, oxfords, and loafers on their toned bodies. The closest man smiled again and said, "Come in, my friends, come in. Wow. You guys are drenched. Gerald, could you please retrieve some towels and dry clothes for these folks? We'll get you guys dried off and settled into your rooms, okay? Oh, Dawson, ol' bean. It's been years. It's so great to see you. And your friends. How in the hell have you made it here and who are your fellow travelers?"

"Well, how we got here is kind of a long story," Dawson replied while taking a towel from the behemoth of a man known as Gerald. "Maybe we can catch up after dinner. Right now, some dry clothes and a nice hot meal would be fab. Oh, and where are my manners? Gentlemen, these are my friends Hugo, Payekha, and Ezinne. Guys, this is Francis, the leader of this little band of scallywags. And this hulk of a man handing out towels is Gerald. He isn't much of a conversationalist but has a heart of pure gold. And there are twenty more of these fine chaps that I can introduce over dinner. Hiya fellas! So great to see you all!"

"Gerald," the ever-smiling Francis stated. "Could you please show our guests to their rooms. And will we be requiring separate rooms or are perhaps some of you lodging together?" Hugo and Payekha glanced at one another briefly before Payekha blurted out, "Separate rooms are fine. No, wait. My mother and I would like a room together, if that's okay."

"Okay?" Francis replied enthusiastically. "Why that would just be right as rain. Which is quite appropriate on an evening such as this. My, listen to the wind howl. It's almost as though nature is telling us what it thinks about this insanity that has befallen us. Very well, then. Dawson, you will have a room next to mine on the second floor. Bedroom twenty-three. I'm so looking forward to sharing a brandy or two with you as we catch up. Oh, I must ask. Just how long will we be blessed by your presence? You are, of course, welcome to stay as long as you wish. We would love to have you join our little family."

"Um, well," Dawson answered. "We were actually only planning to spend one night. You see, our little Payekha here is a bit of a genius. I'm not sure what you fellas have heard about the state of the world, but basically a toxic subliminal message was implanted into everything that was carried by cell phone networks. This message turned everybody who viewed it into violent, um, well, zombies, I guess. And Payekha has developed a *new* subliminal message that will increase people's self-esteem and fortitude. It will allow people to disassociate when they are threatened and stand up against their oppressors. But we have to implant it into the cellular networks for it to have even a chance of working on any survivors there might be. And the only station that can transmit the message is in Pueblo, Colorado. So, that's where we're off to. We're going to Pueblo to try to save the human race from itself. And time is of the essence. So, if maybe we could just bed down here for the night and if maybe you have a spare car lying around?"

Francis stood with his jaw agape for a moment before responding. "Wow. Look at you, ol' bean. You are truly a national hero. You and your friends. Risking your lives to drive across the country to save mankind. I am humbled to be in your presence. This calls for a celebration. Yes! And a special feast! And of course we have some cars for you to choose from. We have a Pinto and...no. That wouldn't work. How about a fine mid-seventies station wagon? That should be roomy enough. It is in fantastic shape and has an 8-track player and that delightful wood paneling along the sides. Oh, how I wish I had been alive during a time that they put wood paneling on a car. It's just so delightfully outrageous. Very well, then. A special visit from my special friends on this special evening. But should you run into trouble, you are all most welcome to return here whenever you wish. Our home is your home. Yes? Grand!

"Gerald, would you show our other guests to their rooms on the third floor. And, oh my, Hugo, is it? Oh, my dear friend, you look like you have been through quite the trying time. Gerald, please show him to his room, then get him to the infirmary. He needs his wounds cleaned and attended to. Robert, could you attend to that? Yes? Splendid. And finally, Payekha and Ezinne, is it? What beautiful names you both have. My, if I didn't know better, I would have mistaken you for sisters. You two will have a room next to Hugo's, if that is suitable. Yes? Wonderful! Sam, could you escort the ladies around while we are waiting for dinner to be prepared? I do hope you like our little slice of paradise. Very well then. Off to your rooms to get dried off and changed! Shall we meet in the dining room in two hours? That should give you enough time to get settled in and perhaps enjoy a few of our amenities. Oh, but just one more thing that I'm afraid I must ask. Do any of you have any weapons? Guns, knives, anything like that?"

Payekha stiffened her spine as brilliant lights began flowing around her. She stared silently at the twenty-two tall vanilla ice-cream cones that surrounded her. She reached into her backside waistline for her spoon. The ice cream immediately melted, and she was once again looking at Francis when he exclaimed, "Oh, you *do* have a gun! Splendid! Just splendid! I only asked because we have quite the armament here and I thought you might be able to use a bit of fire power on your journey. Mankind has always been an angry lot, but they are now quite bitey it would seem. Well, that is just *one* handgun. Should you need anything more, simply ask. Now, enough of my silly rambling and off to your rooms!"

Gerald, Robert, and Sam began ascending the marble staircase followed by Payekha, Ezinne, and Hugo. Their eyes widened with each new discovery in the mansion. The crystal chandeliers. Priceless paintings and sculptures. The finely engraved woodwork. It was the very definition of opulence. Gerald opened a door on the third floor and motioned for Hugo to enter. "Um, I'll just go and get changed real quick, then come and check on you ladies, okay?" he said to the nodding Payekha and Ezinne.

The ladies entered their room and their jaws dropped at the sight of their quarters. To the left next to a grand stone fireplace was a sitting area adorned with lush, red velvet chairs and an ornate wooden coffee table. The walls were tastefully decorated by various paintings depicting the serenity of nature. A wooden built-in bookcase held first editions of classic novels. And the canopy bed appeared large enough to sleep four average-sized people. Or one Gerald.

"Thank you so much for showing us to our room," Payekha said to the towering Gerald. "We won't be but a minute." Gerald left the room and Payekha immediately said, "Alright, Mom. I think this is okay. But I don't want to take any chances. I'm going to stuff my duffle bag up in the chimney and hide it there. If shit goes down, try to get it and get the fuck out of here. Okay?"

"Weeeelll," Ezinne replied. "I don't know if that is necessary dear, but you do what you think is right. These young men seem just fine to me. They are quite polite and have opened their wonderful home to us. That is something that is rare in this world. Especially for White men who are speaking to women who look like us. When they saw our Black faces, they did not react whatsoever. I do not believe they are sexists or racists. Perhaps living in a simpler technological age has allowed their values to be from a simpler, more respectful time as well. And I know how difficult it is for you to trust anyone, dear. How could I blame you for that? Not after the horrors you were put through as a child. And not after what this society has become. I understand your need to always be on guard. But maybe for just one night we can let our guard down. Maybe for just tonight I would like to enjoy a lovely dinner with our new friends. And, most importantly, I wish to spend a peaceful evening with my lovely daughter whom I love more than anything in this world. Okay?"

"Yeah, Mom, of course," Payekha stated in a choked-up voice as she wrapped her mother in a warm embrace. "Yeah, I think we're alright. I was just sure they were going to tell me to hand over my gun. But they didn't. Hell, they even offered us *more* guns. They obviously don't fear *us*, so why should we fear *them*? It is the fear in each of us that leads us to hatred of others. Then suppression. Then violence. You take away the fear, you take away the hatred. That's the entire point of my subliminal messaging. To take away people's fears of one another. To allow people to open up to each other so that we can work together. To allow people to get off of their individual islands and join one another within a caring community. So, I guess I should practice what I preach. Tonight, I'm going to just enjoy being alive. I'm going to enjoy our new friends. And I am going to enjoy being with the most incredible fucking mother anybody could ask for. I love you so much, Mom."

"I love you too, dear," a tearful Ezinne answered. The tender moment was interrupted hy a light rap on their door. "Yeah? Come on in," Payekha stated. The door opened and a white-clad Hugo popped his head into the room. "Hey, I just wanted to let you know that this Robert guy is going to take me to the infirmary and patch me up and change my bandages. But I'll see you at dinner, okay?"

"Yeah, you bet," Payekha answered. "And maybe later tonight, we could build a fire in your room and just hang out and, um, stuff. You know. If you want to."

"Um, um, um, yeah, that would, um, be nice," the blushing Hugo stammered. "Um, okay. Well, I'll see you at dinner then. Oh, and this Sam guy is out here waiting for you. He's going to show you two around."

Payekha and Ezinne's eyes were filled with wonder as they were taken on a tour of the majestic mansion by Sam. "You are, of course, free to wander around without me whenever you might like," Sam instructed. "This is just an introductory tour to help you know your way around. This place is so huge, even *I* still get lost in here some-times. Now this is our botanical garden. Beautiful, isn't it? We have all sorts of exotic plant life from throughout the world. This is also where we grow our fruits and vegetables. People called us crazy when we all went in together and restored this place. They thought we were *really* crazy when we said we were equipping it for the end of the world. I certainly don't mean to gloat at a time like this, but those people aren't laughing at us now. No, they aren't laughing at all. Now if you will just come down this hallway, we have our library.

"You have a lovely one in your bedroom, but as you can see, this collection is quite expansive. Some of the greatest works of literature can be found here. As can encyclopedias and textbooks on pretty much any subject you can think of. And films. Thousands of films on VHS tapes can be found here. We felt it was our responsibility to preserve the art and technology of our fallen species. Well, technology up to 1985, that is. Now this door opens up into our dance hall. We have a DJ stand, turntables, disco lights, and a *very* comprehensive collection of albums from the beginning of recorded music until, um, 1985. All that we were missing were lovely ladies to dance with. Perhaps we could share a dance with you two later tonight. With your permission, of course. I would recommend not dancing with Gerald, however. Not only does he have two left feet, but they are quite big and very heavy."

Payekha began perusing through the racks of records and said, "Huh. Well, you have a lot of shit here, but one thing I'm noticing. Where's the jazz? Where's the blues? Or pretty much *anything* created by a Black artist?"

"Oh, those are probably in another section," Sam responded before quickly changing the subject. "Now, this room is our conference room." Payekha was finally able to fully relax when she looked upon the far wall. Hanging at the end of the long conference room table was a huge golden picture of Dear Leader. That was full of darts. "Well, I must say that I like your choice of artwork in here." Sam chuckled and said, "Yes, we do enjoy playing a game of darts every now and then. And what could make a more perfect dartboard, right? I would say that a shot into his brain is a bullseye, but who are we kidding? He has no brain. What a disappointing dullard he turned out to be. Oh, he was useful to some for a while. But his whole schtick became quite tiresome. If there is a silver lining to the state of the world, it would be his demise.

"Now, this is our game room. Vintage arcade games as far as the eyes can see. Plus, pinball machines, pool tables, and so forth. And the best part? They're all free! You don't have to put a quarter into them. This one here is my specialty. I have the top twenty high scores and... hey. What is *this*? Why, that little scamp, Francis. Look here. He has the number seventeen high score. Well, I may need to correct that after dinner. I believe we have time for one more room before we get ready for dinner.

"This is our recreation area. In here you will find a workout center, swimming pool, and hot tub. Oh, and a sauna. "Weeeelll, I'll be," Ezinne said. "A sauna. My, I haven't had one of those in years. Oh, I don't believe I've ever been so relaxed as when I sat in a sauna. But then, of course, my kind weren't allowed in there anymore. The Regime didn't want Black and White sweat mingling. Or anything else for that matter."

"Well, you certainly are welcome to use ours," Sam invited. "We still have an hour before dinner is ready." "Are you sure? That just sounds lovely," Ezinne replied as tears of gratitude welled up in her eyes. "I must say, young man, that we haven't been treated with this kind of respect in many years. Thank you. Thank you for treating us as equal human beings. Thank you for your hospitality. But most of all, thank you for letting me use your sauna. Payekha, dear, I'll see you at dinner. Momma's going to get her sweat on!"

"Okay, Mom, okay," a giggling Payekha replied. "I want to check to see if my clothes are dry anyway. These are very nice and thank you for them, but they're just a little too white for my taste. Okay, Mom. I'm going up to the room. I'll see you at dinner."

Payekha was escorted by Sam into the dining room and was seated. "Isn't this cool?" Dawson stated. "You're their special guest and get to sit at the head of the table. We're also getting served first. Cool, huh? Why did you change your clothes?" "Um, y'know. I'm just more comfortable in my jeans and black T. And yes, this is very nice. Thank you all," Payekha responded.

Twenty-two faces smiled back at her as they began bringing silver platters and bowls into the dining room. "Um, hey," Payekha began asking. "Where's my mom and Hugo?"

"Oh, they'll be along shortly," Dawson stated as he brought in a large, covered silver platter. "In fact, I'm sure they'll be here by the time the main course arrives. I do hope you like it, Payekha. You *deserve* a feast like this. I've always been in such awe of you. Your strength. Your intelligence. Your self-confidence. And you aren't too hard on the eyes, either. All qualities that I lack. And now, here you are. A true heroine who is trying to save the world is actually here in *my* hometown breaking bread with my best friends. This special dinner is in honor of you, Payekha. And everything you stand for. Actually, I think you just might recognize this dish."

Dawson lifted the cover of the platter, revealing the broiled heads of Ezinne and Hugo. Twenty-three young White men began laughing hysterically as Payekha's shocked mind tried to absorb the horrific scene. Her confused eyes looked pleadingly up at Dawson. He smiled sinisterly at her and yelled out, "Bon Appetit, bitch!"

CHAPTER 22

LITTLE WHITE LIES

Payekha's sullen eyes stared out of her barred windows as man after man forced themselves into her bound and beaten body. They would enter her dark, damp cell and commit atrocity upon atrocity on her as she silently watched out her window. She watched the brilliant green leaves on the outside trees burst into vibrant reds, oranges, and yellows. Then, they turned tan and dark brown. The trees would shed their final leaves of the season and slip into content hibernation before being covered by snow and ice. The warm rays of the sun shined upon them, ushering in a new season as bright green buds appeared upon their resilient branches. And through it all, Payekha just laid there and absorbed the brutal indignities that were being imposed upon her. She was once again a brutalized child. She was once again an innocent, traumatized victim whose cheeks were saturated by her tears.

Her will to fight had been stripped away. Gone was her ability to strengthen her fortitude through dissociation. Gone were the vibrant colors, impenetrable armor, and gallant weaponry. They had been cruelly replaced by the never-ending grotesque image of the broiled heads of Hugo and her beloved mother. And Dawson's sadistic little smile as he haughtily bragged about his macabre plan on the night of their murders.

"What's the matter, bitch?" he had gleefully asked while his friends sipped bourbon and guffawed in the background. "Not hungry? C'mon. Eat a little. Do you want dark meat or white meat? Oh, I *know* you like white meat. Here. Let's just carve a little bit off of Hugo's cheek. He's been perfectly seasoned. There we are. Now open up. I said open up bitch and eat this shit! Yeah, chew, bitch. I'm going to hold your mouth shut until you swallow it. No spitting allowed. There. Good girl. Now, how about some dark meat? Oh, don't her lips look moist and succulent? Mmmm, yeah. A big fat (derogatory term omitted) lip for you. Don't resist! Open up and take it! There you are. Chew it all up and swallow. Your mouth isn't the only thing that you'll be opening up for us tonight.

"Yeah, you're gonna be opening those chocolate legs of yours too. But don't worry. We'll use a condom. We have no idea what type of diseases you (derogatory term omitted) might be carrying. Plus, we wouldn't want to knock you up, now, would we? No, having you reproduce would run counter to our plan. Our plan that we have been working on for years since high school. You see, none of us were exactly lucky with the ladies, you might say. All those stuck-up little bitches had no interest in us. Oh, but they sure as hell would fuck the (derogatory term omitted) and the (derogatory term omitted) and the (derogatory term omitted) now, wouldn't they? Yeah, just spread their lily-white thighs and take on a black mamba. Which got us to thinking.

"What if we were to take over the world? Then we'd get laid as much as we want! I mean, shit, we had just seen Dear Leader do it, and he was an absolute fucking moron! If an utterly insane dullard like *that* could take over *this* country, then *certainly* twenty-three geniuses like us could take over the entire world! But how? We thought and we thought. And then it hit us. Technology. We use technology to tear down society. We get rid of fucking *everybody*, man! Then, we're the only ones left to rebuild and rule. We can get rid of all the vermin and populate the world with White people ruled by us

White men. Just as God had intended. I don't know how God's plan got so far off the fucking rails, but it did. Hitler tried to make it right and failed. Dear Leader tried, but it was obvious to us that he just didn't have the mental capacity to pull it off. He was such a fucking joke to us. No, *we* needed to do it, and we needed to do it right. Tear the entire fucking thing down. Kill everybody. Then, start over. Using technology.

"So, we shunned any technology that was invented after 1985. We had to insulate ourselves against whatever virus or toxin or whatever shit we would unleash upon the world. We weren't sure how we were going to do it, but we knew we had to manipulate people's minds. And to do that, we needed to get into the National Institute of Psychiatric Health. Many of us applied. I'm the only one that got in. And who did meek, kind-hearted little Dawson meet on day one on the job? Why, he met our brilliant Payekha, here. And you told me all about your project to use subliminal messaging to control human behavior. And bingo! Bango! A plot was hatched! Of course, you wanted to strengthen people. I wanted to destroy them. You were so fucking easy to manipulate. Just stand in the corner wearing my little aw-shucks grin. Hold the door open for you. Stupid shit like that. That's all it took to gain your trust and to tell me all about your project.

"And all that I needed to do was whisper into my supervisor's ear about my plan to develop subliminal messages to control human behavior. For their eternal subservience to Dear Leader, of course. He stole my plan and took it to *his* supervisor who took my plan to *his* supervisor and so on and so on. Until my plan was stolen and green-lit by Dear Leader himself and Project Golden Age was born. And, although it absolutely killed me, I knew that I had to have *you* on the team. Hugo and I could do the cell phone implants and algorithm manipulation. But *you* were the expert on the messaging. So, we kept you around. You were the only Black left in the entire federal regime, and one of the few women. But you were brilliant. The rest of your kind were nothing but DEI hires stealing jobs from White men. But you? No, *you* were genuinely brilliant and it fucking killed me to acknowledge that a (derogatory term omitted) bitch could actually best a White man at something. But there it was. If I was going to destroy humanity, a (derogatory term omitted) was going to have to help me.

"As the regime became increasingly hostile towards women and non-Whites, justifiably so, I might add, I had to distance myself from you. But in our progress meetings, I would drop just enough breadcrumbs so you could figure out what we were actually doing. And, knowing you as I now did, I knew you would sabotage it. You would provide us with data that would be so contaminated only a mad fool would release it into the world. Well, either a mad fool or a power-hungry genius, that is. Oh, my lovely Payekha, you played your part so perfectly. You kept giving us increasingly corrupted data. Hugo was so fucking stupid that he had no idea what he was looking at. The mistake you made, my dear, is that you assumed that *I* was that stupid as well. But I wasn't. I knew exactly what I was looking at and I knew exactly what I was unleashing upon the world when I "accidently" hit the 'Transmit' button instead of 'Delete'. I knew it had begun. All I needed to do was get back home in one piece as humanity's base instincts were unleashed and it tore itself apart. And who should once again come to the rescue?

"My heart actually leapt when you came bursting into your office and found us there. What poetic justice. The woman who helped me destroy the world was going to deliver me to my sanctuary. Hugo wasn't the *only* one who knew where the transmission station was. *I* also knew it was in Pueblo. And I knew the route we would take to get there. And it just so happened to be near my hometown where my brothers resided. Lucky me. And lucky that you were so brilliant and had an alternate subliminal message to try to transmit to the world. I just had to play dutiful, shy little Dawson for a little while longer.

"I looked away when you showed your message to us at your house. Hugo looked right at it, and it turned him into a fucking woke pussy. But not me. I stared at your mother the whole time and thought about what a lovely feast she would be for you. And you've probably figured out that I didn't *accidentally* drop my cell phone and it didn't *accidentally* turn on and the Amish kids didn't *acciden-*

tally looked at it. I can't believe you fell for that bullshit story. No, I tied them fucking brats down and *forced* them to watch it. Once their little innocent eyes turned into white balls of rage, I untied them and let nature take its course when their parents came in. They chased me out of the house, and I sprayed the fuck out of them with *GROOMING*. Then I set the house on fire. It was a total bonus when Joshua killed himself by walking into his collapsing home. Man, that was fucking entertainment, right there. And quite poetic. An innocent, honest, hard-working man had been beaten down so much by the ills of society that he was stripped of all hope for mankind and voluntarily marched into hellfire. Some of my best work, really.

"Oh, and I *of course* blew up the car. Just stuffed a long piece of cloth into the gas tank, lit it, and boom. *Oopsy*. Gee, *now* I guess we gotta walk to my hometown that is *conveniently* located just a few miles away. And deliver you to my friends. Why, this calls for a cele-bratory feast! All we had to do was separate you three. Hugo was easy. He needed medical care. And he got it. You see, ever since he watched your inspirational subliminal message, he just wasn't right in the head. So, I removed it. You see that shocked look on his face? Yep, that's the expression he had when I took an axe and lopped his fucking head off. Then, a little ginger, garlic, pinch of black pepper, and voila! Delicious wasn't he? Oh, don't look so sad. You know you enjoy Hugo's head. Which was *another* thing that pissed me off. How could you fuck *him* and not *me*? It was just like fucking high school! Oh well, fuck it. We're going to correct that shortly. Whether you want to or not.

"I remembered you telling me about how your mother was upset that they no longer allowed (derogatory term omitted) into saunas. They were Whites only now, and it was one of the few things that was able to relax her, and the regime had taken that away from her too. Well, *hell*, the sauna had best be on the house tour then, don'tcha think? And the best part about that? She was pre-steamed! Oh man, her flesh just fell off the bone as we were boiling her. Alive. Then, off with her head, a little bit of seasoning, and pop her in the oven for an hour. So tender. Right? Which reminds me. We really need to fumigate that sauna. I'm not sitting in that (derogatory term omitted) bitch's sweat.

"Now, I know what you must be thinking. But Dawson, if you kill everybody on Earth, how does that help you get laid? Good question, Payekha. You always were a smart cookie. Easy. We kidnap the zombie bitches. Or at least the White, good-looking ones. We'll each have our own harem of those insane bitches. We'll drug 'em up, tie them down, and fuck the shit out of them. And then, along comes the offspring. Brand spanking new White babies to re-populate the Earth! Hell, we have five of them locked away in the basement, already. And I just *know* they're going to enjoy the leftovers from our little feast tonight. Oh, don't look so sad Payekha. You've actually done mankind a great favor. You will go down in our history as our matriarch of domination. Of course, we'll have to whitewash that history a bit. We can't have our children thinking that a (derogatory term omitted) played any role in this. Hell, come to think of it, there's no reason for our children to have any idea that (derogatory term omitted) like you ever existed!

"Whatever. We'll just make it up as we go along. That's how all great writing is created anyway. Right now, we are going to take you to your quarters. Yes, you will be beaten and probably tortured a bit. But on the bright side, you're going to get plenty of cock. Big, hard, white cock. For as long as we find you entertaining. And after we're tired of you? Well, you'll make a lovely meal for our slightly irritated, chompy little wives, heh, heh, heh."

Payekha continued to stare solemnly at a black bird that was chirping outside of the barred windows of her cell. Tears began to flow once again as she heard the thick CLUNK of her cell door lock. She shuddered uncontrollably as she heard the morbid sound of the heavy metal door creaking open. She protectively curled her naked frame into the fetal position and sobbed as she heard his disgusting voice once again.

"Well, shit, Payekha," Dawson said as he entered the cold room. "We've got ourselves a little problem. You see, we were able to rape the zombie bitches for the last nine months. And we were able to impregnate them. But do you know what those stupid bitches are doing? As soon as their kid comes squirting out of them, they get all riled up, break their restraints, and eat their own fucking kids! It's fucking disgusting watching them devour their own babies and lick the afterbirth off their purple lips. So, this isn't working. We need to have *real* women to rape who haven't been indoctrinated and who won't eat their own fucking babies. So, we're prepared to make a deal with you."

For the first time in nine months, Payekha felt a familiar spark in her battered soul. It was the same spark that she had felt when she was a tortured teenage girl. The same spark that comes with a glimmer of hope. She uncurled her naked body and stared at Dawson. He was shrouded by black smoke while brilliant colors began circling her body. Her nudity was being covered by a fluorescent purple suit of armor. Her synapses were re-engaged and were firing at a rapid pace as her calculating mind fought through the haze of brutality. "So, what's the deal?" she replied in an assertive voice.

"Well, we need to show these bitches your subliminal message. We can go to town and try to find a computer. You pop in your flash drive, we'll indoctrinate these crazy-ass bitches, so they won't eat their kids, and we'll just keep them tied up and impregnate them again. So, you tell us where your flash drive is and we'll let you live. Not only that, but we'll stop beating and torturing and raping you. We can't let you go, but we'll put you on a really long chain and you can stay in that nice bedroom on the third floor. You'll be fed and treated well. All you need to do is tell us where the flash drive is."

Payekha smiled internally as she contemplated her response. She could feel her purple armor thickening and growing stronger. The circling lights became brighter. The thick, black smog began constricting around her sadistic nemesis. She opened her cracked lips and said, "Um, I don't know where it is. I gave it to my mom for safe-keeping. It was on her when she died. It would be in her clothes."

"Well, fuck!" a furious Dawson shouted. "That doesn't help us at all! We burned all her clothes! Fuck this! You're of no help to us then!"

He reached into his white jacket pocket and retrieved his handgun. "Sorry Payekha, but you're no longer of use to us."

Payekha held an amused look upon her bruised face as she stared at the harmless bouquet of white lilies that the smog-man was pointing at her. She smiled slightly and said, "But I can recreate it. I know that the data on my computer and server was destroyed when the car exploded. But I still have the basics in my head. I created it once and I can create it again. But I need time. Time to heal both mentally and physically. I need to be comfortable. Just put me in that cozy bedroom, get me a computer, and give me thirty days. I just need thirty days to reconfigure everything. And if I don't? Well, then I guess you can blow my fucking head off if you want to. What do you have to lose there, Ace?"

The black smog pulled the white lilies away and rubbed his chin. "Huh, wow, Payekha. Even after months of brutality, you're still smart as hell. Yeah, okay. Thirty days. You've got thirty days. But I want *this* message to be truly one of submission. Don't give me this female empowerment bullshit and don't turn them into violent zombies. I want the *real* shit. I want what you were supposed to be giving us all along. You have thirty days to create a subliminal message to turn every bitch who sees it into a submissive little whore. A submissive little whore who will do *anything* that I say. A submissive little whore who will bow at the feet of their new Dear Leader."

This motherfucker is so crazy, Payekha thought to herself before saying, "You got it. In thirty days, you're going to get all the blowjobs you can handle. Now, go get me a computer. And take me to my room. I want fresh clothes and a real meal. Got it?"

"Thanks Gerald," Payekha stated as the oak door was opened to her elegant stateroom. "You know, of all the assholes who raped me, you were probably my favorite. I mean, for such a large man, you didn't exactly stretch me out, if you know what I mean. Plus, I didn't have to put up with a bunch of gloating and name-calling. Strong, silent, with a small dick. I can appreciate that. Oh, hey. Don't leave before you chain me to the bed. Good boy. Now, if I could have a bit of alone time. I'm going to take a little nap before they arrive with the computer."

The lumbering Gerald exited the room and locked it. Payekha covered her mouth to muffle her hysterical laughter. "Oh man, what a fucking moron," she said as she lifted the bed leg and removed the end of her chain. She dragged her chain over to the fireplace and knelt onto the hearth. "DEI hires my ass. If this were a group of *Black* folks, the first thing they would have done is look for my duffle. They would have tied up any loose ends. But not *these* dumbass White mother-fuckers. They were too high on their own self-importance to even think about it. Until they needed it. All these fascist fuckers care about is their immediate gratification. No contingency plans. Just, I have won and I can't be stopped now. I'm not threatened by anything. It was that imbecilic arrogance that led to the downfall of Dear Leader. And it will be *these* asshole's downfall too. Jesus fucking Christ. I really jammed this motherfucker up there. Ah, there it is. Come to momma.

"Now, let's just see what we have in here. Bottled water. Protein bars. A couple hot pockets. Well, *they're* going to be spoiled as fuck. Three bottles of *GROOMING* and three squirt guns. My handgun and three loaded clips. And sewn into the lining? Ah, there it is. My flash drive. And now for the grand finale. My cell phone. And charger. Now, where's the outlet? There's something that I think I want to show these twisted fucks. Okay, Mom. I'm so sorry for getting you into this. I'm so sorry that I got the entire *world* into this. I started this shit, and I'm the only one who can end it. I hope you have a good seat in Heaven to watch this shit, Mom. Because it's fucking payback time."

CHAPTER 23

JUST DESSERTS

"I assume this will fulfill your needs," Dawson stated as he entered Payekha's room with a laptop computer. "And I got the hotspot that you wanted. Just keep in mind that it is only to be used in this room. No internet in the rest of the house. What? No thank you? It's really fucking crazy out there. It's just quiet. Rotting corpses lying every-where. And wild animals that have taken over the town. I don't know if there are any survivors left in the world, so a little trip to Pueblo would be pointless, anyway."

"Yeah, okay, whatever," Payekha replied dismissively. "Not exactly an option for me now, is it? I'm going to be locked in this room for the rest of my life. Assuming you hold up your end of the bargain, which is fifty-fifty at best. Which reminds me," Payekha continued as she tugged at the chain that was clamped around a bed leg. "Is it really necessary to keep me on this chain? I mean, I get the symbolism you White motherfuckers are going for here, but is it really necessary when I'm in a locked room?"

"Yeah, it is," Dawson answered. "It's *very* necessary. It's a little extra protection in case you get some ideas." "Oh, I've got ideas," Payekha said as she hooked the wi-fi hotspot up to her new laptop. "I've got all *kinds* of ideas and...holy shit! It works! There's still internet! This is amazing. For nearly a year, the human race has been all but extinct and yet its infrastructure keeps humming along. I guess that AI shit really *did* replace humans, didn't it? The entire infrastructure around the world is continuing to be operated by AI bots. Electricity. Water systems. Heat. And the internet. Still all running in top form. Which brings me to my idea. You're going to have to go back to town and get me some more shit."

"You know, I'm not your fucking errand boy," and irritated Dawson replied. "I'm not here to do your bidding. *You* are here to do *mine*! Or have you actually *missed* the symbolism of being chained up in a house run by a group of White men?"

"Oh no, *that* shit hasn't been lost on me," Payekha answered while logging into a website that contained crucial data for her project. "But if you want to indoctrinate those zombie women into being subservient to you, you might want to hear me out. Listen, this isn't going to take me thirty days. It might not even take me a week. I have most of this shit in my head. Sorry, but your tiny little White dicks weren't able to rape that out of me. All I need to do is reconstruct the data in my head, tweak it to meet your pathetic specifications, and implant it into a video or something. But we still have to get them to *watch* it, right? Sure, we could show it to them on my little computer screen here, but that might not be big enough to get their attention.

"But, what about your big, bulky projection TV from the early eighties that you have in your rec room? We could move it to the basement and project my subliminal message on the wall across from their cells. The picture would be huge and attract their attention. We wouldn't have to remove them from their cells. Safety first, right Skippy? All I need to do is hook up my computer to its inputs. Here's a list of wires and cables that I need. Oh, and here's a bonus idea for you, Dawson. I'm throwing *this* shit in for free. You want to be the new Dear Leader? I can make that happen for you. I can tell your pals that the subliminal messaging only works on females, so it's safe for them to watch it. It won't have any impact on them. But that would be bullshit. They'll become just as submissive to you as the women. I just recommend you find someplace to be while the show is playing.

Otherwise, you might end up kissing *my* Black ass. Make sense? So, go get me these wires and cables. You never know when I'm going to hit my breakthrough. It could be in a week; it could be in the next five minutes. But the sooner we show them my message; the sooner you're going to have groveling whores fighting over your shrimpy incel cock. Now get to moving. Boy."

"Payekha, if I didn't need you for this, I swear, I'd slap that fucking disrespect right out of your (derogatory term omitted) mouth. But, goddammit, I do need you. And I like your idea. Fine. I'll go back to town. But you'd better be right about this."

Dawson slammed the door on his way out and Payekha burst into laughter. She lifted the bed post, removed the end of the chain, then sauntered back to the hard-wood desk that housed her new computer. "This is going to be easier than I thought," she quietly muttered to herself. "Now back to my research. Oh shit, how I've missed these stupid fuckin' cat videos."

Payekha's chain was being held by the imposing Gerald as she was led down the concrete steps of the mansion's basement. They entered the cold, stone hallway of the incarceration center. Desperate scabbed and scarred arms were reaching out for them from behind barred doors. Payekha shuddered as she heard the encaged women shrieking at her in rage. "You boys got everything set up?" she asked as she approached the twenty-two other men who were fiddling with the projection TV unit. "Yeah, I think it's ready," Francis answered. "And you're sure we can watch this too? It will have no effect on us?"

"None whatsoever," Payekha answered while beginning to connect her laptop to the projection unit. "I've set this message to only impact people with a certain amount of estrogen." *Yeah, Payekha,* she thought to herself. *Just use big, girly words that these incel fucks don't understand, heh, heh, heh.* "Oh, and boys. I want *you* to watch extra close. I've imbedded a close-up image of a clit in the video. See if you can find it. I'm betting you can't. Alright, I think I'm all set up. Turn on the projector. Hey Dawson. No need for you to be here for this. Why don't you go upstairs and get us a few bottles of celebratory bubbly. It'll make your new little sex toys even more playful."

"Um yeah, alright," Dawson answered. "I'll be back in a few minutes. And then, gentlemen, it will be fun time."

"Okay, here goes nothing," Payekha stated as she began playing a video on her computer. The entire wall across from the holding cells was filled with images of kittens. Kittens playing with yarn. Kittens chasing laser pointers. Kittens staring down cucumbers. And all the while, the women continued to growl and beat against their locked, barred doors.

"Hey! This isn't working!" Francis shouted. "They aren't changing! Dawson said they only needed to watch it for a few seconds for it to take hold!" "Yeah, sorry, sorry, sorry," a snickering Payekha replied. "My bad. Wrong fucking video. Hold on a sec. I'll fix it. Just keep watching the screen." She went behind the projection unit and turned the cat video off. She unplugged the connecting cable from her computer and connected it to her cell phone. She grinned wickedly as she pressed play on a video on her phone, shut her eyes, and covered her ears. "Here you go boys. Now *this* is the real shit."

The women calmed down momentarily as the cell phone projected a video of swaying trees with a ukulele being softly strummed. Imbedded in the soundtrack was Dear Leader's subliminal, irritating voice. He was bragging. He was boasting. He was speaking about being the greatest ruler. The greatest lover. The greatest man to have ever lived. Every few seconds, an image of Dear Leader's opulence would flash followed by an image of the human carnage of his creation. His golden ballroom. Then people in food lines. His garish, cheap gold office. Then people being beaten by his mindless, cruel troops. His hand provocatively placed on the thigh of an under-age girl who was sitting on his lap. Then mass graves being covered with lye. His grandiosity was repeatedly contrasted by the cruel human suffering that he had inflicted upon the world. And it was accompanied by his grating voice spewing non-sensical word-salads of hatred. And then, the video suddenly stopped.

It had stopped because the white-eyed and frothing Gerald had picked up the projection unit and smashed it against the stone wall. It had stopped because the repugnant image and voice of Dear Leader had transformed these men from calculating hate-filled humans into mindless, hate-filled zombies. The crouching Payekha was pelted by flying plastic and glass fragments. She looked up and saw twenty-two pairs of dead white eyes staring at her. The men growled primitively as they slowly approached her. Payekha stood up, reached into her backside waistline and retrieved a gun. A bright blue plastic gun. She smiled at them and said in a mischievous voice, "You've just been *GROOMED* motherfuckers."

"Ah fuck, not *this* again!" Payekha screamed as twenty-two men flooded the stone hallway with their retch. She cowered in the far corner to avoid it, but the regurgitated internal organs landed in the vomit so heavily that she became awash in the refuse. Every few seconds, a gallbladder or kidney or stomach would be ejected from a tortured man's stretched-out mouth. And every few seconds, her beautiful brown face and afro would be splashed by chunky, brown, putrid spew. "Goddamit, motherfucker!" she screamed at the author while the enraged caged women were ripping each other apart. "Stop this shit right now! Stop it! Stop it! Stop it and get on to the next scene! This is fucking gross!"

"Oh, Dawson," Payekha haughtily said as she wiped her chin. "You really were a big pussy, weren't you? I mean, what the hell did you do when you figured out what was going on? What did you do when you figured out that I had betrayed you? That I had made your captured women so infuriated that they tore each other apart? That I had indoctrinated your buddies, then *GROOMED* them? Which caused me to be covered in vomit. Again. That shit wasn't cool. But that's beside the point.

"What did you do? The same thing that *all* you pussy motherfuckers do. You fucking cowered and hid. Yeah, you little incel bullies like to talk big, but when the shit goes down, you're just a bunch of little pussies who curl into the fetal position and whimper for mommy. Oh sure, you had a gun. But you're such a pathetic shot. I'm glad I never gave you a blowjob. You're such a bad shot, you would've missed my mouth and shot me in the eye. Actually, I bet you motherfuckers do that shit on purpose don't you? Just another way to demean and dominate women. What a bunch of assholes. Anyway, whatever.

"I entered your bedroom and you shot at my shadow. I swung my arm and you shot at the stream of vomit. You shot the lamp. TV. Eight-track player. You shot everything but me. And when I approached you and stood over you and dripped your friends' hurl on your thinning blonde head, you just sobbed. You plead for mercy. You actually *plead* for *my* mercy. After what you had done to me. After making me eat my *own fucking mother*! How fucking stupid *are* you? And not only are you a pathetic little pussy, but you also have a glass jaw, as it turns out. Just one uppercut, and you were out like a light. You went down like a French whore at Mardis-gras. You folded like a lawn chair. You, um, okay. You get the point. This is getting sad. Never mind.

"And now, here we are. Just you and me. Just as it has always been since we met. I counted on your kindness and in return, you manipulated me into doing your sadistic bidding. I'm so fucking ashamed of myself. Me, an expert in human behavior, was manipulated by a fucking psychotic incel. Maybe I'm just as pathetic as you are. But I'm not as disgusting," she began concluding as she wiped salsa from her bruised chin.

"*I'm* not a fucking cannibal. But I *do* want to make you suffer. I want your death to be long and drawn out. That's why you're in the sauna. The place where my mother had her final brief moment of joy and hope. You took that from her. You took it from the entire world. And now, my fake friend, I will take it from you. Now, let's just set this to 175 degrees. Shut the door. And I'm going to sit outside and eat my hot pockets and watch life drip out of you, one bead of sweat at a time. I'm going to watch your pasty-white skin turn dark red, like the devil you are. I'm going to watch your flesh bubble and pop. I'm going to watch your eyes explode out of their sockets. I'm going to watch you die a horrendous, painful death. Then, I'm taking that cute 1968 red Mustang convertible that's in the garage and I'm going to Pueblo. Alone. I'm still going to try to save humankind. Not that it fucking deserves it. I'm still going to try to find decent people to share my island with me. Good-bye Dawson. Have a nice sauna, motherfucker."

———

There was blissful silence. There were no horns honking. No traffic. No talking or yelling or laughing. There were no sounds whatsoever to indicate that a human race had ever existed here.

Then, upon closer inspection, one could hear the subtle sound of brilliant green leaves fluttering together in the light, warm breeze. It was as though the Earth was breathing a well-earned sigh of relief. Other sounds began to emerge. Waves calmly lapping upon the shore of a nearby lake. The playful squawks of geese. The bucked teeth of a family of rabbits tearing into their delicious clover. The flirtatious chirps of birds in the trees. A nut falling from its branch and softly landing in the thick brush. The sounds that indicated that nature had persevered despite the best attempts of humankind to extinguish her.

The majestic animals and flowers and trees had endured despite the hunting. And logging. And toxic chemicals that had been spewed into their air and been unceremoniously dumped into their waterways. They had endured despite humankind's lust for dominance over them. Many species had been lost during the humans' tyrannical reign over their home. But many more of them survived. *They* were still *here*. The *humans*, mercifully, *were not*. They had made themselves extinct through their insatiable drive for self-fulfillment. They were now extinct because of their greed. Because of their brutality. Because of their ignorance. And, ironically enough, because of their lack of basic humanity.

The Earth was healing. As was its colorful inhabitants. Then, the ears of a doe perked up. And those of the rabbits. The birds stopped chirping, and the geese cautiously floated silently in their pond. It had been many months since this dreadful sound had been heard. The high-pitched whir of one of their machines. The animals tenuously approached the grown-over pavement and looked to where the sound was coming from. Their hearts sank as they saw it. A single automobile. Driven on this single, lonely road. And behind the wheel, sat a single one of *them*. A female of their despicable species sitting alone in her single automobile being driven on this single, lonely road.

Payekha double-checked the coordinates that Hugo had tattooed onto her arm, looked at a grown-over road sign, and took a sharp right turn onto a winding, pot-holed, two-lane highway. She took her foot off the gas pedal and allowed the 1968 Mustang to coast through the collapsed electric fence that surrounded the cellular transmission station. She turned the ignition off, stepped out of the car, fell to her knees, and began laughing hysterically. It had been all for nothing. The pot of gold at the end of this twisted rainbow had turned out to be a decimated, burned-out concrete bunker. The cell tower lay in the surrounding forest in pieces. The entire perilous journey had been for nothing and all Payekha could do was laugh at her hopelessness.

Her laughing stopped when she heard a large figure lumbering through the nearby brush. She looked towards the direction of the snapping twigs and was confronted by a Black Bear. A gigantic, irritated, and potentially hungry Black Bear. A wave of calm came over her soul as brilliant streaks of light once again encircled her. Her purple suit of armor encased her body briefly, then dissipated into nothingness. Her heart rate slowed, and her mind became unburdened. She looked up into the light blue sky that was adorned with wispy white clouds and smiled. She then looked back into the determined eyes of the snarling Black Bear. Saliva was dripping from his lengthy fangs and massive jaws as she pulled a jar of golden honey from her duffle. She unscrewed the lid and poured the honey over her head. Waves of peace enveloped her as the sticky substance slowly oozed down her hair and upon her shoulders. She smiled once again as she dropped the flash drive into the tall grass and stepped towards the bear. She was delivering her body back to this exquisite nature. And she was delivering her soul to eternal tranquility.

THE END

MS- Oh, *HELLS* no! You are *NOT* ending this fucking thing like this! Sorry to interrupt folks. I'm Maddy, the star of my author's *Hanging Chads* series and I told myself I'd never directly interfere with one of his books, but this ending is total bullshit! I am *NOT* going to allow him to waste your precious time reading this whole fucking thing then end it like this. Like, what the fuck happens? Does she die? Does she live? Does humanity survive? What the fuck happens? Now, for those of you readers who like this stupid fucking ending, just close the book now and move on with your life. Thanks for reading. Hope to see ya in the next one. But for those readers who think this ending is *absolute bullshit,* which is the correct answer by the way, then he's going to write another one. Right, Mister artsy-fartsy dumbass author?

EC- Well, actually this *is* kinda the ending. I thought it was cool.

MS- Nope. It isn't cool. Start typing.

EC- But I thought it would be cool to let the reader use their imagination and determine for themselves what happens. Each reader can struggle with whether humanity can be redeemed or not. Each reader can determine if the human race provides any actual value on this planet or if we are a force of destruction that needs to be extinguished. Each individual reader determines the fate of humanity from each of their own individual islands. Not me. Cool, right?

MS- Nope. It's fucking stupid. People paid actual money for this shit. Write an actual ending. Dumbass.

EC- Fine. Just turn the page then and I'll write an actual ending.

And then the bear ate her face off.

THE END

EC- Happy now?

MS- No! That fucking sucks! Write an *actual* ending!

EC- FINE! I will! How about this?

Payekha was giggling as she was awoken by the playful licks of two bear cubs upon her healing face. "Oh my God, you guys!" She screamed through her laughs. "Stop it! That tickles! And Jesus, you two have just as bad of breath as your father! Fuck, man, I was just sure he was going to eat my face off. I was just giving myself to him. I was giving nature the retribution against us that it had earned for having to suffer through the age of human dominance. I closed my eyes and waited.

"And what did your fucking father do? He just licked the honey off my head. Then your mother joined in. And *you* guys came running. Before I knew it, I had four tongues lapping honey off of me. At first you guys were doing it for food. But then, I realized. You were cleaning me. You were grooming me. You were accepting me into your family. You were showing more humanity to me than my fucked-up species ever showed to you. And if wild bears could show kindness and respect for this deplorable human, then why can't *we*? Why can't humankind understand that we are nothing more than a part of nature and that every living creature on this Earth plays a part in the protection and stewardship of her? Why can't we learn from nature's wisdom?

"Oh, fuck, you guys! You're fucking heavy! Get off me! Okay, you guys hungry? Where's your mom and dad? Down by the stream I bet getting you some nice fish. Come on. Let's go find them."

Payekha was picking berries off a bush while her new family frolicked in the cold, clear waters. She watched them splashing in the stream and laughed at the playfully serene spectacle. Her eyes turned further up the waterway and her jaw dropped as she looked upon a small island in the middle of the water. Fifty yards upstream was a sight that she never thought that she would ever witness again. A small Hispanic boy, a tall Black man, and an Asian woman with a protruding belly were emerging from a small blue tent. They noticed her and paused. The boy wore a large, toothless grin as he lifted his tender hand and waved. The smiling man and woman eagerly followed suit.

Payekha smiled back, waved, fell to her knees, and sobbed tears of joy. This *wasn't* the end. Nature had embraced humankind to ensure that humankind would survive its own folly. And Payekha swore to herself that *this* time, the *humanity* of her species would survive as well.

THE END

MS- Yeah, okay. Not your *best* work, but that's better. Lata Gatas! Maddy out!